HOUSE OF KANU Series

IMPOSTER

KINGS OF GEONGALANN: Book One

ABRAM KLASERNER

This book is a work of fiction. Names, characters, businesses, organizations, places, events and incidents either are the product of the author's imagination or are used fictitiously. Any resemblance to actual persons, living or dead, events, or locales is entirely coincidental.

Book and Cover design by Abram Klaserner

ISBN: 978-0-9964033-0-6

First Edition: May 2015

10 9 8 7 6 5 4 3 2 1

For Carrie, the best adventure I ever took.

CONTENTS

CAST OF CHARACTERS

Fieropa: Woman in whom dwells a ferocious hope

Akosol: Carnal king of Bachar

Regeldam: Wicked king

Onero Seon: Outcast prophet of Bachar

Wylm Kanu: Elite soldier of Bachar

Jugel: Small-town swordsman

Shoshanna: Betrothed of Jugel

Batrachos: Leader of the Nemarians, invaders of Bachar

Hugla Seon: Grandfather of Onero

Yuri Kanu: Grandfather of Wylm

Goor: Beloved son of a specialized blacksmith

The Mugaal: The inhabitants of Arogan Forest

Hamaraz Hywel: General of the Horned Army

Getala: Scout for General Hywel

Jutta Hywel: Beautiful daughter of General Hywel

Kahya: Great hunter and master archer

Kesheth: Father of Kahya

Bagad: Guard in the service of Regeldam

Captain Pilesar: Commander of the White Regiment of King Regeldam's army

Tofir: Intimidating warrior

To Syd and Halym,

This is the first of the books discovered by your grandfather about his grandfathers. He found it while on his journeys. He always told me that the stories in them were powerful and dangerous. He knew that one day you or your parents would want to read them, and he made sure that I passed on his words of wisdom.
"Your history does not make your present;
Your present does not erase your past.
Your future hinges on one simple truth:
Only a life in Rhumaiv will last."

I love you so much.
Stand firm in what you believe.

Your grandmother,
Yahalom

PROLOGUE

Five years before the invasion.

Fieropa stepped into the street and closed the front door behind her, locking it. People did not leave their doors unlocked at night any more, not since the tax increases and the desperation that followed. Her father and mother were sleeping on the makeshift straw mattress in the far corner of the bedroom they all shared. They both were fevered and overcome with fatigue. Madam Seon would be by early in the morning to check on them. Fieropa hated to leave them, but without this job, she could never afford the medicine they needed.

She did not mind working; she had been laboring by her father's side since her youth. She did not mind her coworkers. The owner, Grimsten, could be gruff and harsh, and Rystilla, the other maid, was in need of a tune-up on her moral compass. Nevertheless, she enjoyed the company of both. What Fieropa did not enjoy was the establishment where she worked. Unfortunately, it was the only job to be had, and with her dimpled smile and genuinely pleasant personality, being a bar maid at *The Black Anvil* was enough to help pay the bills and the taxes.

Her father's house was seven blocks from the tavern. The moon was low in the sky and barely a crescent. It was darker than usual. Apparently the lamplighter had not lit the street torches that night. Either that or the oil was being rationed or withheld from this part of the city. The Sixth Ward was often ignored by the wealthy of Naos. Regardless, Fieropa realized she would have to run to work again tonight. Hearing the sound of feet shuffling behind her, she set off immediately.

****

The king sat on his gold-trimmed throne. His forearms rested on cool, polished ivory. Plush, red Sinuvian cloth pressed against his seat and back. Rich, gold-laced tapestries hung from the high cedar rafters. They depicted the history of his kingdom. As a man who cared only about beauty, image, and his own desires, King Akosol sat and considered the fine things around him. He was bored.

He had already tried visiting the concubines' quarters. When he became king a year ago, a call went out that he was looking for a wife. Hundreds of girls, ladies, and women came, hoping to be the one. After dismissing those he found repulsive, Akosol ended up with two hundred and thirty-seven concubines. None of them became his bride. He had decided he did not want the responsibility of a wife. He had considered his harem tonight, but found the eyes of each to be lifeless, scared, or far too willing. Without the sense of adventure, he quickly lost interest.

He had gone to the treasury next and stared at the gold, silver, and gems that filled the room. A significant portion had been acquired in the sale of weapons to his neighbors. A larger stack of gold bars came from the sale of one of his kingdom's border cities. The other coins and scattered valuables were from the tax increase he had placed on his people. He cared little about people, boundaries, or battles- only beauty and pleasure. But on this night, not even that brought him joy.

In the dullness and quiet of the late night, he had considered calling the minstrels, but decided that having people dance and sing before him would only make him feel worse about his current depressed state. He wanted the company of miserable men. He needed to witness the suffering of the destitute. The problem was that he did not want any of his servants or guards with him. With his guards nearby, the commoners would act differently knowing that their king was in their presence. Without his guards, though, mingling could be risky, for the common people did not love him.

As he considered his options, his fingers ran over the hilt of the sword that rested on his throne. He loved this sword. It was a thing of beauty. From the day he first saw it in his father's hand, he had craved it. In fact, it was because of this sword that he coaxed his older brother, then king, to go to war against the Pytecki giants. Akosol knew his brother would not return and that he was next in line for the throne. In fact, being the third son of his father, he had bribed and blackmailed the king's counselors to announce him as the heir to his childless brother.

When his brother's lifeless body returned to the capital city of Naos, Akosol was pleased. He commissioned a great funeral pyre to be burned. During the ceremony he held the sword, the heirloom, in his right hand, pointing it out over the pyre in a kingly manner. It had been hard to suppress the joy that had risen inside him. Finally the Maker's Sword was his.

The Maker's Sword was an heirloom passed down from the first king, Kadosh. According to legend, the Maker himself appeared to Kadosh and presented him the sword. With it, Kadosh defeated a Pytecki invasion and established the kingdom. The weapon was a thing of perfect beauty, second only to a bride on her wedding day, and Akosol took it with him wherever he went.

From hilt to point it was a piece of exquisite artistry. The pommel was twin gold ram's horns encircling and securing a massive pearl. The grip was as the torso of a man in a garment of a hundred tiny multi-colored jewels intricately arranged. The crossguard was two wings of an eagle enveloping and protecting the bearer's hand. An open lion's mouth made up the rain-guard with the blade projecting from the fearsome bite.

The blade was double-edged, and it never dimmed. At rest it glimmered as if freshly polished and lying in the midday sun. Even in the blackest night it sparkled. In the midst of battle, it glowed as if fresh from the blacksmith's fire. The blade did not soften, however, but became harder and sharper as the battle waged.

None could bear the sword save the king. History told of few exceptions. It was a just and merciful weapon. Many thieves and would-be assassins attempted to take or use the blade and fell to an immediate death at first contact. Some who touched or gripped the sword in innocence or ignorance felt the burning portent of its power, but were spared their lives. A few over the centuries had used the sword as a last resort to protect the king and were spared.

Akosol loved this weapon and decided it would be all the protection he needed this night. He also decided that he would have to go to a part of the city where he might not be recognized. The filthy and destitute citizens of the Sixth Ward seemed to him a promising people and place. The rest of Naos referred to that part of the city as the "Sick Ward" because of the rubbish and disease that seemed to plague its inhabitants. Likely no one there had ever seen his face, and that level of poverty and misery was just what he needed to lift his spirits.

****

Fieropa had a very busy night. The men of the Sixth Ward had almost nothing and what they had was being spent at *The Black Anvil*. Her self-righteous friends often judged the patrons of the tavern, questioning how they could spend their last coins on themselves when their families were sick and starving. She did not disagree with the foolishness of the men's decisions, but she did not judge them. For these men, the only relief from pain they ever experienced came at the bottom of a mug.

She pitied them. At times she felt bad taking their money, knowing what it did to their families. She needed her wages, though. Her parent's well-being and health depended on it. With the extra wages and tips, she would bake bread and take it to the wives and children of the men who frequented the tavern. Fieropa understood that she was enabling the men, but helping the sick and destitute is what the Maker wanted her to do.

That is where she found her hope. She had not always known the Maker. In days past, her father had been the type of man who would frequent *The Black Anvil* and other such establishments. On one such occasion, he had gotten in a fight and was injured so badly he could not work for two weeks. She remembered how she, her mother, and her father had gathered around the table one evening, splitting up the last cake of bread. Her father had pinched off less than a bite for himself before giving the rest to Fieropa and her mother to split. It was then that there was a knock on the door.

Weakly, her father made his way and opened the door. There a man stood, cane in his right hand and basket in his left. A thick fur mantle was draped around his shoulders. She did not know it at the time, but the man was Master Prophet Burd Seon. He entered the home and gave the basket to Fieropa. Inside were twelve hot cakes and dish of butter. Fieropa squealed with glee. She went to bed with a full stomach and the prophet spoke all that night with her mother and father.

The next day, and every day after, her father told her about the love of the Maker and a man called Rhumaiv. He told how Rhumaiv had been sent nearly five hundred years earlier to save the people from the oppressive immorality of the horned Mugaal. Fieropa remembers being overwhelmed with the stories and tales, and she wondered when her father would go back to being the drunkard he was. He never did. The passion and excitement he had toward the Maker and Rhumaiv never subsided.

Now, nearly ten years later, she had that same passion and love in her. In the name of the Maker, she tried every night to show the patrons of the *Anvil* and the people of the Sixth Ward the same love, kindness, and hope that Burd Seon, the prophet, had shown her family. As she looked around at the bar and tables set about the tavern, she saw many lives that needed a new hope. The men were all dirty and haggard and bore the slumped shoulders of a hard life. They were all that way, except for one man.

****

Akosol sat at a corner table. He had found an old gray cloak and put it on, noticing only now that his worst garment was a hundred times nicer than what these misfits were wearing. Part of him hoped he did not stand out. The deepest part of him just smiled. Before he left, he had also rubbed dirt all over his face, arms, and hands. His concubines could scrub him down and cleanse his skin during his late morning bath. At his side and under his cloak, his sword was sheathed.

He set his chair in the corner. He did this for two reasons. One was so no one could sneak up on him. The other was so he could see all the locals drink away their sorrows. Their pain made him feel better about his riches. Their suffering strengthened his pursuit of pleasure. Each of the patrons looked exceedingly miserable, and Akosol could think of nothing but his own desires.

He decided he wanted a drink and ordered three mugs of the ale on tap. He began to revel in the warmth and euphoria of his intoxication. As he drank, he noticed the other barmaid. This was not the one who brought him his drinks. This one was different. To be fair, she was different than any of the patrons of the tavern that night. Behind the smudges of dirt and sweat were eyes that sparkled. Her lips were thin and the corners were continuously raised in a persistent grin. Her teeth were exposed by her smile, and from behind them danced the melodious and infectious song of laughter.

Akosol could not take his eyes off her. In fact, now that he had seen her, he noticed nothing else. The joy within her brought the tavern's patrons a hideous hope, and this upset him. He had come to the Sixth Ward, the dregs of his kingdom, to find strength in the suffering of his people. Her misplaced smile and spirit stole his peace, but her beauty eased his pain. As he struggled through this emotion, the vexing barmaid began to walk his way.

****

Something about the man in the corner unsettled Fieropa. To her, it looked like he was trying to look destitute and out of luck. His garment was dirty but of a fine material. His skin was dirty, but she could see streaks and patches of smooth olive skin from beneath. He sat tall and erect, as if he had never had a day of hard labor in his life. What disturbed her most were the smirks and bridled grins he had when observing the other patrons. Nevertheless, she had made it her mission to offer hope to all who entered these doors.

"The Maker bless you, sir. Is there anything I can do for you?"

****

Is there anything that she can do for me? Akosol let that question play through his mind. He smiled to himself at many of the answers he was rejecting before finally saying, "You could join me for a drink and then let me escort you home. "

"That is very kind, sir," she said, "but I have much work to do and have many other lost souls to serve. Is there anything else I can get you?"

That initial rejection stung the king. He had never been rejected before. At least he had never been rejected in action. He did not know what the concubines felt about him in their hearts, but he did not care. They had a duty, and they fulfilled it when required. He composed himself and answered her next question, this time a little more to the point.

"All I want is you," he said. "Give yourself to me, and I will give you the world."

The young lady was taken aback. The smile on her face fled, but this was not the first time she had received such a blatant advance from a patron. "Sir, how about a few bread cakes to soak up a little of that extra ale in your belly. I'll have Grimsten bring them over."

Akosol was beginning to get embarrassed. He would not be rejected this night. Many thoughts began to swim around his head and most of them exited through his mouth as well. "Do you know who I am?" he screamed at the barmaid as he reached out and grabbed her arm. A hush came over the tavern, and everyone turned to look at the man in the corner. Rage burned through him. "You will come with me. I will have you. Do you think you are too good for me? I have had hundreds of women more beautiful and elegant than you, and tonight I will have you."

****

The man was squeezing her arm so hard, she was sure she was bleeding inside. The pain was severe, and his grip was intense. Fieropa could not pull away no matter how hard she tried. She began to yell for help, but she did not have to. Grimsten was at her side in a moment and shoved the man into the corner. He landed with a curious rattling.

The man began to reach under his cloak, but Grimsten pulled his sword and pointed the tip at the man's neck.

****

The tip of the innkeeper's blade broke his skin, and Akosol could feel blood slowly ooze down to his collarbone. He considered still going for his sword. He was quick and his sword was mighty. The fire within him still raged like an explosion, but as he fought the urge to fight back, a strange calm came over him like the calm that comes with the deepest levels of evil.

In that moment, he considered the righteous life of his father, the former king who feared the Maker up until the day that a stray arrow had claimed his life in a battle. He considered his childhood lessons, and he rejected them. Akosol had an unfulfilled desire. A public swordfight was not part of the solution. He lifted his hands in resignation. These people would pay for their crimes against him in the coming days, but tonight, only the lovely barmaid would suffer.

The king excused himself from the tavern and made his way across the street. Silently and patiently, he waited in the shadows of the unlit streets. The anticipation and yearning for what was going to happen left a heavy feeling in his stomach, but he slowed his breathing to help him through the long hours till closing time. A chill of excitement crept down his spine in a slow wave that made his breath taste acidic. The moment of pleasure would come soon enough.

****

"Would you like me to walk you home, Fieropa?" Grimsten asked.

Fieropa once had been a very stubbornly independent girl, but when her father began teaching her about love, Rhumaiv, and the Maker, she learned to see that receiving help did as much for the giver as it did for her. She was certain she would be fine, but yielded to the offer and grace of her employer.

"Yes, Grimsten, thank you, I would appreciate that very much."

****

In the late hour when most of his kingdom slept, Akosol saw the doors of *The Black Anvil* open for the final time that night. Out stepped the vexing barmaid and the burly, soon-to-be-condemned owner of the tavern. It appeared he would be walking her home. The chivalry and kindness of these simple people made the king sick. No wonder they lived in such poverty. How could anyone get ahead in life when they did not look out for themselves first?

Like a common scoundrel in the shadows, the king followed the two. Sensing their direction, he moved on ahead a block, keeping an eye on their path. He found an open door of an empty home. *More like a shack,* he thought to himself. Akosol removed his sword from its sheath and stood just inside the entrance. To his delight, the lady and her guardian walked right by his door.

Waiting till they were one step beyond him, he quickly and quietly stepped from his hiding spot. In one smooth motion, he ran his sword through the man's heart. The bar maid had turned around when she heard her protector drop, but before she could scream, the king had his hand on her mouth, his blade at her throat as he dragged her into the empty home. Then, in the worst desecration of his authority, he completed his plan.

****

Fieropa lay motionless on the floor, her neck bleeding from the cuts she had received. Her attacker was across the room, pacing and brooding. He seemed to be talking to himself but addressing someone else. In her violation, Fieropa thought that she had recognized the man. Master Prophet Burd Seon had taken her father to the wealthy district once, and Fieropa had gone along with them. There had been a parade that day, and the king was on his weighty throne being carried by fifty soldiers. In front of him danced a hundred scantily dressed girls.

The dancers' eyes were peculiarly adorned with thick dark lines painted horizontally and vertically through each. Another painted line curved downward from the lateral corners. Even now, Fieropa could feel a strange, invigorating passion as she brought to mind the symbolization of those eyes. Her glimpse on that day was fleeting, though. The girls were dancing in such a way that Fieropa's father had found it prudent to cover her eyes with his large, calloused hand.

She remembers peaking between the gaps in her father's fingers and looking at the man on the throne behind those provocative dancers. His face was smooth and beautiful, but there was an evil in his eyes. It was those same eyes that had stared at her this night while the man laughed at his actions. They were the eyes of King Akosol.

In that moment of recognition, her pain and fear turned into righteous anger. How dare the man who sat on the throne of Kadosh commit such a heinous act. As the king paced and brooded on the other side of the room, Fieropa rushed to his sword.

****

Akosol was tormented. What should he do now? Did she recognize him? Would it matter? Anger filled him. The desires that had driven him had all vanished and he now hated this garbage that lay behind him. She was a filthy peasant from the Sick Ward. He felt defiled. He had initially intended to just leave, but he felt the need to eliminate her. In fact, tomorrow he would write an edict to eliminate all who lived in the Sixth Ward.

He had just made up his mind when he turned and saw the girl get up from the floor. With determination and effort, she limped toward his sword. The able king easily beat her to the weapon, and stepped one foot in front of her. With the other, he stepped on her outstretched hand and laughed. Appreciating that she had brought clarity to his decision, he grabbed the hilt of the sword.

A pain like lightning shot up his right arm and into his head. He dropped the sword reflexively, still in its scabbard. His hand went numb, and his whole arm dangled lifeless from his shoulder. He could not lift it or feel it. In shock and fear, he stumbled backward against the wall.

****

Fieropa was dumbfounded by what she just saw but did not hesitate to make her escape. She grabbed the Maker's Sword and pulled it from its scabbard. She pointed the blade at the king and demanded his departure. She was unaware that if any other person had grabbed that sword they, too, would be dead or reeling in pain like King Akosol. What spared her life was that she bore the king's seed.

****

Akosol marveled. What had happened to his arm? Why was this girl still alive? Jettisoning his last ounce of wisdom, he disregarded the sword's first warning and rushed her. She swung the Maker's Sword at his head, but he dodged her first parry. Untrained as she was, that uncalculated swing set her off balance. Akosol took that opportunity, and with his still-healthy left arm reached for the girl. He grabbed her hands, which gripped the sword.

This time he could not let go. The pain rushed up his left arm and into his head. Blindness took him first. He experienced the pain and felt the fear of his lost vision, but the sword was not done. Next it took his mind. He became fey like a wild fox, like a fox without vision. He screamed as a man possessed and began to babble and run into the walls.

****

At the point of the Maker's Sword, King Akosol was forced out of the house by Fieropa. He went running and screaming through the streets, tripping, falling, and ramming into walls.

****

When he was found early that morning, he was half-naked and babbling. His mouth frothed, and he was helpless. His eldest son was made king in his place. Akosol spent the rest of his days in the royal stables, cared for like a blind horse. In his days as king, he had beaten and shamed the stableboys. They treated him with more respect. His son was the first king since Kadosh to be without the Maker's Sword, and the Maker's blessing left the palace that day as well. It dwelt hidden in another home.

****

Following her violation, Fieropa had returned to her home. She was weeping and did not present herself to her parents immediately. Madam Seon was supposed to check on her parents that morning, but her husband, Master Prophet Burd Seon, had come instead. He had been shown a vision of what had happened. He comforted Fieropa and prayed for her. He spoke to her parents and explained the situation and what was to come.

The locals took note of the Master Prophet's presence in their neighborhood that morning. They also took note of his frequent visits in the weeks and months to come. The timing was not lost on many when Fieropa began to show. Many tales were spun concerning the prophet and this unwed pregnant woman.

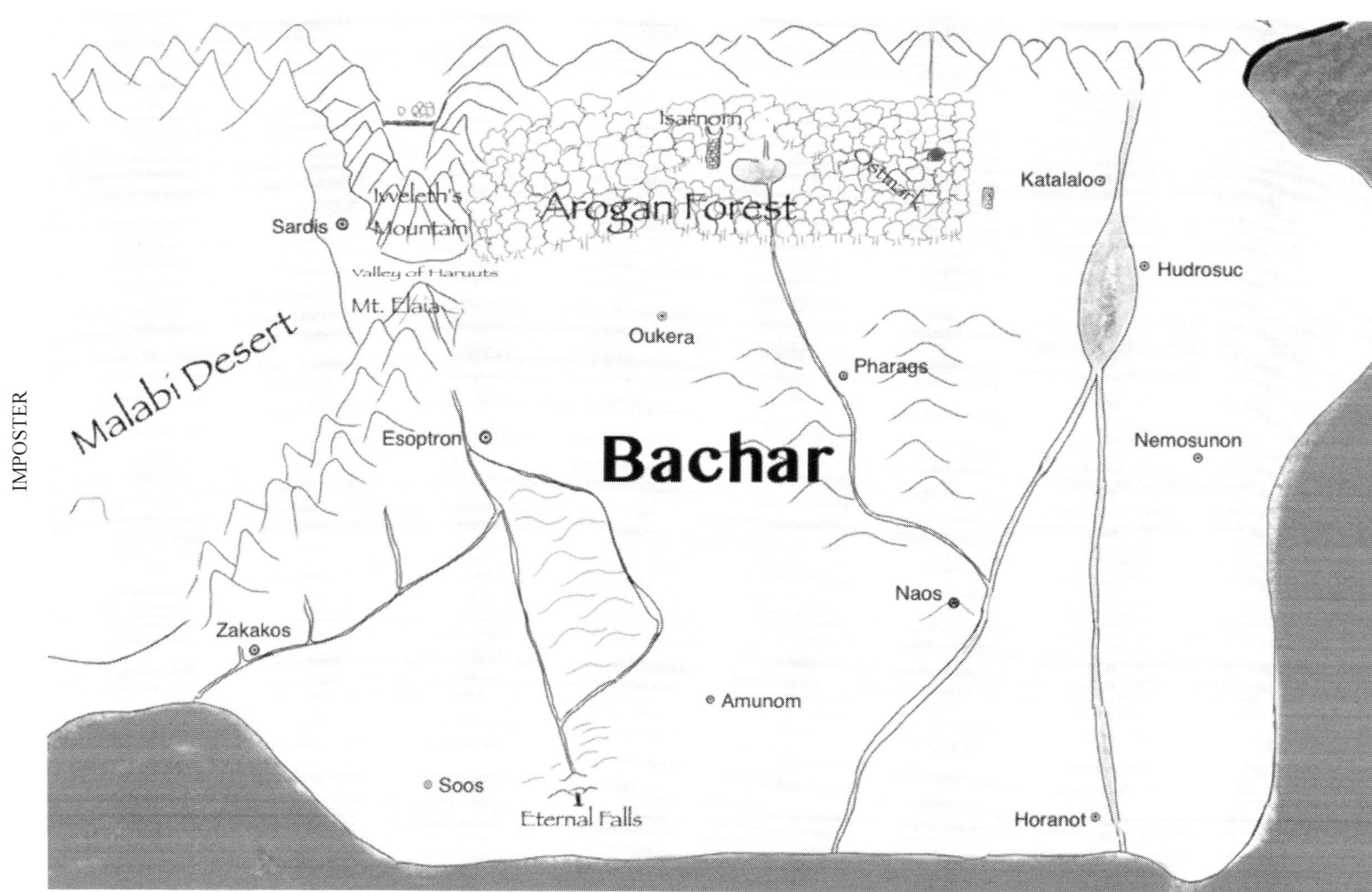
Isarnom
Iweleth's Mountain
Arogan Forest
Sardis
Katalalo
Valley of Haruuts
Mt. Elaia
Hudrosuc
Malabi Desert
Oukera
Pharags
Esoptron
Bachar
Nemosunon
Naos
Zakakos
Amunom
Soos
Eternal Falls
Horanot

1 HOLE

One hundred and three days after the invasion

The being sat on a grand throne. The lights in the room were dim and his face was hidden, all except for a shimmer through the vertical slits of his red eyes. He sat as a king on his throne but did not wear a crown. Instead, he was adorned with the preserved remains of a lion's head. The mandible had been removed and its canines rested on the eyebrows of the presumed king. This was not the head of just any lion, but a white one. By nature or by dye, its fur was like alabaster. The mane was vast and snowy and flowed over the neck and shoulders of the being on the throne.

Beside him, to his right, sat a woman dressed in black. She sat a step lower than the king but held herself with great pride and power. Her hair was as black as a raven and it hugged her pale face.

The king raised his right hand and pointed at the captain before him. His hand was covered by a gauntlet of fur. It seemed to be the actual or fashioned paw of a lion or some other great cat. This time the fur was red, of the deepest scarlet, and the claws extended beyond his most proximal knuckles.

"Send your men through the entire south, to all the towns and villages between the mountain and the lakes." A slight trembling could be heard in the king's voice. He glanced to his left to look at an old man cloaked in a fur mantle. Two officers were detaining the long-bearded man. The king continued. "Cut off the left hand of all males old enough to bear a sword. If you have any doubt of his age, cut off his arm." He looked to the lady at his side who stroked his red right arm in approval.

The king pulled his arm away from his queen and continued his decree. "The quarries of Bor, however, need fresh workers. Take the cages with you. Any able bodied male may be captured, both arms intact, to be put to work in the Pit. Notify me of any that demonstrate the capacity to lead."

"And the women, my king?" The voice of the captain could be heard.

A wicked smile alighted on the ruler's face. "The wives and widows will be left alone." He glanced at his queen, and she returned his wicked grin. "The young ladies and maidens should be brought to the Market."

The captain now joined in those who were smiling. "It will be done as you have commanded, Lord Regeldam. May you reign eternal from your great white throne."

****

"Get up, Onero. Get up now!"

Whose voice is that? Someone was kneeling over him and shaking him by the shoulders, rather violently. Onero slowly opened his eyes. He would have preferred to open them even slower, but the intensity and urgency in the man's voice was foiling that desire. Onero wanted to consider the dream he had just experienced: a white king, a black queen, a red right hand, and amputated left hands. Another hand, the non-dream kind, slapped against his face, forcing him out of that contemplative state.

"Carcasses, Onero, get up! The soldiers'll be on top of us any moment now," the voice barked at him.

It was the voice and intensity of his captain, Wylm Kanu. The word *soldiers* focused his mind quicker than he had intended or wanted. The battle! He recalled a battle, but where were all the warriors? His head was ringing. *Come on, Onero, think. Remember.*

He glanced around. Walls of dirt surrounded him on every side. They rose ten feet high, maybe twelve. They curved at the top toward a narrow opening. Light shone through that opening, providing a limited awareness of his situation. He was in a large hole. Its radius was the length of an average man. Blackness swallowed most of the walls. *Where am I?*

Captain Kanu, his best friend, was still shaking him, and still yelling. Onero listened. Besides the forceful encouragement of Wylm, shouting at him to "get off your sorry butt and look for a way out," he heard the sounds of dying men. The moaning and whimpering of dozens of warriors could be heard somewhere above them. Beneath him he felt the increasingly uncomfortable mound made up of sod, rock, and lumber.

Onero Seon rolled to his knees. That was better. He was glad to get his hips off of the pile on which he had been lying. His head told him that he was not quite ready to stand. *I could stay on my hands and knees all day*, he thought to himself, feeling the pains of the fall that he assumed he just took. In general, he was a few inches shorter than the average warrior, but now felt like he had lost an extra inch or two. Head still ringing, Onero shook it to clear the stars that flitted like gnats in front of his eyes. Dirt flew out of his golden hair which normally fell in waves to the nape of his neck.

Urgency returned to Onero's mind as he saw his friend shuffling and pacing beside him. Wylm was taking inventory of their situation and formulating a plan. His friend had straight brown hair cut short at the neck. His bangs dropped to his eyebrows. Unlike Onero, Wylm was a few inches taller than the average warrior. He was massive in the arms and large in the chest. An arrow was lodged into his left shoulder.

How did that get there? Onero could not recall. *Why won't my head clear up?*

Wylm stepped up to him and grabbed his hand. "Get up, Onero," he said as he hoisted him to his feet. Above them, the wails and groans of dying soldiers provided an unnerving ambiance.

Are those our men? Onero wondered. Just then the sounds of hundreds of pounding feet thudded through the dirt walls. A war cry rang out from an unseen multitude. More than a hint of confidence could be heard in that victorious call.

"Get to the walls." Wylm ordered. "Find an exit point, any exit point. This is Point Zero," he said, pointing roughly east with his open right hand. "You move counter clockwise. I'll go the other way. "

"We have to get that arrow out of your shoulder," Onero offered.

"The Nemarians are nearly upon us. If we don't find a way out of here, we'll both have a collection of arrows in more than just our shoulder," Wylm responded. "Now move."

Of course. The Nemarians. Onero had been part of the last stand against the invaders from Nemar. He could not remember much, but Onero recalled the invasion being very fast and with great purpose, much like the way Wylm was moving about this hole. Onero was now up. His hips and back ached. His friend had an arrow in his arm, so he kept his complaints to himself. "I've found a tunnel alread..."

"Not so loud," Wylm interrupted with a harsh whisper. "Check it, mark it, and meet me at 180 degrees in thirty seconds."

The tunnel Onero had found was roughly at 300 degrees from Point Zero, otherwise pointing north-northeast. It was a very open tunnel shooting off from the hole in which they found themselves. A quick check showed it went at least twenty feet deep, and there was a hint of vitality to the air, suggesting it went even farther. Most importantly, it led away from the battle and to the river and the northeast sea cliffs beyond. He found a narrower passage at 240 degrees as well. His last find was a small opening at 180 degrees. It was three feet high, the width of one man, and seemed to get shallower as it got deeper. A quick check with his sword showed that it did keep going.

"What about that one?" Wylm asked. He was at Onero's side as Onero backed out of the tunnel and came to his feet.

"Not this one, not unless your goal for today was getting a proper burial," Onero reported. "I found a nice open tunnel at 300 degrees from mark. It heads toward the sea and smells like freedom."

"Sounds better than my choices. I found one at 90 degrees, but that would lead us right back to the Nemarians themselves."

"Then the sea it is…"

As they turned around, the light in the tunnel dimmed. The feet of many Nemarian soldiers could be seen around the far side of the hole. An order rang out from one of the soldiers, "Archers ready. Fire!"

Dozens of arrows flew into the tunnel. The nearest ones landed a mere two feet from where Wylm and Onero stood. They were not visible to the Nemarian soldiers above, but they were trapped. Only one option remained: the shallow tunnel.

"Get in!" commanded Wylm.

"But the arrow. You'll never make it in there with that coming out of your shoulder," Onero said.

Wylm grabbed the arrow where it entered his shoulder and broke it off at the shaft. He threw the shaft along the shadowed wall and returned his look to Onero. "Get in. Now!"

Onero dropped his sword, got down, and dove in. Within moments he was on his belly and crawling, the ceiling mere inches from his head. Onero glanced back. Wylm had made it into the tunnel also. Behind him, Onero saw a rope landing on the floor of the hole. "They're in, Wylm."

Wylm looked behind him. His options were limited. He kicked back at the ceiling above their tunnel. Two kicks, five kicks, ten kicks. Finally the dirt and soil began to fall into the entrance. One more kick by Wylm and their hiding place became a tomb. The whole ceiling shifted, and the mouth of the tunnel caved in just as the first set of boots could be seen descending into the hole. Onero could not tell how much of the tunnel collapsed. There was immediate darkness.

"Wylm?" Onero whispered, quieter than he had anticipated. He did not know how well sound traveled through the dirt. "Wylm, are you there?" His voice bounced back to him quickly, bringing with it a stifling silence. With Wylm not answering, Onero came to a sobering realization. He was stuck in a much smaller hole than when he had first regained consciousness.

2 INVASION

Jugel reclined on the slope near the base of the hill. The soft grass provided an ample cushion for his long and lean figure. In front of him, the lake sparkled and glistened as a gentle breeze blew over the waters. The rippling mirror reflected the cloudless sky and the mountain peaks. More specifically, it reflected the snow-capped ridges of Fortress Peak. He loved the sight of those mountains and this peak in general. It meant he was home. He did not travel much, but when he did, he would look back and see the familiar snowy top and think of what he loved most.

What he loved most, just so happened to be lying by his side. The grassy meadow, the shimmering lake, and the majestic mountains were all beautiful, but they were nothing in comparison to Shoshanna. She was his betrothed. In six more days, she would be his wife. They had been lying together on the hillside for many minutes. Shoshanna was cradled in Jugel's left arm. She rested her head on his chest. They were staring at the creation around them. The gentle breeze blew up the hillside and whipped her hair into his face.

He loved her hair. She wore it long like his mother used to. Jugel often wondered if Shoshanna wore it that way for him or for his mother. His betrothed had also loved his mother before her death a few summers ago. In fact, Shoshanna had spent many long days at his mother's bedside, trying to keep the fevers down.

When Jugel's family had moved to town many years ago, his mother had been conspicuously different. She was from the North where hair was worn long. There the women did not work and spent most of their days devoted to their own beauty. When his family moved to the South, it became quickly apparent that Southern women did in fact work. The glory of their hair was a casualty of their labor. It was often cut short to keep it out of the women's faces while they tilled the field or hemmed clothing or helped their husbands put siding on a house.

Jugel's mother was not a vain person, but she knew her husband was partial to her long hair. Not wanting to be thought of as better than others, she worked harder than most women, but kept her hair pulled up while she worked. In time, her reputation supported her, and the other women began to love her. Shoshanna always had loved her, and she modeled herself after Jugel's mother. Jugel did not know if this was the reason he loved her so much or if that was an incidental benefit. Either way, his bride-to-be lay nestled in his arms. He pushed her hair from his face and laughed.

"What is so funny, my handsome warrior?" Shoshanna asked, turning her face toward her lover. "Would you prefer I keep my hair short?"

"If I spend the rest of my life entangled in this bountiful mane, it will be the sweetest imprisonment a husband could want." Jugel grabbed Shoshanna and began to roll across the hillside. Sure enough, he wrapped them together with her hair.

"Now how are we supposed to get out of this?" Shoshanna feigned as if she were a damsel who did not trust her rescuer.

"I have my sword," Jugel kidded.

"You always have your sword. Sometimes I wonder if you love it more than you love me." She did not mean it, and Jugel could tell by the glint in her eye. "Are you going to have it with you on our wedding night?"

"What if we are attacked?" he teased, looking around for a pretend enemy.

"Oh, you will most certainly be attacked." Shoshanna pulled him close, kissed him passionately, and rolled him the other way across the hillside, both laughing as they went.

****

"Wylm?" Onero called for his friend again, begging for a response.

"I'm here," Wylm finally answered. "My foot's trapped, but… There. I'm clear. Can you go?"

"Only one way to find out." Onero began to move. He and Wylm were together again. They were always together, and not merely since the beginning of the war. The two of them were inseparable, but it was not just a military pairing that kept them bound. It was not a life debt nor recompenses either. Rather, they were bound by trust and loyalty and deep friendship. Above all and because of all, they were bound by an oath.

They had been friends and brothers-at-arms since they had begun to crawl. They played together, studied together, and trained together. Swords had been in their hands since coming of age, swinging them at each other as much as at a training dummy. Each had smashed his sword against the other's more than against the enemy's. They had left more dents and marks in the other's shield than the enemy had left in theirs. This was true even after three-and-a-half months of near ceaseless fighting with the Nemarians.

The Nemarians. Onero was finally beginning to remember. With nothing to do except crawl through tight, pitch-black quarters, he began to remember the events that had ushered them into their current situation. Nearly four months earlier, the Nemarians had first set foot on the southern shores of Bachar. In three-and-a-half months of fighting, they had defeated all except a remnant of the Bacharite Army.

Led by their king, Batrachos, the speed and force of this invasion hit like an unsuspecting punch to the abdomen, delivered by an enraged Pytecki. It was said that on that first dawn of the invasion, Nemarian ships lined the southern coast for ten miles. By dusk, they had pressed ten miles inland and spread out along an additional twelve miles of the coast.

The terrible memory of current events was flooding back into Onero's mind. Names and places were whipping through his head. These names and places had seemed very important at the time, but now, as he pressed on, hand-over-hand, knee-over-knee, he wondered if he would ever need to recall these events again. In this hopeless situation, he considered them nothing more than a backstory, one that told how he came to this awful end. Nonetheless, he visualized each detail as it came to him.

On that first day, the Nemarians had overtaken the horse fields of Soos. This act alone crippled the Bacharite cavalry and strengthened the speed of the invasion. Had it not been for the wise actions of the horsekeeper, Sekel Yashar, the whole country of Bachar might have been conquered in only a month. Now it seemed like his actions that day had just delayed the inevitable.

When the Nemarians had come upon his house, Sekel had been in the pasture tending to the stallions. A company of soldiers had stormed his house, with his wife and children still sleeping inside. With only a whip in his hand, he chose the possibility of saving the nameless many of Bachar over the unavoidable death alongside the beloved few of his own household. He had jumped bareback on the fastest horse and rode straight for Naos.

By the next morning, he had reached the Capital. The alarms in Naos were sounded. Battle plans were made. Unfortunately, the majority of the standing army was dealing with a boundary skirmish in the North. It was a full week before the standing army was able to draw any battle lines against the invasion out of Nemar. Batrachos did not wait for them to get prepared.

The great walled city of Zakakos was reached by dawn of day three. The wall was breached at noon on day six. By the time the standing army finally made battle lines at dusk on day seven, they were overrun by the second watch of that night. The Nemarians seemed to never stop. As one battalion advanced, another took its place. By the end of the first week, they had spread fifty miles inland and across the whole breadth of the kingdom of

Bachar. Flying throughout the South were yellow flags in whose center was a large orange oval almost entirely surrounded by a thick black line.

That was week one. Eventually the Bacharite army began to put up a fight and make a difference. It was the difference between warm butter and cold butter against a hot savage knife. Thirteen weeks later, all of Bachar had been conquered except the most northern twenty miles of the kingdom, the plains surrounding the northwest border town of Katalalo.

Onero was glad his memory was coming back to him. Awakening these details brought him some peace. He found it ironic that recalling the destruction of his kingdom and people brought peace to his mind. Considering that he was essentially creeping and crawling his way through a narrow tunnel under layers of earth, he did not scold himself for the thought. Having these memories and thinking upon these things were the only things that kept his mind off the terror of his present situation.

"Are you still back there, Wylm?" Onero called to his friend.

"I'm guessing I'm about ten feet behind you. I would be closer, but you keep kicking dirt in my face," Wylm responded gruffly. "You've no idea how much I'd love to be in the lead right now."

"I'd be happy to stop and let you crawl past me or even over me," Onero answered sincerely. "But I do not think there is room for two bodies at the same point in the tunnel. I cannot tell you how many rocks have scraped against my back. Luckily most of them were smooth. Can you imagine if they were sharp? I probably would have lost a gallon of –"

"Onero, shut up," Wylm interrupted his loquacious friend. "The fact that we haven't died yet means that there's air coming from somewhere into this dank, soil prison. To ensure that you don't waste it all, will you please shut up?"

Shut up. The words of his friend triggered another memory: the memory of how they had ended up in that wretched hole which had led to this miserable tunnel. The Nemarians had been pressing through the whole kingdom. All of the Bacharite army had fallen except for a couple thousand foot soldiers. Those remaining had made their stand in the far north of Bachar in the plains of Katalalo. What had been purposed to be a retreat had become a necessary battle. With the Pantokrator River to the east, the Great Mountains to the north, and the Forest of Arogan to the west, the Nemarian army to the south had hemmed them in.

The battle had started at dawn five miles south of the Watchtower. It was on the same site of an ancient battle that had taken place centuries ago between the armies of Bachar and the treacherous Mugaal of Arogan Forest. The Mugaal had been crafty and industrious in the days of the ancient battle. They had dug many war trenches that were deep and thorough, running from the forest to the river. It was an intricate maze with many tunnels. Years after that ancient battle, soldiers of Bachar had been sent out to fill the old trenches of war.

For some men, who are wicked of heart, when the master is not looking, the work is not done well, Onero thought to himself.

Commander Hamyn Kanu, father of Wylm, had been slain in battle ten days ago. Most of the ranking officers had perished as well. Wylm had been the highest ranking officer left. When the war started, he was captain of a small battalion and loved it. There were no battle plans to draw up, no strategy to be made, only swing, parry, thrust, parry, cleave, then lead the men to do the same. Wylm was good at what he did. Some said he was the best fighter and the best soldier. For this final skirmish, though, Comrade Wylm Kanu had to command the troops in the most desperate of situations.

Onero knew that Wylm had hated the thought of being the commanding officer, but that had mattered little then. The Nemarians quickly outflanked the remaining Bacharites. Wylm had known that hand-to-hand combat was necessary to stay close to their fighters. Otherwise they would have all been eventually taken out by volley after volley of arrows. When the Nemarian soldiers kept coming, Wylm had realized that his men would have to push for an escape route. They would have to overcome either the torrent waters of the Pantokrator River or the deadly shadows of Arogan Forest.

Until six months ago, Wylm had never cared much about scary stories or the supernatural. He had paid them no heed and had found all such tales as a way to intimidate or influence the weak minded. Only after their recent adventure in Embor, had Onero seen even a hint of fear in Wylm. Despite that, Wylm had decided that, even though the unknown haunts of the forest were more survivable, the river was more likely to lead to freedom. The last surviving soldiers from Bachar had made a push toward the Pantokrator River, but they had been cut off and surrounded.

They had been standing side by side on a small knoll in the open field, a few miles south of the watchtower. There had not been a house or building in sight, though there apparently had been once. Small planks of wood could be seen under the torn sod, and this had seemed to bother Wylm. Even as the enemy had begun to circle the knoll, Wylm had continued to glance at the planks. Onero recalled Wylm was curiously far more distracted in battle than he ever had been before.

The battle had been fierce that day, and the Nemarians had seen the fury of Wylm and his men. To avoid more losses, they had set up archers in an incomplete circle around the knoll. They backed away from the twenty-two warriors that remained of the Bacharite army. A final push through the Nemarian lines was not going to happen.

Onero could still see the faces of the twenty men that stood with him and Wylm. Their names were hidden from him, but their faces were vivid. They were grim and full of anger. None of them were yielding or admitting defeat. Onero cringed. He felt shame as he juxtaposed the faces of his fallen comrades with the words he had spoken to Wylm at that moment.

"I will dine with you at the Maker's table this day, Wylm," he had said.

"Shut up, Onero."

"It has been the greatest honor to fight by your side and to count you my dearest friend in life."

"Shut up, Onero. You're not dying this day."

"But Wylm…"

"Carcasses, Onero. Shut your trap, or I'll take you down myself."

At that moment, a hundred archers had launched a volley of arrows in their direction. With his right foot, Wylm had hooked Onero's leg then brought the elbow of his sword-wielding arm against Onero's chest, knocking him to the ground. In his shock, Onero had hooked Wylm's arm and pulled him down with him. When they had landed, there was a *crack* instead of a *thud.* Sod and splinters had risen from the ground as arrows rained from the sky. One arrow had found Wylm's left shoulder. After that, they had continued to fall.

3 ROLLING IN GRAVES

Many years before the invasion.

Yuri Kanu sat at the corner table. The noise of the tavern was louder than usual that night. That was good. It would keep others from overhearing his conversation. Yuri was a grand warrior and commander of the king's army. This night, however, he did not feel so grand. He raised his head. Coming through the doors of the tavern and making his way to the corner table was his dearest friend, Master Prophet Hugla Seon, whose mind and wit was the sharpest in the kingdom. Yuri and Hugla spent as much time together on the battlefield as they did studying the writings and prophecies of the ancient fathers.

Yuri and Hugla were not only friends, but they were also brothers-in-law, husbands to royal sisters. Their wives were granddaughters of the righteous king Emporai, who now rested with his fathers. Both the warrior and prophet had earned his bride's hand to the delight of their father. They had both worked hard to reach the pinnacle of their respective professions, and each had earned their authority by merit and grace.

Now they served under the reign of an immoral king, an impetuous man who lived in contempt of his Maker. He was an angry ruler whose kingdom was continuously crumbling in his less-than-capable hands. In his wrath and folly, the king often condemned the first face he saw after receiving any ill-favored news. Many times that was the face of the Master Prophet. On most of those occasions, Commander Kanu had been charged with the execution of his best friend. Through cunning, wisdom, and prayer, they had been able to avoid imprisonment, banishment, and death, until this night.

"I see you have called me to the tavern again, Yuri. Does this mean you were charged with carrying out my execution yet another time?" Hugla greeted his friend as he took his seat.

"Not exactly," Yuri responded, pushing a mug of beer across the table to Hugla.

"You know that I will not drink that. It could lead to actions unbecoming of a seer," Hugla Seon stated as he looked curiously at the face of his troubled brother-in-law.

Yuri frowned. "Perhaps tonight you will make an exception."

"Now I am intrigued," the Master Prophet said. "I still will not drink the ale, of course, but I am quite intrigued. So go on, my friend, spit it out. What has gotten you so worked up? The Maker has hidden it from me."

Yuri Kanu grabbed his beer and downed the remaining contents. He slammed the mug on the table and reached across to grab the one in front of Hugla. "The chronicler has been reading the histories of our benevolent ruler," Yuri said, speaking the word *benevolent* with an excessive amount of sarcasm. "The master of the guard informed me that your multiple verdicts of execution have been coming up in the readings. The king is enraged over his judgments not being carried out."

"So am I then to be executed?" Hugla questioned, not with fear, but with the desire to gather information.

"No," Yuri replied. "The king has realized that it was I who always stayed your punishment and tricked the king into leniency." Yuri paused. He brought the mug to his mouth and guzzled half that pint as well. "The king has decided to send me on a mission as a reward for my cunning."

"I thought prophets were supposed to be mysterious while soldiers were frank and direct," Hugla quipped.

"Then let me be frank." Commander Yuri Kanu paused again to finish his mug. "Soon I will be heading directly to my death."

"Alright, enough with the dramatics, Yuri. What is this mission that has you so out of sorts?"

"Arogan," Yuri said with a dreaded hush, each syllable carrying with it the inevitability of doom. "I am being sent to the Horned Realm as a spy."

"When?" Hugla asked.

"At the end of the week."

Hugla sat back and thought. He knew this was a futile exercise. No spy had ever returned from the Horned Realm for at least two hundred and fifty years. His being sent to the land of the Mugaal was a way for the king to sentence him to death without showing to the public that he was trying to be rid of him. It would appear to any that knew of the mission that he was honoring the commander of the armies of Bachar.

A chill went across Master Prophet Hugla Seon's neck. He grabbed the goat-skin mantle that lay across his shoulders and pulled it over his head. Yuri had seen him do this before and what came after was usually amazing. Hugla's eyes were closed, but Yuri did not rush him. Slowly the prophet raised his head and looked at his friend.

"I and my descendants will guard and protect the life of you and your descendants above all others, save the king."

"Hugla, you have always been there for me. I do not doubt your loyalty. What do you mean by these words?" Yuri was confused by the proclamation of his friend. To be honest, he had expected some proclamation of judgment on the wicked king, or some oracle of victory for himself. He was in no way expecting what he heard.

"I will go with you to the Horned Realm. I will bear my staff alongside your sword." Hugla looked with love into the eyes of Yuri. "The words I speak are dear to my heart, and apparently dear to my spirit. The House of Kanu is a great house with a remarkable future. The House of Seon is honored to call you our friends. We will be even more honored to make your name great. The well-being of the house of Kanu will be our burden and our privilege."

Yuri was touched by the words of his friend. He felt the same passion of loyalty and devotion that Hugla had just expressed, and he had just downed two pints of beer in the past ten minutes. "Your words have touched my heart, my friend, and to you I return them. I and my descendants –"

"Yuri wait," Hugla tried to stop his friend from making a rash oath, but a Kanu is not easily swayed once he has made a decision, especially when he has had too much ale.

"Do not try to be more honorable than me, Hugla. These words are also true to my heart." Yuri paused and recalled the phrase. Hugla no longer tried to stop him. "I and my descendants will guard and protect the life of you and your descendants above all others, save the king."

****

Crawling and creeping through a pitch-black tunnel was beginning to take its toll. Time was lost. Direction was lost. All that remained were the inches in front of him and the friend behind him. Onero could not remember ever being in such utter darkness. Even in the blackest nights, there is always some light once one's eyes have adjusted. Now there was nothing.

The severity of the darkness began to play tricks on his mind. He marveled at the extent that hope was related to light. As he pressed on, hand-over-hand and knee-over-knee, the perpetual thoughts that had kept him distracted were beginning to wane. Dread and dismay began to invade his soul like a Nemarian onslaught. He had to keep moving. He had to keep thinking. If he did not purposefully keep his mind occupied, then nothing could help him. Fear would surely overtake him much quicker than the servants of Batrachos overtook his beloved kingdom of Bachar.

For the past five years, since he had been expelled from the House of Prophets, Onero had learned to manage his own thoughts. When his mind was quiet, he would quickly sink into gloom. With perpetual positive thinking and mind-building exercises, he was able to keep a positive outlook on his life. He made it a practice to keep his mind busy with useful things. This helped him shut out the depression that stalked him, and it helped him to remember the many things he had learned during his days of training.

For most of his childhood, he had studied the Writings and Prophecies. When his father helped Fieropa and hid her secret that she had borne the King's child, Onero's whole life changed. He and his father were shunned from the House of Prophets. They were banned from the books and scrolls that only the prophets were allowed to read. Onero had mourned the fact that Maker would no longer speak to him, a prospect that he had eagerly been anticipating.

Now that Onero had been ostracized, he spent many hours recalling and reciting the words and stories of the ancient texts. No longer having access to the writings, all Onero had was his memory. So he kept his mind busy to remember those words and to prevent himself from dwelling on his unwelcome fate. The fact that his life was torn away from him challenged his belief in what was right. That unrest in his soul kept him perpetually on the brink. When he was not speaking or purposefully thinking, unwelcome thoughts would slip past his defenses and he would all too quickly sink into depression.

As Onero considered his tendencies to plunge into despair, he came upon a gap in the wall to his right. "The tunnel splits off here, Wylm. What should I do?"

"What're our options?" Wylm asked.

"Straight or right?"

"Stay straight. Always go straight," Wylm answered in a lecturing tone. "Don't you remember anything I've taught you? If you branch off, you forget your purpose and set yourself up for going in circles and losing your way. You know how I hate it when a person deviates from what they've set out to do, from what they've promised to do. 'I and my descendants…' You know the rest."

That last phrase was supposed to be a jab towards Onero's father, but Onero ignored it. The war had been too fierce and the battles too often for Wylm to have previously made these biting remarks, but in the nothingness of this tunnel there was nothing for him to do but to think and brood. Onero hoped this would pass. If Onero tried to argue, it would just take too much energy and would anger his friend. Wylm was not a person whom you wanted angry unless you were on his side.

If Wylm was anything, he was purposeful. Just like he had said, when he made a plan or made a promise, he would not deviate until goals were achieved and all was saved. The two of them truly made a great team. Onero appreciated all that Wylm had done for him. If there was one person in the entire world with whom to be trapped in an unpleasant situation, it was Wylm.

Their current situation was not the first adventure they had experienced. Onero had fought bravely by Wylm's side on multiple occasions and had even held his own, but there was no greater fighter in all of Bachar then Wylm Kanu. Onero knew it. Wylm's late father, Commander Hamyn Kanu, had known it as well. No one else seemed to observe or appreciate what this young man was capable of doing.

Onero knew very well what he could do. He had gotten into many situations over the past five years where the only thing that stood between him and death was Wylm Kanu. Whether it was nature, beast, man, giant, or witch, Wylm Kanu gave up his well-being on at least five occasions to save the life of his only friend. Onero would have done the same for Wylm, but Wylm never needed saving.

Despite all that Wylm had done and all the adventures and adversaries he had overcome, he had never risen in the ranks of the Bacharite Army like his father and grandfather before him. His father's friends did not like Wylm. He was crass with his words and arrogant with his speech. If he disagreed with a decision, he verbalized his opinions without regard to the politics or emotions in the room. Wylm thought only of the problems before him and the steps necessary to overcome the problem.

He did not care for politics or diplomacy. If a direct order went against what he thought was right, he would disobey it. Wylm used to argue his side with well thought out points, but commanders and dignitaries spoke too much of appearances and the art of not being offensive. Over time, he no longer made his case. He would simply make a plan and carry it out.

It got to the point that many captains and lieutenants, as well as senators and governors, insisted that Wylm be expelled from the army. The only reason he was not was that his father, Hamyn Kanu, was in charge and loved him. More than that, Hamyn believed in his son. Onero knew this by the importance of the missions Wylm was given. However, Wylm never heard those necessary and deliberate words of encouragement from his father, and judging the heart of a person was not Wylm's strong suit.

So Wylm was sent to the Borderlands in the southwest of Bachar beyond the walled city of Zakakos. There he and his men patrolled the nefarious lands that bordered the Malabi Desert and the Realm of the Pytecki. More than once they intercepted messages or halted the illegal trafficking of goods or people. Many parents of young girls were eternally grateful to Wylm and his men for their effective deeds. It is not known what the Pytecki clans do with these daughters of men, but during that time many were saved from the hands of Bachar's most wicked residents.

Though his methods were effective and his victories praiseworthy, the demeanor of Wylm Kanu was difficult for his soldiers to handle. Never did he offer compassion to any of his men. If a soldier had a death in the family and wanted to go home to bury his dead, Wylm would not allow him to return to the squadron. "The dead are dead, and there's no longer any hope that you can give them. Your nation needs you right here, right now. If you're willing to betray your nation over the death of your mother, then I don't want you," Wylm would respond.

If a soldier came back from battle with a grievous wound, Wylm would lecture him the whole time he was bandaging the wound. "Why didn't you dodge instead of parry?" Or he would say, "Didn't you see the size of that tree? Didn't you consider that would be the best place for someone to ambush from? Why weren't you considering the plan of our enemy? If you can't see the whole picture, what good are you to me?"

His men did not love him, but they respected him. He was always victorious. He never lost. He never received a grievous wound. He always saw the whole picture, at least in the immediacy of their situation. Wylm also lived by his words. When his mother died three years ago, he did not leave his command. He did not shed a tear for her until he returned to Zakakos during his leave three months later. His soldiers saw this and gave their all for him. Men do not have to love their leader when they are winning.

Onero was different than those soldiers. He actually loved Wylm. He and Wylm had been friends ever since he knew what a friend was. He recognized all of Wylm's flaws. He knew he was a broken man who craved the spoken blessings of his father. Perhaps that is why he felt for him more in the late years than in the innocent years of their youth.

The former Master Prophet, Burd Seon, was always encouraging. He told Onero often that he loved him and was proud of him. Even after the scandal five years ago, he still spoke love despite the shameful words the nation piled on him. By mouth or by letter, Burd Seon told of his love for his son and his love for his Maker. The second part baffled Onero, but it was because of both that Onero still had love for his difficult friend.

At one point, Wylm had been exceptionally detached from the emotional needs of his men. One of the soldiers had died from a snake bite during a long pursuit of an elusive band of human traffickers. Wylm had declared that there was no time for mourning and no time for a burial. The soldier who had died had been his most tenured and loyal warrior, aside from Onero. Every man left him that night, except Onero. Onero always stuck with him through the best and the worst. Wylm never thanked him for staying, though. He never thanked him for anything.

"Okay, Wylm, straight it is." Onero bypassed the tunnel to his right. He was surprised that he was holding himself together. *Keeping my mind busy has been really helping*, Onero thought to himself. He wanted desperately to talk to Wylm, but anticipating Wylm's response kept his words in check.

Wylm had been more caustic and irritable than usual. Having never been a lover of small talk, it had made him especially irritable since the recent death of his father. This was not entirely surprising. Most sons are broken up after the deaths of their fathers. Unfortunately, Onero had borne the brunt of Wylm's anger. He knew why, and he knew it was not his fault. The occasional friendly conversations they used to have had become almost nonexistent. Here in this tunnel, he figured the less he spoke to Wylm, the less snarling he would have to endure from his contentious and injured friend.

The other reason he had not been speaking was to conserve air. That fear was fading though. For as long as they had been in the tunnel, they had not felt faint nor felt the struggles of air hunger.

In the darkness, cramped as they were, Onero could not tell what time it was or how long they had been crawling. He suspected it was three or four hours at least. The question nagged at him for a little while before he finally decided to break his silence. He decided to forego his previous hesitations and speak to the lighted ale-grenade behind him.

"What time do you think it is, Wylm?" Onero asked. His voice was weaker and higher pitched than he had intended.

"You're finally speaking again, huh?" Wylm responded with a non-answer. "I think you've just set a personal record for longest amount of time without attempting a conversation. Were you conserving air or just trying to avoid me biting your head off?"

"Conserving air, of course," Onero gave a partial truth. That was the trouble with having a life-long friend. They know everything about you, including what you are thinking. "But I figure since we made it this far without difficulty, the available air must be sufficient."

"You'd better speak for yourself when it comes to *without difficulty*," Wylm retorted.

"What is the matter? Is it the arrow? Is the pain too much?"

"No, I was referring to my air quality."

Onero was now concerned about his friend. "Perhaps you are losing a lot of blood. I learned that when the body loses too much blood the ability to perform activity lessens, leading to shortness of one's breath. Do you think you have lost too much blood? Do you need to stop? I can attempt to dress the wound. It will be difficult to maneuver in this space, but we cannot lose you down here. That would be –"

"Shut up, Onero. Carcasses! Shut up." Wylm shouted his exasperation. "It's not the tunnels. It's not the loss of blood. It's you. You are the reason for my poor air quality. You are reminding me of the reason I chose to not join the charioteers. You should consider more vegetables in your diet."

Onero laughed. It felt good to laugh. *When was the last time?* he wondered. Wylm joined him, and for a few moments they enjoyed a lighthearted chuckle.

"Five hours," Wylm said.

"What?"

"My guess is we've been in this tunnel for five hours," Wylm clarified. "While you were busting through barriers of personal silence records, I was counting and timing my steps, so to speak. I'm guessing my right knee is moving forward twice every three seconds. For one hour, according to my timing, I didn't do anything but count. I'm guessing we've done that one hour span five times."

"You are remarkable, Wylm."

"I know."

"So how far do you think we have gone?" Onero pressed.

"By my calculations?"

"I would not trust any other."

Onero meant that. Wylm was amazing at strategy and as nimble with an equation as he was with a sword. Over the past few months, his tactical calculations had been exceptional, even in the thrall of battle. Onero considered for the first time that this improvement seemed to happen right around the time Wylm stopped sleeping so well. He wondered if the two were related.

"I figure every time my knee goes forward is one foot, so every time my right knee goes forward is two feet from where I started." Wylm was just now working this out. "I'm estimating my right knee advances twice, or four feet, every three seconds. It seems we have kept a fairly steady pace since we started… so we are likely going eighty feet every minute. That is 480 every six minutes, and 4,800 feet per hour."

"So at five hours –" Onero was trying to help with the math - "that would be, uh, two zeroes, then ten, and carry the four."

"About 24,000 feet," Wylm grunted out the answer, showing evidence that he was beginning to struggle.

"What's wrong, Wylm?" Onero asked. "Is it the arrow?"

"Yes, but I'm fine," he answered. "I'm guessing we've crawled about four and a half miles, if my estimations are correct."

"Do you think we are still heading west?" Onero questioned. He knew that all Wylm could give him was mere speculation. It was impossible to know in what direction they were heading or even if they had been down here five hours, two hours, or two days.

"I'd guess so," Wylm answered.

Onero considered this for a moment. "I do not know whether to feel hope that we are potentially getting somewhere, or to lose hope since there has been no exit or escape in all this time. Of course, that is assuming there is an exit to this thing. Do you think we should have taken one of the side paths? What if one of those was the exit?"

"Just keep crawling, Onero." Wylm's voice did not reveal any sign of hope. In fact, he seemed to be a little more labored in his speech. Each sentence began with a small grunt, which was seemingly necessary to expel the remaining words. "What was it you said on the battlefield? You 'will dine with me at the Maker's table'? Forget that. We may be crawling all the way to Ivveleth's Mountain. We may end up eating breakfast with the evil queen herself."

"Don't talk like that, Wylm. That's not funny. "

"Maybe we'll go farther than that. Maybe we'll make it to Sardis. Maybe we'll find where your father is hiding."

Onero did not want to hear it. "Stop it, Wylm."

"They had an oath!" Wylm interrupted. He would have been yelling, but the fatigue of the day and the wound to his shoulder had taken its toll. "He left him, Onero. Your father left mine. For how many years was he by his side? How many years of peace did your father *protect* mine. Then the war came, and he abandoned him. He up and ran. Our grandfather's would roll in their graves."

Wylm was not finished. "'I and my descendants will guard and protect the life of you and your descendants above all others save the king.'" He recited the oath. "Guard. Protect. The *honorable* Burd Seon ran away, Onero. Your father took his mistress and ran. He left my father to die alone on the battle field. He should have been there." Wylm's words were slurring. "He should have died with him. He should have…"

The pause was accompanied by the abrupt *thump* of Wylm's head striking the dirt. Onero could not turn around, and even if he could, he could not see through the blackness. He paused and listened. He could hear breaths, but they were shallow. Surely the wound to Wylm's shoulder had finally completed its task.

4 OATHS IN THE DARK

The hot metal glowed a deep red in the blazing furnace. Heat blasted back toward them. It was hotter than normal. Young Goor watched as his father turned the blade in his hand. This was going to be the finest piece in the collection. Another few days and it should be completed.

"Why is this one taking so long, Daddy? Why is it?" Goor asked as he handed his father a rag soaked with ice-cold water from the spring.

"This is a special sword, my son," his father answered. "It is for our coming king, the great Shachal." He set the blade on the anvil, wiped the rag quickly over the severely heated metal, and then made two deft strikes of his hammer to shape the blade. Promptly he returned the piece to the furnace.

"When is he coming, Daddy? When is Shachal going to set us free? When is he?" Goor took the rag and dropped it back in the bucket. The water was already becoming too warm. He would have to run to the spring to get more.

“I believe soon, my son. The prophecies do not say for sure, but I think soon.” Goor’s father verbalized his hopes. “I do not believe he will tolerate this current imposter much longer.” The blade was heating up again, nearing the perfect glow. “I need you to freshen the water now.”

Goor grabbed the bucket and ran deeper into the cave where the cold spring waters flowed out of the rock. He thanked the mighty Shachal for this gift of a home: a hill that gave both a fiery furnace and an icy spring. He ran as fast as he could, trying not to spill the water. Two things spurred him on. First, he loved spending time with his daddy. Even greater, he loved hearing stories about Shachal.

Goor rushed into the room where his father was working and placed the bucket on the floor beside him. “What makes you think that Reg—“

“Do not speak that name, my son,” Goor’s father stopped him. “That imposter is a worthless being, not deserving of having his name spoken, let alone to be sitting on the throne.”

“I’m sorry, Daddy. I am. ” Goor hung his head.

“My beloved boy, you are not in trouble. You meant well, and your heart is pure toward Shachal, our savior.”

“Thank you, Daddy.” Goor decided to try his question again. “How do you know that the Imposter is not Shachal? How?”

Goor’s father pulled the blade out of the furnace and set it on the table beside him. He pulled up a stool, sat, and beckoned to his son. Goor ran over to him and sat on his lap. “Let me tell you about our lord and our god.

When he returns, you will know it is him because he will be white. Shachal was always set apart from all others because of his appearance."

"Is he huge?" Goor asked in wonder.

"The stories say he was larger than most when he first reigned, but that may have been tales exaggerated because of the greatness of his deeds." Goor's father grabbed his face and gently turned it toward his. "When Shachal returns, he will not be what you expect. All that the prophecies have told for sure is that he will come from the mountains, he will be white like the snow, and his courage will know no bounds."

"I hope he comes very soon. I hope."

"If he does, young Goor, you must serve him with all your heart. All of your devotion must be towards him. You must make his name great, and in return, he will do the same to yours."

****

Onero rose up on all fours. The tunnel was higher here than at other points. He searched his tack: no rope. Of course there was no rope; they had dressed for battle, not adventure. Options ran through his mind, but there were not many: drag Wylm as far as possible along this progressive tomb; leave Wylm and save himself; or stay here with Wylm and die together as friends.

I and my descendants will guard and protect the life of you and your descendants above all others, save the king.

It was not a difficult decision. Only the logistics were proving to be a challenge. Without rope, how could he perform the task? The answer came to him. It was unfortunate, but the best option. Onero backed up in the tunnel and took some relief in his discovery that he could back up overtop Wylm at this point in the path.

With legs outstretched, straddling Wylm, and his right arm extended, hand by Wylm's head, Onero reached his left hand under his face-down friend, grabbed Wylm's tunic by the right shoulder, and rolled him onto his back. If he was going to move his friend's body along the tunnel, Wylm's face and wounded shoulder could not be dragged through the dirt. Next, he loosened Wylm's war belt and inched it up under his arms.

Wylm's body was prepared for transporting, but now Onero needed a rope. He began to take off his own boots and trousers. This proved to be the most difficult part. Despite being higher than most other places, the tunnel still limited his ability to comfortably slip out of his clothes. Finally he got his trousers off but could no longer reach his boots. Trying not to waste precious energy, Onero crept forward, took one pant leg and tied it around Wylm's war belt. The other leg he tied around his own.

Now came the test. Onero crept forward in the tunnel to restart his journey. He did not get far. Wylm's unconscious body stopped him in his tracks. Onero tried again and put forth considerably more effort this time. Finally they moved. Always the scholar, Onero's mind traveled back to the science lectures from his days of education. He knew that if he did not stop, it would be easier to keep going.

The long, difficult crawl became even more difficult. And he did not know how much farther he had to go. Onero plodded along. Each movement was a struggle. He could not stop. Wylm's life was waning. He took his mind off despair. He prayed for strength, and then twenty-one words marched repeatedly through his mind.

I and my descendants will guard and protect the life of you and your descendants above all others save the king.

They had heard a rumor ten weeks earlier that the former Master Prophet, Burd Seon, Onero's father, had been seen leading a small company westward. Burd was seen entering the house of an alleged harlot. He left the house moments later with a young boy in one arm and the prostitute holding his hand trying to keep up. She carried with her a small bag and a long object wrapped in linens and strapped to her back. Many eyewitnesses reported the trio stopped by a few other homes before hurrying off to the royal stables. The horse master, Sekel Yashar, was there. He gathered a dozen horses and outfitted the haggard bunch.

Reports and rumors stated that Onero's shunned father placed the young boy on the largest stallion then hopped on behind him. Sekel Yashar bowed before the master prophet then sent them on their way. Burd Seon, the boy, the prostitute and ten others headed west toward Mount Elaia and the Valley of Haruuts, then Sardis beyond that. So what had begun as a scandal four or five years earlier had escalated.

The whispers on the street had gone like this: Burd Seon, Master Coward; Master Prophet has illegitimate son; the prophet and the prostitute. Had the war not been so intense, surely the whole kingdom would have been discussing it. The disgrace and humiliation of the Seon name would have worsened. *They already excommunicated me*, Onero thought. *What more could they have done?*

Sekel Yashar had come to Onero as a messenger. He had found him one week later with Wylm and his battalion. They were on the front lines defending a strategic valley twenty miles from Naos. Onero recalled watching the horse master leave the tent of Commander Hamyn Kanu before coming to him. He handed Onero the already open note, gave him a hug, and then rode quickly to the west. Onero read the message. "*I've gone to Sardis … save the king*".

Onero considered the words as he continued to crawl. *Save the king.* That was the part of the oath that had Wylm in a fit. He did not realize that Burd Seon was doing just that. Onero's father had left his place on the battlefield beside Commander Hamyn Kanu to save the life of Fieropa's son, the heir to the throne. When the horse master, Sekel Yashar, bowed in front of Burd, he was really declaring allegiance to Fieropa's small child who had been seated in front of Burd.

Wylm did not know this, nor could he ever find out. Onero's father was a man who abhorred secrets for the rot that they cause in those that keep them. Yet, he had insisted that "no one on this side of the Great Mountains" could ever be told that Fieropa's son is the true heir to the throne of Bachar. "The future of Bachar depends on it," he had said. Dutiful son that he was, Onero kept the secret. In less than two months, that secret was already eating at his closest relationship. Much in the same way the scandal that this secret ignited ate at his mother's health, leading to her early death three years ago.

I and my descendants will guard and protect the life of you and your descendants above all others, save the king.

An oath is an oath and should not be stated flippantly or contemptuously. So Onero would keep it even if he did not understand it. Why did their grandfathers include their descendants in the oath? Did they have the right to do that? Their sons, Burd Seon and Hamyn Kanu were also dear friends and repeated the oath on their own accord. Ultimately the same was true for Onero and Wylm. What Onero wondered, though, was whether the oath of one man was truly binding on the actions of that man's descendants?

That was the second to last purposeful thought Onero had in those tunnels. The strenuous demand on his body, stifled air, and lack of food and water had finally culminated in complete fatigue. He collapsed. He did not even attempt to pick himself back up. He had progressed to absolute exhaustion and had not left even the chance for a second effort.

Despite the blackness that already surrounded him, things still became dimmer. One final thought drifted through Onero's mind before he succumbed to the inevitable: *We will end the day better than our brothers-at-arms. At least we will be buried, buried together, the way it should be, Seon and Kanu.*

5 A GOOD TRADE

The warrior took his stance in a valley between two peaks. His sword was gripped tightly in his right hand. He stood like a man devoted to a cause, like a lion defending his pride against a challenger. He gritted his teeth and let forth a roar of challenge to his unseen foe. The ground shook in response. His ancient enemy was approaching.

A seasoned fighter, with a moment before battle, he checked his gear. In his right hand he gripped a sword, a plain blade of the strongest metal, its hilt wrapped in leather. It was perfectly balanced in his hand as he twirled it in a deft circle. In his left hand was a wooden staff, a little taller than a man. He spun it over his head and snapped it back to his side. He checked the simple helmet on his head. It was without dent and without shine. Its only marking was an unknown symbol at its front. Sitting secure atop the helmet was an ornamental crown of a brilliant rare metal, within which was set a precious stone, blue and glistening like the clearest sky. The warrior followed the light of that stone, but still the enemy did not present itself.

Battle not yet upon him, he continued his process. Across his shoulders, fastened with a simple button, was a shaggy fur mantle. Around his neck was a gold necklace with a small vial, its contents appearing dark red. He tucked the vial under his war tunic. Next the warrior repositioned the leather gauntlets around both his wrists. They were stained a dark green and etched with the same symbol that emblazoned his helmet. Last of all he, felt for his shield, which he had secured behind his back. It was a simple round shield, covered in red leather. He ran his finger over the leather, still moist from its recent oiling. Satisfied with his gear, he did not bother with the other sword that was fastened along his back under the shield.

Suddenly the ground trembled again causing the warrior to snap to attention. The mountain peak across from him began to quake. Then it burst. Rocks and stone became deadly projectiles, and the air filled with dust. Darkness began to descend upon the warrior. Clouds of dust pulsated around him, kicked up by some unforeseen force. He shifted his stance to brace himself, for even before the fighting started, he was already losing his footing.

Then the sound started. It began as a shrill cry of evil piercing the air. Quickly it turned into a victorious cry of freedom as if from some wretched beast, chained for millennia, now finally escaped. As the warrior reset his feet, the pulsing air stopped, and for a moment, the sound paused. Then, through the darkness, from merely feet away, a loud guttural taunt bellowed from the evil that stood before him. The noise shook the warrior and he closed his eyes at the sulfuric smell that escaped the lungs of his foe.

****

His eyes opened. At least he thought they were opened. It was dark. Of course it was dark. How long had it been dark? How long had the air been stale? How long had it been since he could stretch his arms and legs? He had to keep moving.

He was on his back. Onero reached up. The ceiling could not be found. He reached down for the belt that was connected to Wylm. It was gone. How far back did he lose him? He remembered dragging his friend until fatigue, and then he did not remember anything else. He had to find Wylm. Onero rolled over to get off his back. For a moment, he fell. The sudden impact and immediate pain in his head, elbow, and knee told him he was no longer in the tunnel. Onero took a deep breath. The air was fresh. The room seemed open except for the table on which he had apparently just been lying.

Where am I? Where is Wylm?

Onero further explored the room, his hands stretched out before him, searching through the darkness. It was a small room, but after spending a day or so in the tunnel, it felt huge. The walls were about eight feet apart. On one side was a windowless door without a knob or handle on this side of it. Across the room was what felt like a boarded-up window. Onero felt a tarry substance applied along the seams, presumably to block out all light.

A dark, dank tunnel for a dark, dry prison cell. *A good trade,* thought Onero, but not good enough. He was relieved that he was wearing his pants, but his boots were seemingly still in the tunnel. Going to the window, he knocked on the boards. They were thick and felt strong. His fist and elbow would not withstand the assault. He searched the room for a stick or weapon. Nothing. He felt around his ankle for his hidden knife. It was gone. He gave a high kick to the boards. Not a budge. Two more kicks. Nothing. His feet throbbed.

Suddenly, there was a commotion outside his door, someone yelling, boots scuffling. There was an intense *thud* against the door, and it flew open. Onero had to hop back to avoid the door catching his nose as it swung toward him.

"Onero?" It was a one word, part question, part command, that could be translated, "Onero, if you're in there, then speak up and get over here. We're in grave danger." Onero knew that tone anywhere. Standing in the door was Wylm Kanu. His shirt was off. As Wylm turned to glance back into the hall, Onero could see the birthmark of the Kanu family centered on his left shoulder blade. The darkened skin resembled a sword and a shepherd's crook forming an '*X*' about a square inch in size. Despite their unknown time in the tunnel, Wylm's chest and torso were clean, as was his face. Fresh upon his left shoulder, higher and lateral to his birthmark, was a carefully placed bandage.

"I am here, Wylm," Onero responded immediately. "I see you have escaped captivity again. Does that make three times or four?"

"Five," Wylm replied. "You forgot about our scouting trip to the desert. And I see you were getting comfortable with your new surroundings again. Yours is the fifth door I kicked open. Thank the oath I found you when I did. We don't have long. I released a few other prisoners while looking for you, so that may buy us some time."

"Thank the oath," he had said. Did that mean he would not have come looking if they had not pledged loyalty to one another. Onero chided

himself for even thinking in this way. Wylm came for him, did he not? And there were more pressing things to worry about, like escaping.

Wylm waved Onero toward him. Onero followed. They took a left into the hallway. The light was dim, and neither one had any idea whether they were getting closer to escape or deeper into their captivity. Onero considered the other prisoners. They would know which way to go, or at least they would provide a distraction and cover.

"Open the other doors," Onero suggested to Wylm then told him his plan.

"Smartest thing you've suggested since the war began." Wylm was never the most uplifting of leaders. For the majority of their lives, he and Onero's conversations had often been laced with excessive sarcasm and playful taunting. However, since Burd Seon escaped to the West with his small caravan, Wylm's mood did not allow him to receive the same level of teasing.

They began kicking open doors on either side of the hallway. Most of them had prisoners; none of them were Men. They were Mugaal, every one. At the first door, a large Mugaal approached the threshold. Like all Mugaal males - they had never seen a Mugaal female - he had large horns, about six to eight inches in length, which pointed skyward. They emerged from the side of his skull, above his ears. He had thick untamable hair that was more like a goat's than a human's. His nose did not come to a point and drop drastically to his upper lip, but the portion around his nares gradually progressed into his upper lip. It was difficult to tell where the nose stopped and the lip started. Finally, his beard hung long and distinct from his chin. Mugaal did not grow full beards, as their hair typically grew only on their chins. This one's was long and poorly groomed.

In a matter of two seconds, the Mugaal's countenance changed four times. First he had a look of cautious hope. Then, upon seeing his saviors, looks of anxiety and hatred wrestled across his face. Finally, upon seeing that his freedom was unhindered, the deep-set eyes and furrowed brow of self-preservation took over.

For each prisoner they released, a similar response was received. "Don't let your guard down, Onero. All we need is for one of these wretched Mugaal to decide we're not friends, and we'll have a fight on our hands."

Overall, the plan worked. Wylm and Onero followed carefully behind the many newly-freed prisoners. When a guard or soldier could be heard detaining the escapees on ahead, the two of them would pause or duck into a room for cover. Eventually, they made it to the anteroom, just inside the main gate. It was locked, of course. There were now three prisoners at the main gate, trying to break the lock.

Five Mugaal guards came from behind and surrounded the unarmed prisoners. One of them was the large Mugaal who they had first set free. The guards rushed the prisoners, but the large one's quickness was as great as his size. He relieved the guard of his sword and, with the help of his fellow escapees, soon did the same with the other guards.

"Where's the key?" the large Mugaal demanded. Each guard held his tongue. "Get me the key now, or one of you won't be going home to his family tonight." The guards still remained speechless, and in response, the large Mugaal kept his word and eliminated one of the guards. At the sight of their friend motionless on the ground, the other four hurried to the guard's room and grabbed the key.

From there, the three Mugaal prisoners escaped unhindered and headed south out of the gate. As soon as they left, the remaining four guards sounded the alarm. That was Wylm and Onero's signal. They rushed from their hiding spot, blasted through the guards who were beginning to shut the gate, and headed north, opposite the escaped Mugaal.

6 AROGAN

The prison where they had been held was deep in the eastern portion of Arogan Forest. The Mugaal called that area the Ostmark. Very little was known about Arogan or any of the Mugaal Realm. A treaty was made long ago declaring that the citizens of Bachar would not cross into the forest, and the Mugaal would not leave the forest. That accord had been kept until four months ago when the Horned Army had made raids along the northern border of Bachar.

Over the years, a few heroes of Men had made attempts to scout out the forest, but most were never heard from again. The last known successful escape from Arogan was hundreds of years ago when the Mighty Three of King Kadosh had marched into the realm to retrieve an heirloom for the king. Those deeds of legend are well told among all the children of Bachar.

The forest was thick and difficult to traverse. Onero and Wylm both wished some weapon had become available during their escape. After going a mile or two, they paused briefly to make a plan. Ducking behind a particularly massive tree, surrounded by rampant undergrowth, they discussed their circumstance and listed out their options.

Onero started. "I have no boots, you have no shirt, and we both are weaponless." He bent over to pick up a long branch off the ground, and then pulled off the twigs to make a staff. "I am pretty sure we are in the Ostmark. I got a brief glimpse of one of the mountain peaks through the branches, and it was a peak that overlooks the eastern realm. Going south just takes us back from whence we came. To the west and north are more Mugaal. To the east we should find our freedom. It cannot be too far until we get back to the open fields north of the watchtower."

"All true, but going east is no good," Wylm replied. "At the speed of the Nemarian invasion, they've surely pushed much farther north already. As far as we know, they'd not yet invaded east of the Pantokrator River and the best place to ford is in the far north, about ten miles south of the mountains. There's one point in the river where an army could ford fifty abreast. East will bring us sure captivity, and I don't feel like making it six escapes any time soon."

"Then let us make our way west." It was Onero's turn. "If we can make our way to the edge of Arogan Forest, perhaps we can get through the Valley of Haruuts or even up over the mountain ranges north of Ivveleth's Mountain. Perhaps we can make it to Sardis."

"Curse Sardis!" Wylm barked. "I am not interested in Sardis, a refuge for cowards and harlots. I am not interested in seeing your father." He paused and brooded, and by the look on his face, Onero knew not to interrupt him. "And your father does not want me to see him either. Curse Sardis and curse your father. Curse the coward!"

Onero had enough. In one quick move, he brought his simple staff around and swept Wylm's legs, knocking him to the ground. The motion continued fluidly as he brought the same tip of the staff to Wylm's throat as he lay flat on his back. "That is enough about my father, Wylm." He could not defend his father completely since that would require full disclosure. "You do not know what happened. You were not there. But you and I have an oath, and I am right here, right now, by your side. And nothing will break that oath." He dropped the staff from Wylm's neck, turned around, and began to walk away. "I will never break my oath."

Something struck him in the back of the head. Onero wheeled around in a defensive stance. A pinecone came hurtling at his face. He deftly batted it away. Wylm was laughing. "Passion. Finally. Now come get these briars out of my back." Onero went over and helped him up. They had been best friends essentially since birth. This was not the first time that an impassioned fight was over and done in the matter of moments.

"Forgetting my anger for the moment," Wylm spoke calmly as Onero pulled more than a dozen thistles from his shirtless back, "Sardis is really not an option. Even if we made it into the west, the Nemarians have surely passed through the Valley of Haruuts by now. The fear and superstition that reportedly halted their forces between Mount Elaia and Ivveleth's Mountain are only hindrances, not barricades. It's doubtful that Sardis still stands. Even if it did, the Mugaal are keen and industrious. No man has survived a visit to Arogan since the Three. The chance of making it to the west of the Horned Realm is slim. Our only chance is to attempt to traverse the Mountain to the north. We are fortunate they haven't yet found us."

He did not know it, but Wylm was speaking a lie at that very moment. They *had* been found. A scout, named Getala, had been watching and listening to them. He was the best of scouts and personal assistant to General Hamaraz Hywel. Considering their situation, these two escaped prisoners would need to raid the nearest homestead for clothes, boots, and perhaps provisions. It just so happened that the next home to the north of them was that of the General.

Keeping low, Onero and Wylm made their way north. The call of a bird chirped from a tree close behind them. Wylm lead the way in hopes of trampling any thorns and barbs for Onero, who was still bootless. Anxiety began to rise in Onero's chest. His breath felt metallic, his hair stood erect, and his senses increased in acuity. The forest was quiet, too quiet. Wylm was being more cautious, more hesitant that Onero had ever seen.

Onero was beginning to feel overwhelmed, beginning to panic. Watching Wylm skulk through the forest was not helping. If the greatest warrior he knew was leading the way in fear, how was Onero supposed to feel? He was just a shunned prophet, needing rescued more often than the princesses in the children's tales he used to read. He knew he had to quickly get his mind thinking about something else, or he would become unraveled, even if that something was the very thing that caused both he and Wylm's apprehension.

He thought back to his readings, the books and scrolls he used to read before that privilege was stripped from him. Onero recalled the teachings about the Mugaal. They were an industrious people, skilled in the mind as much as in strength. Compared to men, they excelled in these two areas, but they lacked heart and soul. History or myth told of Mugaah, one of the grandsons of the first father. He was the brightest and quickest of his brothers and felt he could overcome any foe by the skill of his might. He listened little to wisdom and relied merely on his own abilities.

One day, he was hunting with his brother in the forest that is now called Arogan. Mugaah had ventured onto Ivveleth's Mountain, a forbidden place, where Ivveleth herself had been imprisoned at the dawn of the world. As soon as Mugaah stepped foot on the base of the mountain, she called to him from deep within his heart. In his lust and pride, he rescued the evil Lady of the Night. She transformed him into his idolatry and gave him horns of strength. He took her in marriage and had many children. They were called the Mugaal.

Over the centuries, they had been a thorn in the side of the patriarchs and ancestors of the Bacharites. At one point, almost five hundred years ago, the Mugaal had nearly destroyed Bachar. With the help of the Lady of the Night, they had intermarried with men and seduced a large population of Bachar. It was the lowest point in Bacharite history. Hope had never been so sparse. Despair had never been so prevalent. Never, that is, until this latest invasion by Batrachos and his Nemarians.

In those days, over a half century ago, a man had come out of the desert, west of Sardis. His family had escaped to there when the Mugaal first began to reign in terror. The man came back with his uncles. His mother was known, but no one could tell of his father. The man's name was Rhumaiv. Armed with the nine tools of the Creator, he approached the Mugaal. However, instead of fighting, he handed himself over to them. In their immorality, they sacrificed him to Ivveleth somewhere deep within the woods of the Ostmark.

It is said that at the moment of his sacrifice, a shockwave went out into the entire world. Nine out of every ten Mugaal were instantly destroyed, as well as all of those beings that were part Man and part Mugaal. The prophecies suggest that one like Rhumaiv will come in power to rescue the people in the last days. Some believe it will be Rhumaiv himself.

The ten percent of Mugaal that survived renounced their worship of Ivveleth. Instead, they worshiped their own might and creation. They cut down much of the central forest and quarried rock from the mountains to the north. With these materials, they built the city of Isarnorn. Three hundred years ago, the Mighty Three of Kadosh brought back word and description of this great city. It was a hand-crafted marvel unlike anything a Man had ever seen before or since. They said its beauty rivaled the sight of snow-tipped Mount Elaia against a deep pink sunset.

In the midst of the city of Isarnorn is a tower of the same name. The greatest mathematicians in Bachar predict its height around five hundred feet. It is the home of King Bardaz Berogeis and his family. Some say the Mugaal king watches over his entire Realm from atop the tower. It can be seen from Naos and Zakakos on a clear day.

Besides their city and buildings, the Mugaal are also rumored to have made many great weapons of war, although none had ever been seen south or east of the forest. The northern districts of Bachar often tell of explosions along the mountain faces in the Horned Realm. It is assumed the Mugaal are testing their great weapons.

Three hundred years ago, nearly two hundred years after the Day of Rhumaiv, the righteous King Kadosh of Bachar set up his kingdom. His army was great. It was at that time that Kadosh and the then ruler of the Horned Realm made a border treaty. In those days, the Mugaal people were relatively few in number and their imagination and labor had gone solely into the splendor of the city and tower.

Onero's anxiety was beginning to subside. As he followed Wylm with greater peace, he continued to meditate on the people of the Horned Realm. If it was true that they had such great weapons of war, what kept them from attacking Bachar? Surely they were not a righteous people. The Bacharite army had been weak for at least twenty years, ruled by impotent and immoral men. Onero considered it a miracle that the Mugaal had kept to the treaty for three hundred years.

Finally, Wylm and Onero came upon a homestead. The home was large but simple. It was built closer to the trees than Onero had expected of a Mugaal home, especially due to its size. It seemed that someone of importance lived here. They had expected that all people of affluence and status lived in the great city of Isarnorn. A hundred feet or so beyond the house was a clearing. The trees were noticeably thinner, and more light came in from that direction.

Their trek through Arogan required speed and stealth, but a stop at this house was a necessity. What they needed were boots and a shirt. If they came easily upon a weapon or food, then their situation would be better still. Wylm chose a window on the second floor.

"If I were to build a house, I'd put my bedroom window there," Wylm said.

The logs that made up the outer walls were easy to grasp and the window was open. Onero considered how easy it was to break into the home of these overly trusting Mugaal. The room was unpopulated, and Wylm had proven to be correct. They found clothes and boots that were close enough to a fit. Wylm found a knife under the bed. Things were going so easily that they decided to not push their luck and forego the risk of getting food.

Shod and clothed, they headed back to the open window. A small contingent of horned soldiers could be seen approaching the house about a hundred feet away.

"Carcasses," Wylm spat. "We've been found, and I think they saw me. Get moving. We've got to find another exit."

They rushed out of the room and tried the doors on the other side of the hallway, but they were all locked. The only other option was downstairs. Wylm and Onero dashed down the hall with respective knife and staff in hand. They bounded down the stairs, four to five steps at a time, till they came to the first floor. At the bottom of the steps was the sitting room.

There, directly across from the stairs, were two occupied chairs. For a moment, Onero only noticed the person in the chair to his left. He was a chiseled and foreboding Mugaal in full military dress. Flanking him and guarding every door were armed warriors of the Horned Army. Onero glanced over his shoulder back up the stairs. There stood a Mugaal scout with an arrow nocked and aimed between Wylm's eyes. They were surrounded again, outnumbered and poorly armed.

Onero turned to Wylm. "If I get the shortest one by the door, can you take the rest?"

7 THE WHITE LION

With a quiver of arrows over one shoulder and his unstrung bow in his hand, Kahya kissed his wife and walked out the door of their simple home. He considered it a perfect home. It had a kitchen, a sitting room, and two small bedrooms. Ideally, his four children would all share one room while he and his wife slept in the other. In fact, that is how nights normally started, but eventually at least one of them would end up in his bed nestled in beside his wife. Kahya would pretend to be jealous, but the children demand their mother. He yielded every night, relishing the fact that they adore their mother so much.

"Thank you for this here good life," Kahya said aloud. No one was with him. No one was near him. Besides his wife and his children, that was his favorite companion: *No one.* There was not much he enjoyed more than solitude. He walked down one side of the ravine, jumped across the creek, and climbed up the steeper far side. He loved having a home on the slope of the ravine, near the life-giving waters of the mountain creek. The folks in town called it a gorge, but they were prone to exaggeration.

The town sat within a wooded area, with a narrow forest road leading to it, but the trees and underbrush in that part of the forest were not thick. Kahya considered that a domesticated wood, and that was not good enough for him. He needed to be deep in the forest. That was where he found peace, being close to creation. There was something about the simple way of the forest with its massive trees and abundance of wildlife. He preferred this setting. He preferred the simplicity of relying on the gifts of creation and the skill of his hands. Hunting in this forest made him feel like his first forefather, Emabbir.

Kahya sat on a stump and set his quiver beside him. He pulled out one arrow and inspected it from point to feather. The remaining arrows received the same assessment. This was his ritual, never trusting that his past works would ensure his future quality. "Them there is some good arrows," he pronounced over his projectile of choice. Then he grabbed his bow and strung the horse-hair cord. The string had been a gift from his father, who had recently moved to the capital after Kahya's mother had died.

Footsteps rustled in the distance behind him, approaching quickly from the other side of the ravine. Kahya nocked an arrow and turned slowly. The noise was far enough away, and he did not want to draw attention to his position. What he saw put his mind at ease. One of the women from town was running toward his house.

Feeling fortunate that he left the house when he did, Kahya turned around. "Nothing worse than hearing those town women babble," he said to himself. "It's like they never have nothing to do."

Kahya did have something to do, though, hunt. There was nothing like a good hunt. Today's was going to be different than others. Rumors had spread that some foul beast had been seen close to one of the nearby homesteads. It was not any game or domestic animal that anyone had ever seen. From what the forester described, it may have been a bear, but no bear had been seen in these parts for a hundred years. "It can't hide from me," Kahya said to himself.

As he considered the details his neighbor had told him of the beast, his wife called to him from the house. She beckoned him to come home. No fear or anxiety could be heard in her voice. This was unlike her. She was not the kind of wife who always tried to keep her husband at home. She recognized the role he played and let him be the husband he needed to be. That is why her call was subtly alarming. "No way she's calling me in to listen to that there town gossip."

He made his way back to the house, leaving his full quiver and now unstrung bow just inside the door. The woman from town was in a chair in the sitting room, a cup of tea in her hand. "Mornin', ma'am. May the strength of Emabbir find you this day," he resigned a greeting to his guest. His wife was standing beside her, holding their youngest child and bouncing up and down on her toes. Kahya wondered if the bounce was to calm the baby or in response to the visit.

"Come in here, Kahya," she beckoned. "A letter came in from your father."

Kahya's father, Kesheth, had been tired of forest living. When his wife died, he found himself unwilling to do all the things necessary to maintain his home. Desperately lonely and overwhelmed, he went on a vacation to the North. While there, he found the women to be most appealing, with long flowing hair and skin untarnished by physical labor.

Before long, he found himself working in the king's castle as one of the guards in the throne room. The king had discovered his skill with the bow, and after being made to prove himself, Kesheth had been rewarded with a well-paying job, the wife of his choosing, and a servant to manage their home. Every so often he would send a letter home. It would arrive in town and someone would run it out to Kahya.

Kahya walked to his bride, and she handed him the sealed roll of paper. Slipping his knife from his belt, the forester cut through the seal and unrolled the expensive parchment. He read the note slowly. Reading always came slowly for him, having never spent much time in the classroom. He was an uneducated man in regards to books and words. His intelligence came through tales and stories and through big green eyes that saw what most people missed.

He furrowed his brow, rolled the letter again, and turned to the woman from the town. "Thank you, ma'am," he said. "Your efforts are much appreciated. Have a great day."

"Kahya!" his wife scolded him. "Don't be so rude."

Kahya tried again. "Begging your pardon, ma'am. That there is a beautiful dress. I hope your tea was to your liking. Now, can I walk you out?" Kahya was a polite and kind man, but he needed to be alone with his wife and that as soon as possible.

The woman from town was quite offended and did not hide her disdain. "Well I never…" she started as she handed his wife her cup of tea and walked out of their small house, slamming the door behind her.

His wife was irritated and embarrassed. "What has gotten into y—?"

"Sit down." Kahya was not the kind of husband that interrupted his wife. He loved and cherished her, but this was too important for a petty argument. "Just sit down."

She obliged, still angry, but she had never heard him speak to her like that. Kahya read her the letter, struggling through most of it. His wife listened in shock, hand over her mouth for much of it, her mind racing many times, causing her to miss some words. When he was finished she spoke up. "Did he say he was in the room when the prophet spoke?"

"Yes, ma'am."

"Do you think it was the same prophet that was… you know?"

"I can't say for sure, but I reckon so."

"Do you think your father will get in trouble if anyone finds out he sent that letter?"

Kahya did not answer that question. His silence spoke loud enough.

His wife halted her anxious interrogation. She always questioned the wisdom of her father-in-law's decision to move into the North, but Kesheth did not deserve what he was surely about to suffer. There was one more question about the letter, though. There was something she thought her husband missed. "On the bottom of the letter, there was one more word. I don't think you read that last word. What does it say?"

Kahya unrolled the paper again and sounded out the word in his mind. Immediately his stomach churned. "Run. It says RUN."

****

"Again!" the king bellowed from his throne.

The guard drew back his whip and flogged the shirtless male before him. The one being punished let out a cry. He held his hand up to the king for mercy, whimpering as he did.

"Again!" the king said, never one to be considered merciful. He was fed up with the ineffective work of his advisors. There had been a revolt at the labor camp yesterday. The prisoners were tired of their care and treatment. They had banded together to overtake their captors and escape.

They had killed five guards and injured ten more. Before anyone could stop them, thirty prisoners had begun their climb out of their incarceration. Only at the last moment had some archers arrived to stop them before they had reached the level ground. Twenty prisoners had died. The other ten had retreated to their confinement.

At the foot of the king's throne knelt the advisor of forced labor, the one who was supposed to manage these things. This fool begged for mercy. His poor plan had led to fifteen less guards and twenty less prisoners. On top of that, the remaining guards had beaten the other ten prisoners so much that they would be useless for another week. More workers would be coming soon, but the need for laborers was now. None of this was helping his plans, and it angered him.

"Strike him again!" he commanded again, then turned his words at his advisor. "You are a fool. Have you no respect for me? Have you no respect for my glory? Must I manage every decision in my kingdom?" They were all rhetorical questions, and he expected no answer. The only response his advisor had to give anyway was a broken whimper.

"Here is what you will do starting tomorrow," the king declared. "Increase the archers on the walls. Make a lesson of anyone who even feigns rebellion. Lengthen the work days. The prisoners will not have the energy to even think of escape. Finally, take special care to ruin the life of Bor's most recently acquired prisoner, since he has taken it upon himself to try to ruin mine." He looked to his guards. "Drag him out of here."

The guards obeyed, leaving a streak of blood across the stone floor. The throne room doors were opened, and another pair of guards brought in another being awaiting the king's judgment. His face was bloodied from interrogation. The guards cast him at the foot of the throne.

"This is Kesheth, one of your throne room guards," the guard on the right proclaimed.

"I know who he is," the king said. "What is the accusation?"

The same guard continued. "Three nights ago, you cast out of this very throne room an ill-speaking prophet, Lylyth curse him. You then made proclamations regarding his profane oracles. That very night, Kesheth was overheard discussing his opinion with another. He said that he thought the king's actions cruel and unjust in ordering the maiming and dismemberment of so many of his subjects."

"How do you know this?" the king asked. "To whom did he make this proclamation?"

"To me, my lord," spoke Bagad, the guard on the left. "I am the one he told, and there is more."

"Go on."

"I and some other guards went to his house to arrest him for words of treason against you and your judgment," Bagad continued. "When we arrived, we saw paper, pen, and an ink jar on his desk. There was also evidence that he had used his seal. There were drops of fresh wax on the top of his table. We questioned him as to whom he had written. He told us he was writing a letter to his nephew, who lives in the northwest of the kingdom near the land of the Roes.

The king was getting annoyed at this lengthy explanation. "And what is wrong with that?" he asked impatiently.

"In truth, your excellency, Kesheth is from the southeast foothills," Bagad answered. "He has a son who still lives there. He talks about his son and his grandchildren often."

"How do you know this?" the king questioned.

"Because he and I have been dear friends since he came to Kefeer ten years ago."

The king stood from his throne. "Is this true, Kesheth? Does a member of my personal guard betray me by sending warning to his son in the South?"

Kahya's father stood silent before his accusers. Often he regretted not getting to see his grandchildren grow up, and he missed his son and his lovely daughter-in-law. Today, though, he had no regrets. Today he knew that sending that message on his fastest horse would be the salvation of his family.

“Do you not answer your king?” the question bellowed forth with increasing rage. The king had risen and descended the steps until he was standing directly in front of Kesheth. “Bagad, take your knife and slit this traitor’s throat.”

Bagad hesitated. He was loyal to his king above all his friendships, but being the one to execute his best friend was not what he had anticipated.

“Do you also dishonor your king? Would it help if I reminded you of the reward for catching and reporting a traitor? You will have the wife of this traitor and another of your choosing from the Bride Market.”

Those words from the king were all Bagad needed to hear. Loyalty to his relationships had always been important, but loyalty to his king and, more importantly, his own status, weighed heavier. He considered how his status would improve with the addition of two more wives. Long he had turned his eyes on Kesheth’s wife with her dark brown eyes and long tawny hair.

In his lust, Bagad slit his best friend’s throat.

King Regeldam approached and smiled. “You have done well, Bagad. Now continue to please me and go to the prison in Bor. There you will make sure that my special guest does not forget his words against me.” He took his red right hand and ran it across the throat of Kesheth’s lifeless body. With a wicked grin, he brought the bloody finger to his mouth. “Let it be known that this is what happens to any who betray the White Lion."

8 A GRACIOUS DEATH

The immense Mugaal in the chair in front of them sat tall and erect. He was adorned in formal military dress. There were three braided cords off his right shoulder and two off his left. If Wylm had guessed correctly, the Mugaal was likely a general. He was larger than Wylm, but not as large as the Mugaal they had help escape from prison earlier that morning.

The lady beside him was of middle age. Onero had never heard or read of any Man's description of a Mugaal woman. If this lady was any representative of Mugaal women in general, then they were beautiful creatures. Judging by the lady's example, female Mugaal do not have horns. Their hair is not coarse and shaggy, but rather long and thick on their heads only. Her nose, however, set her apart from the women of Bachar in that it did not meet abruptly with the upper. However, it did not blend into the upper lip like a Mugaal male. It was somewhere in between.

Onero and Wylm each considered their options and independently came to the same conclusion. There was nothing to do but stand there and take what was coming to them. They surveyed the soldiers around them and the archer behind them. Not one of them was making a move. Realizing that the soldiers were under orders not to take aggression, first Wylm then Onero turned to face the one who would have given those orders.

As he sat in his chair, the general displayed the utmost confidence. He was obviously older than either of them, but looked like he would not back down from any fight, even being unarmed as he was. "My name is General Hamaraz Hywel. This is my wife Tamaz. Welcome to our home."

Is this really happening? Onero wondered. He and Wylm had just broken into this person's home, endangering his family. Did he now really welcome them?

"We were twelve hours from having this meeting anyway, but the sons of Men are a hasty breed. Master Commander, you will find your shoulder to be well healed and carefully sutured. My servant, Getala, has your last dosage of medication to prevent infection. He is the one behind you, with the bow."

Wylm turned to look at the scout, who acknowledged Wylm with a wink. Wylm was not amused.

"Your faithful servant will find his boots beside him there at the bottom of the stairs," the general continued gesturing to the spot three feet from Onero where, sure enough, his boots sat.

Wylm chuckled at the *servant* reference; Onero was dumbfounded at everything else. They were both speechless, which was fortunate, since the general was not done speaking.

"Thanks to your antics, we lost a good guard today at Libbiorn Prison. His wife and family have been informed, and benefits will be given. We shall erect a pillar in his name." The general bowed his head for a moment, then again looked at the two perplexed men in front of him. "You came into Libbiorn three days ago. We did not bring you to the prison. You came to the prison."

The general paused a moment to let those words sink in then continued. "In our preparations for war with the Nemarians, we came across a secret tunnel in the prison. I sent my servant, Getala, to check out the tunnel. Four hundred feet in, he came across Master Servant, followed by Master Commander. Master Commander woke up two days later, even with infection setting in. Very impressive, sir," he said turning to Wylm. Then looking at Onero, he continued, "And Master Servant awoke on the third day. You were both nearly recovered and ready for your journey."

The questions had multiplied, and Onero could no longer hold them back. He did not know what to ask, but that had never stopped him from speaking before. He opened his mouth to see what would come out. "What journey? Who are you? Why are you being so kind? Why are you so freely telling us Mugaal secrets? Do you really think you can defeat the Nemarians?" Then he paused, feeling no better for having displayed such exasperation in that mindless flow of words.

The general looked to his wife, then looked back to Wylm and Onero and smiled. "I will answer all your questions, although maybe not to your liking and definitely not in the order you asked. My name, as I said, is Hamaraz Hywel. I am general of the Horned Army. As important, I am the devoted husband of my wife and the loving father of my son and two daughters."

At the mention of his daughters, Onero glanced around the room and saw two young ladies along the back wall of the sitting room. They were the most beautiful women of any race he had ever seen. The apparently older of the two was looking directly at Onero and held his gaze for longer than a glance. Onero was not used to this sort of attention from attractive females. It was Wylm's physical prowess that drew attention among the maidens of Bachar. Onero blushed and grinned, completely forgetting the words of the general for a moment.

General Hywel saw this reaction and recognized the cause of Onero's distraction. "Jutta, take your sister and go to the other room." The seemingly older sister grabbed the hand of the younger and walked through a wide opening on the side of the room to Onero's right. She grinned sheepishly as they went, looking embarrassed but not ashamed. Then she stole one more glance at Onero.

Wylm saw this and quietly burned within.

The general looked back to Onero, who was blushing much more than a moment ago. "Now that you have met my daughters, I will continue. Three of your questions will be answered with one story. You see, we Mugaal are great and powerful and are afraid of almost nothing. We are, however, afraid of your god. Our people have not forgotten the Decimation of Rhumaiv five hundred and twenty-three years ago. The devastation was inexpressible and our elders have made sure that it is not forgotten. In fact, there is a clearing less than a mile to the north that stands as an eternal witness to the sacrifice of Rhumaiv."

"Because of this fear of the power of your god, manifested through Rhumaiv, my people signed a border treaty with your people three hundred years ago. We have kept to this treaty, all the while increasing our military power. We have been biding our time, waiting for a new enemy to arise or for your kingdom to fall from the grace of your god." The general was a fine orator and expressed himself as if he had been rehearsing these words.

"When the spies of Batrachos came, King Bardaz Berogeis, lord of my people, believed the opportunity to advance our kingdom had finally arrived. He knew of the rebellion of your recent kings and believed that your god was no longer with you because of their immorality. He therefore was not afraid to break the treaty. He conferred with the Nemarian emissaries and purposed to cause a border skirmish, thus distracting the Bacharite army in the north of your country as Batrachos swept across the South."

General Hywel answered many of Onero's questions, but one still remained: why was he so freely telling Mugaal secrets? Onero did not have to ask again, though.

"Again, you must be wondering 'why is he telling us all of this?'" the general continued. "The answer is complex and simple. We are afraid to kill any Man. The last time that we killed a Man who entered our kingdom – that being Rhumaiv—ninety percent of our pure brethren were destroyed. We are afraid to kill any more. Nonetheless, we cannot send men back to their kingdom once they have seen our secrets. So we send all captives through the Mountain Pass to the lands of the far north. The pass is guarded heavily by the people of that kingdom and, thus far, all expeditions have ended amidst the mountain. This may be a death sentence, but it is death by another's hands, not death by the hands of the Mugaal."

This struck Onero as peculiar. There sat the general, who appeared to be hospitable and gracious, yet he announced to them their impending death.

He had the arrogance to presume that Wylm and Onero should be grateful that their deaths would not be dealt by the Mugaal.

The servant, Getala, came up behind them and handed Onero his boots. To Wylm he handed his shirt, freshly laundered, along with his last dosage of medication. *Why are they concerned about infection if he is supposed to be dead before he gets to the other side of the mountain?* Onero vexed.

Wylm had been reading between the lines, seeing past the grand speech of this presumptuous Mugaal before him. When he realized that the general had no intentions of killing them personally, he transformed from a surprisingly grateful guest to a boorish, obtuse nuisance. "May your kindness and hospitality come back to you four-fold when the Nemarian army invades your land, kills your women and children, and burns your forest to the ground. May they provide you with a cold, dark cell where you can lie shirtless, while healing from your wounds." Wylm feigned refinement, trying to sound just as pretentious as the general.

"Your manners are unwelcomed here, Master Commander," General Hywel tried to interject, but Wylm was not finished."

"My name's Kanu, Wylm Kanu, and this man with the staff isn't my servant, he's my friend, Onero Seon."

"Did you say Kanu and Seon, warrior and prophet?" The general glanced to his wife then back to Wylm.

"I did not say 'warrior and prophet', I said 'man with a staff'. And if you are done interrupting me, Hamaraz, I will continue." Wylm's words amused Onero. The general had gone too far with his smooth tongue and had irritated the most irritable man south of the Great Mountain. Normally Onero would have been considering how he would have to smooth this situation out, but this time was different. He was particularly enjoying this rant.

Wylm continued with a near growl. "The Nemarian army has been battling my fellow Bacharites for over three months, and we haven't so much as slowed them down. They'll annihilate this kingdom as well, and there'll be fewer survivors at the hand of their brutality than there were at the grace of Rhumaiv."

The general's patience was thinning, but his pride was not. "The Mugaal will not be defeated. We have prepared three hundred years for this opportunity. Victory will be ours. I swear it."

"On your daughter?" Wylm challenged.

This caught the general off guard. It caught Onero off guard as well. He looked to Wylm, but Wylm was staring directly into the soul of General Hamaraz Hywel. The general's wife put her hand on his arm. General Hywel brushed it off. She looked to her daughters, who had snuck back to the large doorway. Anger toward this brazen man burned in their countenance, but as their father delayed in answering, their anger began to turn toward him as well.

Wylm was not yet done. "If you are so confident in the Horned Army, swear on your daughter. Jutta, is it?" Wylm asked, turning his eyes to the older of the two girls. The look of the younger daughter to her sister confirmed he had chosen correctly.

Hamaraz Hywel was furious. He had entered the confrontation with great confidence and poise and had these two men on their heels with curiosity, but this man had challenged him and his ideals in front of his family, servant, and the most loyal contingent of his army.

An oath should never be made flippantly or hastily, or in the heat of passion, but General Hywel made one nonetheless. “I swear on my daughter, Jutta, that the Mugaal will crush Batrachos and his Nemarians.”

Silence. It was only for half a second, but if felt like a minute. Tamaz Hywel slapped the face of her husband and stormed through Onero and Wylm on her way up the stairs. Jutta Hywel went running back out the side door, her sister following her.

The general stood, flames dancing across his eyes. “Getala, prepare them for their journey,” he commanded as he approached, stopping when his nose was two inches from Wylm’s. Wylm was still armed. “And let him keep the lady’s knife.” He then marched to their right into the adjacent room, but his shoulders slouched as he passed under the threshold.

9 EYES OF FIRE

Wylm and Onero were outfitted with proper attire, a tinderbox, and three days ration of food. Onero was allowed to keep the staff he had fashioned in the forest and Wylm was allowed to keep the knife. They were set on two horses and were surrounded by a contingent of the Horned Army's best horsemen, armed to the horns. Getala, the scout and servant to General Hywel, was to go with them.

"Wait," came a call from the house as Getala was giving final orders to the soldiers. "Wait, Getala." Jutta Hywel was running from the house. She approached Getala and put her soft hand on the neck of his horse. "Wait, Getala, I have something for the exile."

"Does your father know you are here?" Getala questioned her gently. Wylm heard the sound of hidden adoration in his words.

"My father does not even know I exist," Jutta expressed sharply, casting an ill look at Wylm as she said it. Wylm grinned. Her beauty mesmerized him, and the unraveling of her father delighted him.

Jutta then approached Onero. She reached behind her neck, unlocking the clasp of her necklace. Then, with both hands, she reached it up toward Onero.

"Thank you, my lady," Onero said, but as he reached for the necklace, she pulled it away. It took a moment before he realized she intended to put it around his neck. Wylm groaned audibly. Onero bent forward on his horse, but still could not get his head low enough to reach Jutta's outstretched arms. He climbed off the horse and stood before her.

As he stood only a foot from her, he was taken aback by her beauty. He had expected that being this close to her would expose features that betrayed perfection. Instead, the opposite was true. The attraction he had felt from across a room paled to what he was experiencing at this moment. Even her smell reminded him of the wildflowers that grow in the meadows south of Zakakos.

Jutta stepped closer and placed her necklace over his head. The pendant was four horns intertwined to look like a flower. Jutta grabbed his hand "So you will always remember that, even though it looks otherwise, there is goodness and beauty in Arogan that is still redeemable." Jutta leaned forward and kissed Onero on the cheek, then quickly turned and ran back to the house.

Speechless, Onero looked at Wylm.

"If you don't mind, I'd like to ride off to our deaths now," Wylm said, eyes burning through Onero. He was clearly annoyed by what had just transpired.

After a few hundred feet of riding, they entered an expansive clearing. The Mugaal referred to as the Decimation of Rhumaiv, the result of the death of Rhumaiv over five hundred years ago. About a mile in diameter, it was a large circular void right in the middle of the dense forest. There was no vegetation. Even the trees on the edge of the expanse lacked limb or leaf facing the inside. The ground was scorched and parched, with large dry cracks from the ground contracting upon itself. In the very center of the void was a small circle of life, three feet in diameter. The spot was overwhelmed with lilies in bloom.

"Those flowers bloom year round," explained Getala. "Snow never falls on this sacred spot where Rhumaiv was slain, not even in the worst of winters."

Getala paused and closed his eyes as he sat on his horse. He tipped his head. Onero was surprised at the deference that this Mugaal showed toward the one that was slain here.

Onero wondered about the title of *Decimation* that the Mugaal gave to this place. Though a word that intimates severity, it really only meant the destruction of one tenth of the people. In actuality, ninety percent of the Mugaal had died that day. Onero knew this, and he figured the learned Mugaal knew this as well. He wondered if not all the Mugaal were as humble as the general's servant seemed to be. He wondered if this proud people ultimately thought little of their losses that emanated from this place.

Getala spoke up again. "It is said that Rhumaiv was sacrificed with his own sword. It was a fantastic blade of heavenly beauty and power. Months after the Decimation, a few brave Mugaal survivors came to this spot and found the sword stuck blade down into the soil. For two hundred years, no one could pull the sword from its spot. One day, many centuries ago, it went missing. Some of our spies believed they had seen the sword carried by one of your kings a few years ago, but when the king became fey, the sword disappeared."

Getala was done with his history lesson. The journey to the mountain would be a hard half day's ride. They continued north, with Getala leading the way. At dusk, they came to the base of the mountain. The horses were tired, having stopped only once.

Onero was awed at the sight of the mountain. He had never been all the way to the base of the Great Mountains before. In the place where they stood, the mountain did not reach down gradually to the plain below. Instead, it rose sharply into a hundred foot sheer cliff. Vertical columns could be seen on the face of the rock, evidence that the Mugaal had purposed for it to be unclimbable. In the midst of the rock face was a fissure, splitting it from top to bottom. They were still too far away to see how wide this gap was.

Before they actually reached the mountain and the gap, the company came to a massive wall. Each end of this thirty foot high wall abutted the sheer face of the mountain. It formed a semicircle with a one hundred foot radius centered at the gap in the mountain. The wall was ten feet thick and forty archers marched along the top. At its most southern point was a single, narrow gate. It was only wide enough to pass through sideways without a pack. No horse or forward-facing person could travel through it.

"The wall was not built to keep in the exiles, but rather to keep out any invaders from the North," Getala explained. "On the other side of the gate is where you will spend the night. The archers will watch over the area all night. Torches burn along the whole inside wall, and there are pyres throughout the field. You will be warm and safe tonight. By noon tomorrow, you will no longer be considered citizens of your kingdom but invaders from the North. Our archers are ordered to fire on you as soon as the sun is overhead. May the power of Rhumaiv fall on you, Masters Seon and Kanu."

Wylm and Onero pulled the gear off their backs and stepped sideways through the ten foot deep gateway. Despite darkness falling, the field before them was well lit. From the glow of the fires, the rock wall beyond reflected an orangish-red except for where the Mountain Pass vertically cut a thin black expanse. It looked like the eye of a large feline staring angrily at them, taunting them, beckoning them to take their chance with the world beyond. Tomorrow morning they would awake to walk to their deaths.

10 BETWEEN THE WALLS

He was awakened by a roar. It was a deep roar, like the sound of many waters. Coming into focus before him, blazed the large eye of some great cat. It flickered in the darkness, lit by either a surrounding flame or a fire within. He did not know. It was a dreadful, terrible eye, but he could not look away. Stars filled the sky behind it. Soon the stars began to move and reorder. They merged and joined until the distinct face of a lion was evident around the eye. The eye blinked, and he realized it was actually looking at him.

Long he stared at the flickering erubescent iris and then at the long, dark, vertical pupil that split it. He saw a glimmer in that darkness, showing further life and intent in the mysterious, fearsome eye. He stared at that glimmer. It became larger, coming into focus. He realized that it was not a single point of light but a scene or moving image of some story.

There were lions. Many strong and virile lions surrounded a few old and cachectic ones. Amongst the old lions was a young lion that had only three paws, the two back and the front left paw. Still it was resilient and agile. The stronger lions pounced on the few and killed the older lions, then dragged the young lion, wounded, to the feet of a huge cat that was surrounded by many lionesses, including a black lioness that paced behind it. The young lion arose. Its front left paw turned gold with claws of steel. It struck and killed the huge lion.

Then, emerging from the mountains, sprung a fierce beast that was like a lion. It was huge and white as snow. At its side was another black lioness. It dispersed or killed the first band of strong lions and surrounded itself with others. The one with only three legs ran and hid until he could find more help: other three-legged lions, an eagle, a ram, a buck, a man, and a little ewe lamb.

Meanwhile, the white lion-like beast kept growing larger and larger. Its fortress grew with it, becoming impenetrable to any great force. The black lioness laughed at its side. The white beast was searching back and forth throughout its kingdom, looking for something. Finally it stared into the eyes of the dreamer, hate flashing across its face as it let out a tremendous roar.

****

Onero woke early that morning with a start. His respirations were fast and shallow. It was still in the last watch of the night. On the plains, the sun would be up in an hour, but this close to the forest, it would be at least two. He imagined how cold and dark it would be in the pass. He glanced to the mountain. The *cat's eye* still stared at him as it did the night before. It had influenced his dreams.

It had been difficult for him to get to sleep with the fatigue and emotions of the previous day wrestling with his mind. He had been fitful. It had not helped that the torch lights played such a trick on the face of the mountain. Onero tried to put that out of his mind. He wanted to put that dream out of his mind as well, but the randomness of it haunted him. In truth it bothered him that he had been having these strange dreams ever since he struck his head a few days ago. *That was the third time I struck my head this year,* he thought. *I really could have used a physician after I fell in that hole.*

Onero turned over to check on his partner, not surprised to find that Wylm was already awake. He was sitting on a rock by one of the pyres in the middle of the field. As Onero drew near, the smell of roasted lamb invaded his nostrils. Wylm was preparing the meat that had been packaged for them for their journey. Onero joined him by the fire. No words were exchanged at that moment, only the knowing looks that in front of them roasted their last meal before the end.

Once their breakfast of lamb, and bread was finished, Wylm finally broke the silence. "No sense waiting for the sun. It won't reach into the pass until midday anyhow. I'd rather have many miles under my belt by that time." They grabbed their water canteens, packs, and weapons; Onero had his staff, Wylm his knife. Wylm went over to the wall and grabbed two torches. The archers on the parapet raised their bows, arrow nocked, and yelled at Wylm to put them back.

"It's not noon yet," Wylm derided. "Are you going to kill us? You wouldn't want to be responsible for the death of another ninety percent of your people, would you?"

Oh how I would hate to be at war against him, Onero thought to himself.

The air cooled with every step as they got nearer to the pass. The torch flames flickered in the movement of air. On the face of the mountain, to the right of the entrance, were markings. From twenty feet back, it looked like writing, but a few more steps revealed they were tally marks. "Twenty-three," Onero announced, having paused momentarily to count them. "I wonder what it means. Maybe it is the number of people who have entered." Wylm made a vertical slash and diagonal slash on the last set of tallies.

The rest of that day was rather uneventful, unless stories of stubbed toes, narrowing gaps, and breezy tunnels can be considered eventful. The fuel that the Mugaal had developed for the torches was very long lasting. They truly were an industrious people. Onero felt the sense of despair rise up within him. So much was going wrong. Comfort was not found anywhere. The one on whom he could always rely on was angered with him, or at least, with his family.

Depression and darkness were starting to tug at Onero again as he watched his best friend plod along before him. Recently, their time together had brought tension and irritation. Onero found himself preparing responses to potential future arguments. Along with this came the unsatisfying taste of resentment toward his best friend. He knew he was not being fair to Wylm, and his frame of mind was not helping. *Come on, Onero. Think of Wylm as the hero that he is.* He glanced at the high rock walls beside him. They reminded him of one of Wylm's most recent feats.

Onero recalled back to the latest time that he was rescued by Wylm, before the Nemarian invasion. It had been a cold early spring evening near the southern slopes of the Guardian Mountain ranges. Wylm and Onero had set up camp near the base of the mountain, just high enough to see any travelers who may be trying to sneak through Giant's Pass, but not so high that they could not hurry down and stop them.

They had travelled over Folly Peak to get to the Bachar side of the mountain from the desert side earlier that morning. Rumors of a Pytecki raiding band a bit farther south had led to the decision. In individual combat, Wylm could actually defeat at least one Pytecki giant and maybe up to three. Many of the locals, however, had been reporting eight to twelve of them. Locals were known to exaggerate, but still that would be too many. Thus Wylm and Onero decided to bypass that portion of the Malabi Desert as they made their way back to Bachar territory.

Not until they had made camp that evening did they realize that Onero had left the tinderbox at a resting site about an hour or two up the mountain. Wylm had been furious. Except for his limitations of showing respect to his officers, Wylm was a perfect soldier. He maintained his person and his gear as directed, and he never made these kinds of mistakes. Onero offered to head back up the mountain to retrieve the box, and Wylm allowed him, mostly because he was going to send him up by himself anyway as punishment for his lapse in judgment.

It had been a long hike up the mountain, but eventually, without any incident except for a bloody knee, Onero made it up to the camp and retrieved the tinderbox. Pausing only a moment to catch his breath and relieve himself, he started back down the mountainside. It was about the tenth hour of the day. On the way back to their base camp, he took a slightly different route. It started out as an easier path with less danger in the terrain. Then, while stepping out to see if a smooth angled rock would be safer and easier than taking the path, Onero slipped and fell backward.

He had been slow to arouse, much like after falling in the hole near the watchtower. When he had finally come to his senses, his head throbbed, and he was seeing double. Twice Onero had vomited, but still felt ill. As he looked around, he had seen that rock walls surrounded him. They were high, at least ten feet above him. A screech owl, perched atop one rock, scolded him. No ceiling had been seen, but the unadulterated view of the night sky shone over him. Double vision had prevented Onero from appreciating the view as he would have on any other night. He continued to look for a door and had found that the rock walls surrounded him on three sides except for a small wood door on one wall and another wall being made up of mostly large wood planks.

On that cold, wretched evening, he banged on the wall and began to scream for help. His cries had been met with the howls and barks of what sounded like many wolves or feral dogs. Instinctively, Onero had jumped back from the wall. His foot had slipped on something, possibly a loose stone. For the second time that day, Onero had struck his head on the rocky ground.

For a full day, he had stayed in a drowsy state, going in and out of consciousness. A few memories came to him as he later tried to recall what had happened. The small door had opened. The howling became louder until it turned to growling and then whimpering. A man crawled through the small door. The only vivid memory he had was Wylm leaning over him and calling his name.

After that, he remembered being carried by Wylm, having been flung over his shoulders. Then there had been an uncomfortable bouncing as Wylm ran. He ran for a long time. Many turns were taken. Despite all those turns, wall after wall persisted in Onero's memory. Within those dark halls, the bodies of many wolves had been strewn about.

Onero did not remember anything after that until he woke up the next morning in the lower camp. Wylm was still asleep, tossing and turning.

When Onero went to wake him, Wylm had screamed, a look of terror coming over him.

Onero wondered about that night as he followed Wylm through the pass. Wylm never talked about it. For days, Onero would ask for details, but Wylm gave none. Before long, he would yell at Onero if the evening in question ever came up. Whatever happened that night, Wylm was never the same. He would shudder at an unforeseen shadow and grab the hilt of his sword at the sight of any raven. *Really he changed more that night than the day he heard my father had left for Sardis,* Onero thought.

Wylm spoke up. "It's been dark overhead for some time now." He pointed high up the pass, where the faintest sliver of sky could be seen. "We'll stop here to sleep and continue in the morning."

The travelers made camp. The path was narrow enough that two people could not comfortably sleep side by side. Instead, Onero and Wylm slept head to head with the torches at their feet to deter any creature that might call that narrow gap home. Unlike previous nights, Onero had no dreams as he lay in the midst of the mountain.

11 THIS TOO SHALL PASS

There was a rap on her bedroom shutters. The room was still mostly dark, and only the faintest light could be seen through her west-facing window. It was too early for anyone in the town to be up and about. She pulled her covers tighter around her and listened. The noise came again, but this time a little more forcefully. She reached for the club that her father had given her. Her knuckles whitened as she fearfully squeezed the narrow grip.

"Shoshanna," a voice whispered outside the window.

She lightened her grip.

"Shoshanna, it's me. Come to the window."

She knew that voice. She let go of the club, and it fell to the floor. She scolded herself for the *thud* it made. Surely it would wake her father, but what did she care? This was her wedding day, and her lover was outside her window. Shoshanna bound to the window and threw open the shutters. There he stood, with a single flower, a lily of the valley, her favorite.

"Jugel, it is our wedding day. You are not allowed to see me." She stood at the window and placed both her hands along her hips. Her tone made her lover back up a step in unexpected shock. "But I am so glad you did." She took the lily from his hand and jumped out of the window and into his arms.

Jugel caught her and spun her around. He held her and gently brushed her wild hair away from her face, revealing her glorious smile. She was laughing loudly. "Keep your voice down, my love. You will wake your father."

"And what will he do, ground me?" She laughed some more.

"Perhaps he will do nothing more than tell your mother." Jugel feigned a look of fear in his eyes. "And if she finds out I broke tradition by seeing you this morning, I might not live to exchange our vows."

"Be nice to my mother," she smiled.

"I always am," Jugel responded. "If I was not, she would burn a hole through me with those fearsome eyes."

Shoshanna smacked Jugel in the shoulder. "How many years will it take for me to mold you into a good, tame husband?"

"Good is what I strive to be every day." Jugel slipped in a quick kiss before he continued. "But do not expect to ever tame me."

“I have never known you to be anything but good, and I have come to realize that you will never be tame.” She grabbed his face and kissed. “I do, however, expect you to be a little more tolerant of my mother.”

“As long as I can have my sword with me.”

She smacked his shoulder again then kissed him with great passion. Fortunately, it was still quite early. Had any neighbor witnessed them, the whole town would have heard of their scandalous embrace. Shoshanna pulled away one last time. “Today is a day we will never forget. In a few short hours, our world will be turned upside down.”

Jugel was breathing louder than he knew, overwhelmed by his passion for his soon-to-be wife. “I'm afraid the next time I kiss you, my heart will not be able to handle the emotion. I will be undone.”

Suddenly a knock came to her bedroom door. Jugel lifted Shoshanna back into her room. She closed the shutters and scurried to her door. She opened it to find her father standing there.

“I thought I heard noises,” he said, peering around the room. “Are you alright?”

“Yes, father. I just cannot sleep from excitement.” Her heart pounded inside her chest, yearning for the touch of her lover. She knew she was telling her father the truth.

He saw her heavy breathing and the lily that she had set on her bed. He looked to Shoshanna and cupped his hand to her face. “Soon, my dear. Soon you will be in his strong embrace.”

He left the room, and she shut the door. She hurried back to the window and opened the shutters. Jugel was not there. She looked this way and that but did not see him. She called for him, but he did not answer. Slowly she made her way back to her bed and laid her head on her pillow. She clutched the lily to her chest and smiled. Excitement filled her as she considered the day's upcoming events. She felt as if the whole kingdom would be watching as she and Jugel stood together in the town square holding hands, as they ushered in their future.

****

Onero and Wylm woke early and ate some bread. Onero appreciated the opportunity to eat another breakfast. They continued their journey almost immediately. Three hours later, they looked overhead to see that the mountain side was quickly coming down toward them. They were approaching the end of the pass. This realization stirred in Onero a wrestling between hope and anxiety. Anxiety soon won. A hundred feet ahead, they saw the first body.

It was lying among a pile of rocks. At least three of those rocks were resting on top it. The man had been armed with a sword. Wylm grabbed it for himself. The next four bodies were found in a similar manner, lying amongst medium-sized rocks that had no doubt rained from above as a series of intentional projectiles. Wylm checked every man's weapon and was soon armed with two swords in their scabbards, one in his hand, a spear on his back, and a shield on his arm. Onero carried a sword in one hand and his staff in the other.

They pressed on. The body count continued to climb, but the cause of death progressed to arrows as they neared within two hundred feet of the end of the pass. They began to move much slower and more carefully.

Wylm occasionally traded out his weapons for finer pieces. Eventually he was satisfied with what he carried and ceased from scavenging the weapon-laden corpses and skeletons. Onero also picked up a shield as they stepped warily toward the light of day, shields in front of them.

Onero glanced above his shield and could see the end of the pass, a mere two stone throws ahead. Only two more bodies were left. By his count, that was a total of twenty-two bodies. *One different than the tally marks at the beginning of the pass,* he thought to himself.

Their senses had reached maximum acuity by this point. They felt they were a moment away from death with every step, but no attack came.

As they were coming upon the last two bodies, a hiss sounded in front of them. A large brown snake coiled at their feet, angry and poised for a strike. Wylm swung at it with a sword, but it recoiled and then struck at Wylm's feet. He was able to move, but tripped on a rock on the narrow path and fell backward against Onero, knocking them both to the ground. In the chaos of the moment, Wylm had dropped both of his swords.

The snake struck again. This time, Wylm caught it with his hand, stood, and threw it forward. It struck the rock face. With the strength of his throw, Wylm had twisted his torso and managed to get the tip and tail of his spear stuck on either side of the pass. He could not get free or turn his body to face the once again approaching serpent.

The snake coiled itself upon a rock in front of them, preparing for another confrontation. Strangely, it did not curl its tail underneath it to assume the striking position. Instead, it began to coil from the top down, making many turns of its head along its tensed, muscular body. It was as if it were taunting the pair of men with whom it dueled.

As it curved and twisted, Onero rose to his feet and noticed a symbol on its skin across the back side of its hood. It looked to him like an angry left eye, pierced through the center with a thick vertical line. It did not appear to be a mark of happenstance, but a symbol of distinction. He had no time to ponder this, though, as the snake tensed for another strike.

At the moment the serpent vaulted, Onero dove overtop the incapacitated Wylm and grabbed the snake just as it was inches from Wylm's face. He rolled as he landed and came back up to his feet to throw the snake even farther down the pass. His motion was abruptly stopped. The staff in his hand had gotten wedged between the rock faces just like Wylm's spear had.

He glanced back at Wylm to confirm the ridiculousness of this coincidence. Wylm, however, was staring at the staff, face ashen. Onero realized that it was not his own staff that was stuck, but there was a staff in his right hand, the same hand that had caught the snake.

Incredulous, he let go of the staff. It remained stuck between the rock walls. With effort, he dislodged it and examined it; it was wood. What was happening? He threw it to the ground in disbelief. It bounced and rested where it landed, wood on rock. A dancing thought partnered with an old memory, and Onero approached the staff again.

He grabbed it midshaft and gripped it tight with confidence. Sliding his hand to the tip of the staff, he angled it down so the top made contact with the rocks below. To Onero's amazement—and Wylm's horror—the staff became a snake, starting at the head. Wood turned to skin as he continued to lower it. Finally it was all serpent again, except for the four inches of wood tip that he still held in his hand. When he finally let go, the snake turned and faced Onero.

"What on Ivveleth's Mountain is that?" Wylm finally spoke. He had seen the brutality of war. He met the strongest, fiercest, and most ferocious in battle and had defeated them all. He had stood with Onero against twenty men and had come out victorious, slaying eighteen of the twenty himself. But Wylm Kanu had never seen anything like this, and it scared him. "Carcasses, Onero. What is going on?"

Onero knew. He knew, but he did not believe it. How could it be real? What were the odds? He had held this staff before, never with permission, but he had held it. His grandfather would set it by the front door during visits. Onero would sneak over and grab it. With two hands, he would pick it up over his head, look to the sky, and proclaim some curse of frogs or locusts. His grandfather always caught him before he could finish the curse. A prompt scolding and lecture would follow. Then Onero had been hugged for minutes on end until he knew how much his grandfather loved him.

"Do you know what this is, Wylm?" Onero begged. "Do you know whose this is? And that means…" He did not finish the statement but looked down at the two bodies lying in front of them.

"I swear to Rhumaiv if you don't tell me what is going on…" Wylm began a threat.

"His staff, Wylm. This is my grandfather's staff, the staff of the prophets, the staff of Seon. And if this is the staff of Seon, that means…" They were trading unfinished sentences.

Wylm now looked at the two bodies in front of them, finally understanding what Onero was thinking. With a forceful motion, he freed his spear from the walls and hurried to the two bodies. Brushing aside the cobwebs, rocks, and dirt, he saw the sword and light armor of his family on one of the corpses. The sword was simple but strong.

On its pommel was engraved the sign of the house of Kanu; it was an intercrossing sword and shepherd's crook. The hilt was wrapped in red-stained leather and was long enough for just one hand to grip it. The crossguard was simple iron that came to a beveled point on one side and curled toward the blade on the other. The iron blade was double-edged. It was remarkable in that its fuller, which grooved through its midline on either face, was stained red, a skill known by no man south of the Great Mountains.

The blade had been given to one of the Kanu patriarchs hundreds of years ago. They had been shepherds. The story went that one day a man came into the field where the many brothers were keeping the sheep. He announced that he was looking for warriors to serve the king. The older brothers laughed and went back to their duties. The youngest son, still a boy, volunteered and knelt very low to the ground. With this very sword, the stranger had tapped the boy on either side of his head.

The legend further told that when the sword had made contact with the young Kanu boy's left shoulder blade, his shirt burned at that spot. When the scarring and blistering had finally healed, a mark was on his shoulder, a sword intercrossed with a shepherd's crook. Wylm, of course, did not believe in this nonsense. He hardly believed the story of the sword's history in the first place. He picked up the sword and stared at its pommel. His left hand reached behind his back to try to scratch his shoulder blade, which had suddenly begun to itch and tingle.

As he and Onero disencumbered their grandfathers' bodies of their armor and weapons, Wylm noted that the body of Commander Kanu was closer to the opening of the path than that of Prophet Seon. Wylm also noted that his grandfather had six arrows in his front legs, abdomen, and chest. The prophet had one arrow between his shoulder blades, pointing from back to front.

Already irritated by the new tingling along his left shoulder blade, the smolders of rage were fanned by what seemed another example of imbalanced devotion and valor. "Another prophet turns and runs while the Kanu family fights with honor and valor," he snapped, his voice dripping with poison at the word *prophet*. "Where is the guarding? Where is the protecting from the house of Seon?" He stood, burning at Onero, accusing him of betrayals that had not happened, raging at him for treacheries not committed. "Like father, like son. There is no loyalty in the house of Seon."

Onero had been caught off his guard. He had just bent over to pick up the serpent-staff when Wylm began his verbal attack. As Wylm snapped at him, unrestrained by reason or wisdom, Onero surveyed the bodies, finally understanding the situation that propelled the words. He held his tongue. Wylm would not be calmed by words, and the tolerance Onero carried toward Wylm's outbursts was waning.

Wylm waited for a reply and became angrier when none came. His shoulder blade continued to itch. He backed up to the wall and rubbed his back against it. The sensation did not cease. Wylm threw his sword down at the rock. The itch stopped, but the anger did not. "Go." He turned to Onero.

Onero said nothing.

"Go!" He said again, screaming this time. "You lead the way. For once in three generations, let a Seon die before a Kanu. Salvage your family's dignity. Honor the oath in a way your ancestors never did. You go first."

He turned away and began to take the light armor from his grandfather's corpse.

Onero marveled at the instability of his friend. Ever since his father had traveled to Sardis, their friendship had been on an ever narrowing precipice. Wylm's rage and jealousy were ever growing. He was becoming less and less able to hold them back. In regards to the oath, Onero had resolved he would never falter. He picked up his gear, sword in his left hand, and his grandfather's staff in his right. He would not leave Wylm, but he would give him some space. South of the mountain, Wylm had been a dutiful soldier and dear friend. As Onero neared the mouth of the pass, he had a persistent question. *What was going to emerge from the mountain?*

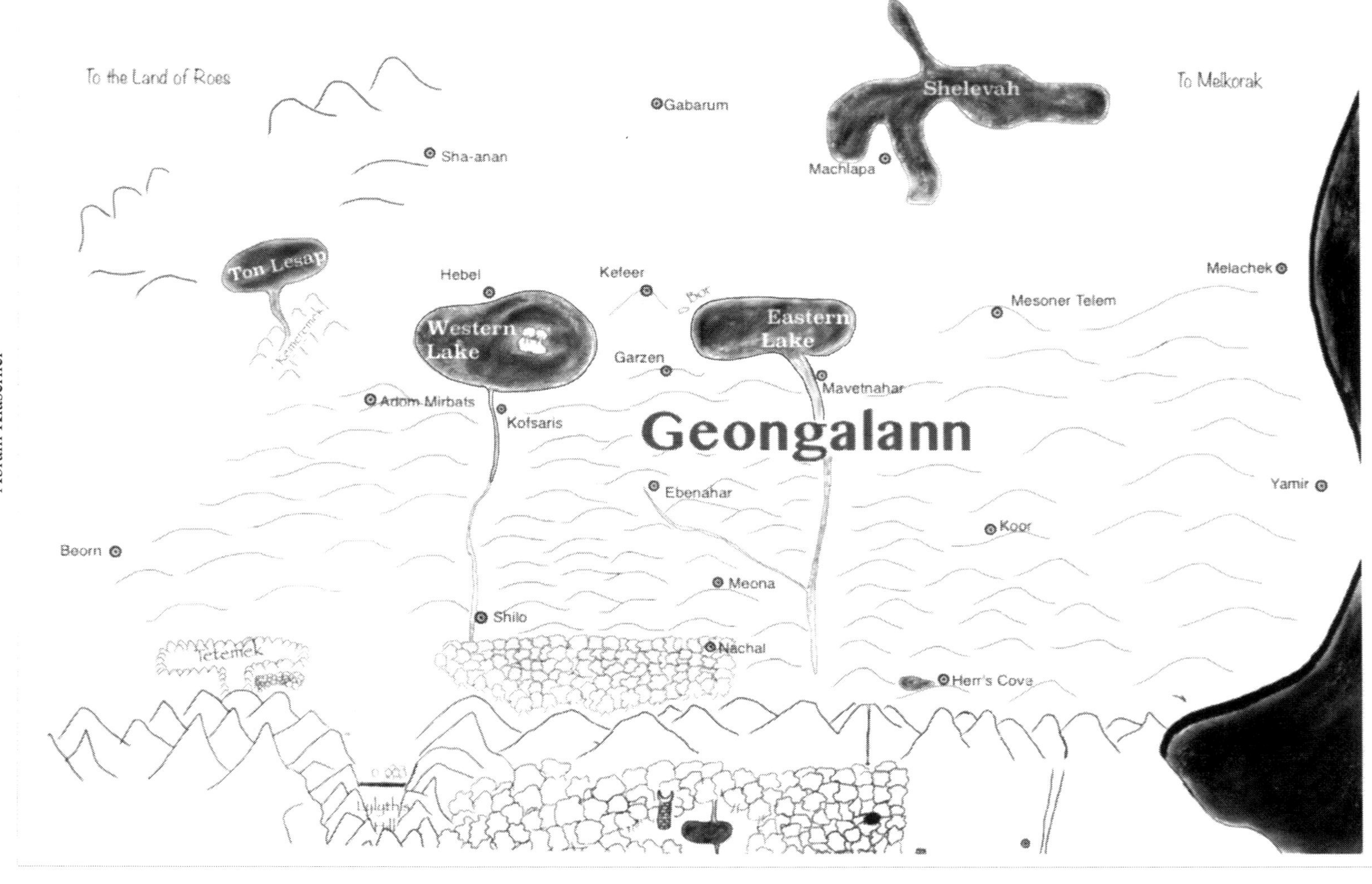
To the Land of Roes
Gabarum
Shelevah
To Melkorak
Sha-anan
Machlapa
Ton Lesap
Hebel
Kefeer
Melachek
Western Lake
Eastern Lake
Mesoner Telem
Garzen
Mavetnahar
Adom Mirbats
Kofsaris
Geongalann
Yamir
Ebenahar
Koor
Beorn
Meona
Shilo
Nachal
Herr's Cova

12 SMOKE AND FOG

Wylm stepped out of the mountain pass, wearing the armor of his ancestors but leaving the sword behind. The itching sensation would have driven him mad. Instead, he wielded two other swords from former warriors who had died in the pass. Armed with experience, skill, and an inner wrath which Onero had fanned, he had been ready for any attack from any person or creature.

No arrows had flown. No blades had crashed upon him. Nevertheless, Wylm had indeed been struck. As he looked around this new world, north of the mountain, a strange sensation struck his soul. It was one that he had not felt since childhood: Wonder.

He recalled that his parents had taken him as a boy to the Eternal Falls in the south of Bachar. Memories rushed in of when he'd cornered that last rock ledge and had seen the falls for the first time. He'd been overwhelmed with awe and wonder on that day. The beauty of unseen creation had stopped him in his tracks.

The same feeling rushed over him now. The expanse of creation before him was truly awe inspiring. Seldom did Wylm pause to take in such beauty. He was usually too busy about his affairs, achieving goals, and planning missions. Onero had always been the romantic. Right now, though, for once, he joined in appreciation of what his friend often tried to point out to him.

Here he stood in a place where he'd never been. This was a whole new land, a new country. In fact, it was a whole new realm. As far as he knew, since the days at the beginning of time, no person south of the Great Mountains had ever viewed this land. Wylm stopped to take in the scope of it.

The world around him was beautiful. The exit from the pass was quite high up the mountain. Spread out before him and below him were tall, rolling hills, a thousand of them. Those closest to him were thick with trees. As the hills rolled north, the covering progressed to mostly grass and the occasional tree. This went for miles on end. Laced between many, like shimmering blue ribbons, were rivers wide and narrow. Far off in the distance was a reflective glimmer, which Wylm supposed was a lake or two.

The sky was free of clouds and full of life. The whole scene was like walking into a new beginning. Again Wylm thought back to that boyhood trip to the Eternal Falls. The physical nature of the falls set them apart from any other waterfall he had ever seen. The fast icy water escaped from the side wall of the cliff and seemed to shoot out twenty feet before it descended. Then it dropped a mighty drop. There were no gentle descending slopes in that area of Bachar, and this was no exception.

The falls dropped for two hundred feet before they came to the level of the ground below, although that was not where they stopped. There was no pool or river on the surface that took the water across the ground to the southern sea. Instead, the water plunged through a crevice and submerged deep into the earth. From there, it pooled and then flowed south. It did not emerge again until the underground river flowed into the sea about twenty miles farther south.

Wylm was always fascinated with the Eternal Falls. They seemed to have no beginning and no end. It was like a fresh start. The past no longer mattered and the future was not affected by what happened during its descent. Power and glory defined its brief existence as it plunged into the depths.

"Beautiful," Wylm said to himself, describing his current surroundings and his memories of the falls. He began to walk down the hillside and came upon Onero, who had paused to take in the view as well. *New beginnings*, he thought to himself as he considered how his emergence from the pass was like the falls emergence from the cliff side. "Pretty country," he said to Onero as he passed him, intentionally bumping into his shoulder. "New world, new rules. Consider yourself released."

"An oath is an oath, Wylm," Onero yelled after him. "I have never betrayed our friendship or our oath, and I never will." He was exasperated, having had this conversation before, and not enjoying having it again. "I will guard and protect you and your descendants above all else, save the king."

"We'll see," Wylm called back as he walked down the mountainside. He took a deep breath to take in the smell of this new world. Smoke invaded his nostrils. It was coming from below him and to his right, beyond the hill at the mountain's base. The smoke rose black and thick. *Apparently not everything's good in this world,* he thought, turning to head that direction.

As he began to descend the mountainside, he heard a loud yell, like the roar of a lion. The hair on Wylm's neck rose. It was a sound of anguish and anger from a voice of confidence and familiarity. It seemed to come from the direction of the hill where the smoke was still rising. "Sounds like pain and rage," Wylm muttered, speaking his own emotions out loud. "I can relate." He meant the words. Pain and rage wallowed in his own heart: rage at the betrayal of the Seon family against his own; pain at losing his father and the loyalty of his best friend. Onero had not betrayed him yet, but the actions of his father and grandfather essentially showed that one day he would. "A person can't escape his family," he muttered again.

Taking another step, he called back to Onero, "I'm heading over there. Feel free to join me if you like." With his swords, he cut his way through a briar patch that was in his path. Then he looked back to Onero. "I may need protection."

How could Onero ever understand? He always considered himself more righteous just for sticking with Wylm, but Wylm had done so much for Onero. *How many times have I saved him?* Wylm thought. He then listed for himself all those times: the traitor soldiers; the Pytecki raiders; the waterfall; the smugglers; and the Raven Witch of Embor. It was the last one that bothered Wylm the most. Onero did not even know the whole story, and Wylm planned on never telling him.

Wylm thought back to that night when Onero had gone back up the mountain to retrieve the tinderbox he had left there. *He still thinks that wolves were the worst thing in the hills that night.* When Onero did not return at the expected time, Wylm had gone searching for him. The mountain air had become exponentially colder that night the higher he went, and the risk of Onero freezing to death was very real. Wylm had found Onero's trail leading from their last stop together before they had descended. The trail lead to a rocky cliff and stopped. *The clumsy fool had slipped down the ledge,* Wylm remembered.

Carefully Wylm had made his way down the unforgiving slope. At the bottom were markings indicating that someone had been dragged. He followed those tracks through a rocky crag until the trail stopped. It had gotten too dark at that point to identify any additional markings. The temperature kept dropping, and he was getting concerned about losing his very best of friends. Actually *concerned* was not the right word. He had been flat out scared. Onero had always been there for him. In fact, he was the only one who had truly always been there for him.

After Wylm had walked a few more paces, a thick fog or mist began to rise from the ground. His vision had become limited to no more than a foot in front of him. Suddenly two large eyes stared at him, inches from his face. He had drawn his sword and yelled out reflexively. The owl before him let out a terrible screech, flapped its wings, and clawed Wylm's face before flying away. The branch on which it had been sitting rose up and nearly hit Wylm's jaw.

Just then, wolves had begun to howl nearby. Wylm had yelled for Onero but got no response. The fog had become thicker with despair. The temperature plunged like hope. He had called again, but this time a scratchy and withered voice spoke back to him through the haze.

"Who disturbs the residents of Embor?" the woman's voice had asked.

"My name's Wylm. I'm looking for a friend who's lost," Wylm had replied more hesitantly than he would've liked to admit.

"This is Embor," the withered voice had called back. "All is lost." The way she said those words had made Wylm's knees tremble. "The Raven Witch rules this place. If your friend is lost, she has made sure he will never be found."

"Take me to this witch." Wylm had never had much use for myths and magic. "She'll return my friend, or she'll taste my blade. Where is she?"

The fog had pulled back just enough to reveal a small path. Standing twenty feet away was a bent old woman with ferocity in her eyes. "I am right here."

As Wylm thought back to that night, he shuddered at the memory. He continued down the mountain slope towards the rising plume of smoke. Despite the already intense heat of the morning, a chill ran across his neck. He shook it off. Just the thought of that wretched woman sent a fear through his gut. *If I could face her, I can face anything,* Wylm thought to himself. He glanced at Onero behind him and wondered whether what he had done for him was really worth it, for a Seon. *Cowards and backstabbers.*

They were nearly at the base of the mountain. It had been a steep descent. As the ground leveled, Wylm saw the smoke rising from behind the hill before them. For the moment, he would stick with Onero. He wanted to be around when Onero broke the oath. Onero would not have the satisfaction of Wylm being the first one to balk. A gentle breeze whisked down the hill, washing them in smoke.

Wylm turned to Onero and gave him a half smile. "Looks like the adventures continue, for now."

13 HEIRS APPARENT

Regeldam strode through the streets of Kefeer. His personal guard surrounded him without making him feel suffocated. It had taken many years and many floggings before they finally understood what was too close and what was too far from their king. Today they were quite busy rustling and holding back the citizens of his capital city.

Much construction was being done all around him, and he had not been out to see the progress in quite some time. Naturally, he was not pleased. His glory was waiting on the rebuilding of Kefeer, and there were still many months of work left to be completed. This was the second time in a week he was unhappy with his advisor of forced labor. He doubted he would give him a third try.

He was on his way down the main corridor to view the new banquet hall. It had been built with expensive timber from hills in the southwest of his kingdom. The trees had been the livelihood of the citizens there, but he knew they were honored to give up the only resource they had for his glory. *It's a shame I will need more timber after today*, Regeldam thought to himself. He looked as one of his guards allowed a lone soldier through the perimeter.

"Your sons are gathered, your Excellency," the soldier relayed, standing at attention before his king.

"Are they all present?" King Regeldam asked, annoyed that the soldier merely stood at attention and did not kneel. Nevertheless, the information was of vital importance, and he let it pass.

"All except your heir-appointed, my Lord. He is serving as an emissary to Melkorak."

The soldier was merely relaying the facts, but still Regeldam could sense the fear within him, having given his king a report of unfinished work. Regeldam waved off the news and suppressed his joy at the young lieutenant's anxiety. "I have sent my messengers for my heir," he responded, then paused and turned back. "Speaking of messengers, has the one returned from Captain Pilesar?"

"He has, my lord."

"Well, fool, what did he reply?" He was irritated that he even had to ask this follow-up question.

The anxious soldier pulled a note from beneath his breastplate. "The message reads, 'Tell the king there are two, not one. The first is Dehion, from the east side of Kefeer. Her son is a butcher there. The other was Reaschi of Gabarum. Her son is lieutenant Hiram, one of the king's personal guards.'"

Regeldam stroked his chin with his right hand, the red fur of his gauntlet rubbing against his soft black beard. This always soothed him. "Tell my personal assistant about the butcher. He will know what to do. And bring Lieutenant … what's his name?"

"Hiram, sir."

"Hiram. Of course. Bring Lieutenant Hiram here to me."

"Yes, sir."

The soldier saluted his king then genuflected in deference. Regeldam smiled in pleasure. However, the soldier did not leave but stayed standing at attention before the king until Regeldam became irritated. "What is it?" he barked.

"Concerning those of your sons already gathered in the hall, my lord, should we begin the ceremony?"

Regeldam paused. It was a good question. The soldier would not be punished for his breech of protocol. "Have they been drinking? Are their spirits high and their muscles soft?"

"All but the children have had their share of wine, your excellency."

"Very good." He nodded. "Be sure the soldiers know that none of my sons are to leave the banquet hall. Not one!" Regeldam stroked his chin again, but this time it was not the red fur that soothed him, it was the control he was taking over his destiny. "The ceremony may begin. Burn it to the ground."

****

Khichterik read the note presented to him. He was sitting on the many layers of whale and bear hide that covered his throne of ice. Wrapped around his shoulders was his royal robe made from the pelts of three white tigers and trimmed with furs of the arctic fox. His right hand gripped his spear, a horn off an arctic whale. It was a trophy of his youth when he had torn the tooth from its bearer during his warrior's quest many years ago.

"What is this?" he boomed at the servant who had handed him the message. "Is he trying to start a war?"

The servant bowed his head and presented the facts. "The emissaries from Kefeer also brought with them twenty pounds of silver, not a few precious gems, and two beautiful young women."

Khichterik, king of Melkorak, pondered this, and then gestured toward the thick ice doors of his throne room. "Very well, bring him before me."

The crown prince of Geongalann was ushered before the Ice King. He stopped at the base of the throne and nodded in deference to the massive being who reigned over the Ice Realm.

Khichterik stood and opened his arms in welcome. "Greetings, prince of Geongalann, son of King Regeldam, heir to the throne in Kefeer. It profits my kingdom greatly to have you stand before me as an emissary of your people. May the blood spilled here today be all that is spilt between us for a generation."

This turn of phrase brought up the crown prince's head. "Begging your pardon, King Khichterik? I do not understand."

The king of Melkorak pointed his spear at the prince and his attendants. "Kill them all."

****

"Lord Regeldam, you called for me?" Lieutenant Hiram said, having been ushered into the throne room before his king.

Regeldam nodded as his loyal body guard approached him. "As you have likely heard, a terrible tragedy has befallen my family."

Confusion flooded Hiram's mind. "Yes, Lord. It is most dreadful. Is there anything I can do?"

"Hiram," Regeldam held up his hand to quiet the seasoned protector. "I knew your mother when I was a young man." He paused to let that sink in and then clarified, "You are my last remaining heir. Thank you for your service and protection these many years. Unbeknownst to you, you have been safeguarding the life of not only your king, but your father as well. Now you are the only male left in this world who can call me *dad*." Regeldam rose from his seat and descended the stairs of his throne. "Come, approach me, my son. We have business to attend to."

Hiram approached the king with an emotion he had never felt. He had often dreamed about this day, the day he would meet his father. Now it had finally come and it was overwhelming, like a childhood story. Surely all those boys from his youth would regret the names they called his mother.

He would make them pay one day. Not today, though. Today he would bask in the reality that he had finally met his father.

King Regeldam opened his arms to his newly-discovered offspring. “Embrace me, my son.”

Hiram approached and held his father. Tears began to form in his eyes, and he did not try to stop them. This was the greatest moment of his life. Then the blade of a sword entered his abdomen and exited behind his left kidney. He looked up and stared at the one who gave him life, the one who now took his life as well.

“You have served me well, my son,” Regeldam said as he dropped Hiram’s limp body to the floor, leaving his sword in the abdomen of his last surviving heir. He turned to his servant. “Retrieve and clean my weapon.” Then he turned to his queen, who had been seated on her throne behind him. “Come. Let us celebrate the security of my kingdom.”

14 WEDDING DAY

They came to a lake on the other side of that first hill, nestled in a valley between it and another hill. An underground mountain stream fed the lake. The waters were still and gave off a perfect reflection.

Onero stared at the reflection. Wylm stared at the source. A village lay on the far side of the lake. Thick black smoke bellowed from over half the houses, which were smoldering in ruins. Many had already collapsed upon themselves. Women could be seen running. A child was wandering in a daze behind one of the houses. A woman darted out of some tall grass, scooped up the child, and ran back into the grass.

Wylm quickened his pace to a jog. He loved a good fight. They were about a half mile from the town. As they drew near, Wylm pulled his two swords from their scabbards and made sure the spear on his back was ready for battle. Onero had his sword in his left hand and staff in his right, but switched them as he got closer.

Wylm and Onero entered the town. No one met them. No one could be seen. As they strode through the middle of the street, they eventually spotted a group of men farther up the street. They appeared to be soldiers, arrayed in armor and iron swords. They seemed to be surrounding something, or someone. The soldiers were yelling and ordering and barking commands. Wylm and Onero were too far away to tell, but it seemed to be more taunting than ordering whatever it was amongst the soldiers.

Another hundred feet brought much more clarity. A garrison of about fifty soldiers surrounded ten males from the village. Amongst the males was a single woman dressed in a white gown. The villagers had made a ring facing out to the soldiers. Most of them were old and gray. Their hair was long and very thick. The majority were armed with shovels, rakes, and pitchforks. One had two lumber axes. Another, the youngest, had a sword.

It was the youngest that caught Onero's eye more than any other. He stood in defiance of his oppressors. The older men all stood a step behind him and looked to him when they were not looking at their attackers. He held a magnificent sword in his right hand, leveled at his hip, but poised and ready to strike. His left hand was moving back and forth, sometimes out in front of him, beckoning the soldiers to come join the pile of the dead at his feet, while at other times it was reaching behind him, touching the outstretched hand of the woman in white.

It was in this beckoning motion that Onero notice this young man was not actually a Man. He was male, but not Man. At the tip of each finger was a claw. This was not just a sharpened fingernail, but a thick and pointed claw. His arms were quite hairy. Onero had known men who were exceptionally hairy in the arms and body, but a glance at the rest of the company in front of him proved that this was not an exception but the rule.

These men appear to be another abomination of Ivveleth, Onero thought to himself, comparing them to the Mugaal. He referred to them as *men* because he did not know what else to call them. Based on the soldiers and the young man defending his freedom, the whole race was quite large. All were as massive as the large Mugaal they had helped escape from the prison just a few days ago. Even the older men, who had bent backs and limited nutrition, had atrophied to a size still larger than Wylm, who himself was considered an impressive man.

Most of the men had facial hair. It was not coarse like a Man's beard, but soft in appearance like the well-tended hair of a lady of the royal court. The majority tended to have a dark complexion to their skin. The youngest's jaw was set in boldness and his lips were separated to display gritted teeth, and Onero thought at least one tooth was a little longer and sharper than the others. A shallow cleft in his upper lip was centered under his short wide nose. His hair was like a thick flowing mane. *Of course like a mane. These men are lionish,* thought Onero.

With this thought weighing in his mind, he heard the muffled cries of deep sorrow restrained by fear. Off to the right, sitting in front of a small home, a group of elderly women were huddled around many ailing lion-men. Most of the males were older. Some were young. Each was cradling his left arm and wrapping it in his shirt or the skirt of the woman assisting him. All of these garments were blood stained. One uncovered his arm and held it up as the older woman attending him tied a rope tight around his left forearm. Distal to the rope was an acutely traumatized limb, void of a hand. It appeared each lion-man had suffered the same grievous wound.

Off to the left came another chorus of cries. These were not curtailed by fear, but were propelled by a lack of hope. A horse-drawn cart was leaving the village. It was about six feet wide, eight feet deep, and housed a large cage with thick bars. In the midst of the cage were young women. Onero guessed the nine women in the cage were between fifteen and thirty years of age. They were being abducted, and only ten men with eight farming tools, two axes, and one sword had any chance of stopping their departure.

Wylm and Onero approached the chaos, Wylm leading the way. His lust for adventure drove each step. He loved a good fight, and this seemed like a good enough cause to bear arms. Onero saw his friend's purposeful stride and weighed the situation. If Wylm acted, the surrounded men had little chance of living more than a few minutes. They were not warriors, and they brandished no weapons of war, save one. Thus, Onero made the decision to speak up while lives could still be spared.

"We'd like to speak with your commander," he said with a forced confidence, betrayed ever so slightly by a little crack in his voice.

The whole village turned quickly to the new voice. Every person was surprised by the authoritative words, and even more surprised by the sight of two short, pale-skinned warriors. A presumed officer barked a command, and a contingent of ten soldiers came and surrounded the two new faces.

"Carcasses! What are you doing?" Wylm whispered gruffly to Onero. "Do you really think this is going to work?"

"I'm trying to save the lives of the villagers," Onero answered in hushed tones.

"You idiot, you've ruined our chance at a surprise attack."

The leader of this band of soldiers approached them on foot, flanked by eleven soldiers. "I am Lieutenant Yaash of Sha-anan, leader of the Third Claw of the White Regiment of Lord Regeldam's army. Who are you, and what is your allegiance?

"We are warriors of a kingdom south of the mountain. We wish to ascertain what crime has been committed by these villagers to deserve such heinous treatment." Onero strived to display an assurance that he did not actually possess. Wylm's words would have rang truer, but to no peaceful resolution.

"The men of Herr's Cove have come into the king's displeasure. The women are soon to come into his pleasure. Now, insolent fools, drop your weapons and give yourselves up. One small warrior and one man with a stick do not pose a threat to us, even if you are as pale as the sprites of Lylyth's Hill." Yaash turned to his soldiers. "Subdue them and cut off their hands. By their own admission, they are from the South."

Onero began to speak again, but Wylm let out a battle cry, and in one circular motion he decapitated two soldiers and ran another two through with his swords. Leaving his sword in the abdomen of one soldier, he grabbed his spear and hurled it at the lieutenant, pinning him to the man behind him. Retrieving his first sword, he then quickly dispatched with two more soldiers who had closed in too near.

Had he been a mere spectator, Onero would have been impressed with Wylm dropping eight men in five seconds, but three of the remaining four soldiers were closing in on him. Onero was skilled, but nothing like his friend. It took a little longer, but he eventually felled two of the soldiers while Wylm took care of the other two. Onero turned and saw that the ten armed villagers had taken advantage of Wylm's initial distraction and had begun to fight as well.

The young man with the sword had quickly added to the stack of bodies beside him, and the man with the axes was holding his own as well. The eight older fighters in the circle had managed to slay five more soldiers, but the trained soldiers quickly rallied and killed four of the fighters from the town.

"Get to the captives!" Wylm ordered.

Back in soldier mode, Onero obeyed his ranking officer and made his way over to the remaining captives. He slew three more soldiers in his approach, but three of the older men had died by the time he got to them. They continued to fight together and lost another man in a matter of moments. All that remained in the circle to fight were Onero, the young man with a sword, and the one with two axes. Both of the latter were quite skilled, warriors of valor.

The lady in white still stood with them. She stayed behind her presumed lover, keeping out of the way of anyone swinging a blade. Soon the four of them were backed up near one of the burning buildings. A soldier took a fierce swing at the young warrior and knocked his sword back hard. As his arms arced toward his beloved, he let go of the sword to keep from striking her. It landed in the smoking wood and flames of the burning home. Onero quickly gave the man his sword and began battling with only his staff.

In the meantime, Wylm had rushed to the wounded men. A contingent of soldiers had broken off to quash any potential reinforcement to this insurrection, whether they were capable of battle or not. In other words, they planned to kill every person in the town, even if they were already mortally wounded. Wylm had seen this and stopped the soldiers, taking the first out with his retrieved spear and then slaying the other five before they got there. By the time Wylm had joined the others, it was four against twelve with injured reinforcements preparing to scavenge dead soldiers for a weapon.

The young lion-man with the sword let out a war cry. It was the loudest noise Onero had ever heard from an individual. It was the authoritative roar of a lion calling his comrades to arms. The soldiers hesitated in their advance and the four warriors took advantage. The feeling of impending victory rose in Wylm, Onero, and all the villagers. That feeling lasted for only a moment.

A bugle sounded from the far hill and a volley of arrows whistled through the air. The wounded villagers, who had all been rummaging for weapons, were all pierced by the flying darts. Most of the women who had cared for them met the same heinous death. Onero, Wylm, the two village warriors, and the lady in white still stood.

Horse hoofs and military issue boots were heard stamping, pounding, and rushing from the edges of the village. Reinforcements had come for the soldiers and the remaining soldiers from the original fifty retreated to meet their help. Another salvo of arrows flew toward them. "Get down!" Onero yelled, looking for Wylm who was out of reach but already hitting the deck.

A cry went up from the commander of the soldiers, ordering them to cease firing. Wylm stood, still armed with both swords. Onero stood, too, and stepped by Wylm's side. Beside Wylm was a pile of bodies. The warrior with two axes was lying on top of the young man. He, in turn, was lying on top of the woman. Soon the young man twisted from under the other, helping his beloved to her feet. The other warrior had taken half a dozen arrows to save the life of the younger. Wylm gritted his teeth. The young man arose with Onero's sword in his hand, his beloved behind him.

"Drop you weapons," the captain ordered.

Onero looked at the more than sixty soldiers armed with swords or bows. Only three remained to fight them off. Everyone else was dead or incapable. The only other survivors were a few older women and whatever mothers and children were still hidden in the woods and high grass. Onero dropped his staff. The young man quickly followed suit and dropped the sword that Onero had given him.

Wylm was annoyed. He had never surrendered. He had been captured before—five times before, to be exact—but he never surrendered unless that was part of the plan. This time, there was no plan. He found himself in a strange land surrounded by savage creatures. His plan would have been to rush the captain and take out as many of these beasts as he could on his way out. Unfortunately, there would be no one alive to sing songs about him except for these two cowards at his side. Finally, he put down his swords.

The soldiers swarmed them and bound them. The captain strode before them and chuckled. "Perhaps King Regeldam was right to listen to that crazy old fool. There is some fight yet in the southeast foothills. Perhaps I should say there *was* some fight."

One of the soldiers, who had been present for the initial skirmish, was holding the lady in white. He called to the commander. "Captain Pilesar, what of this pretty thing? The cage of girls from our detachment has already left for the Market, and the cage accompanying your reinforcements is quite full. Should I put her in there or take her on ahead to meet up with the other women from this village?"

"Neither," Captain Pilesar grinned. "She is a thing of rare beauty and a great reward for King Regeldam. He will be quite impressed to learn that she cost the lives of nearly forty of his soldiers. Bind her and secure her on a spare horse. Take her quickly to Kefeer. She will make a welcome addition to the king's harem."

The young man from the town lashed at the captain. "You worthless…" Rage boiled inside him, but those were the only words he could manage. He jumped to try to kick the captain, but the soldiers holding him from behind yanked him down hard to the ground, knocking the wind out of him.

Captain Pilesar and the soldiers laughed. As they laughed, Onero looked down to the ground. His staff was not lying among the weapons at his feet. He suddenly felt something long and musculature curl up his leg and slip under his loose tunic. It rested, wrapped in a few coils around his waist.

"Shackle them behind the cage of women," Captain Pilesar commanded. "I think they will enjoy the one hundred mile walk back to the Kefeer."

15 A SECOND DREAM

He awoke with a gasp. Air. He needed air. The darkness was pressing in around him. Breathe. He had to breathe. There it was. Air. It was coming easier now. The darkness was passing. His lungs were opening.

It was a dream. A dream? How long had it been since he last had a dream? He remembered having one other dream when he was a boy. His great uncle had told him the tale of how the Mugaal had once been defeated by a Man named Rhumaiv. The story had left him spellbound. On that very night he had experienced his first and only dream.

That had been a good dream then, when he was a boy. He had dreamed of a horned creature, like a ram, leading the Mugaal to mighty victories. It was because of that dream that he had built his home so close to the Decimation of Rhumaiv. That place reminded him of the power of a strong leader. It reminded him of his dream.

This night, General Hamaraz Hywel did not have such a pleasant dream. It was over now. He had finally caught his breath. He was surprised how fortunate he felt to be alive. Was it possible to die because of a dream? Was it possible to suffocate from a lack of air in one's nightmares? The burning acidic feel in his lungs made him not doubt the possibility.

He reached beside him to wake his wife. She had often asked about his childhood dream. Countless times he had retold the story. She had never had visions in the night. In fact, he had never met another Mugaal who had ever had even a single dream. This night he considered them lucky. Hamaraz tapped the blankets beside him, trying to wake Tamaz. She was not there.

How many nights, he wondered. His wife had hardly spoken to him since those two men from Bachar had come through five days ago. She was still mad at him for the presumed oath he had sworn. "It was not an oath!" he mumbled to himself. Of course he would not give up his daughter. That bullish Bacharite had irked him. The man had challenged his leniency and gotten him to say words he did not intend to say. But he would not give up his beloved Jutta ever. That girl was his joy, she and her sister.

He had spoken the words he did because he had truly put his faith in the might and ingenuity of the Mugaal and the Horned Army. Now, after waking from this nightmare, he was not so sure. He got out of bed and went to look for his wife. She had been staying in the girls' room, sharing the bed with one or the other of them. This protest of hers was the worst she had ever done, even worse than three years ago when he had forgotten her birthday. How long would he have to wait till she spoke to him, let alone share their bed again?

Hamaraz opened the door to the girls' room. It took a moment for his eyes to adjust to the darkness, but he found her. She was lying beside Jutta. Her arm was draped over her elder daughter, and she was facing the back of her head. The general quietly walked over to his wife and tapped her on the shoulder.

"Tamaz. Tamaz, I need to talk to you."

She did not stir, let alone respond.

He tried to shake her gently. "Tamaz, darling, wake up. I have something to tell you."

This time she had turned her head by the end of his sentence. "What do you want, Hamaraz. I'm sleeping."

"Wake up, darling. I need to talk to you," he pleaded.

She turned her head back to face Jutta's hair. "I will not wake up at this time, nor do I wish to talk to you." She turned to him again, her right nostril curling in contempt. "And I am not one of your soldiers that you can tell me what to do."

"No, you are not, my love," he agreed, "but you are my wife, and I need to speak to you."

"Don't remind me," she spat. The words stung like an arrow in his side. "I will speak with you in the morning."

"I had another dream," Hamaraz offered.

Tamaz turned and sat quickly on the edge of the bed. The movement startled Jutta, and she awoke.

"Mom?" Jutta questioned drowsily, not fully awake.

"What did you see?" Tamaz questioned her husband.

"I will tell you downstairs over tea," Hamaraz answered his wife.

"Da- General?" Jutta questioned her father. She was obviously more awake now, having halted her natural tendency of calling him "Daddy." Since the incident with that pesky Bacharite, she had been calling him "General", not even acknowledging him as a parent.

"Go back to sleep, Sweet Girl. I need to talk to your mother. She will be back up shortly. I love you."

Jutta did not respond.

Tamaz bent down and gave her a kiss on the cheek. "I will be back up. Your father had another dream."

Jutta at first looked interested in this dream, but she feigned indifference. "I love you, Mom."

Hamaraz and his wife went to the kitchen downstairs and brewed a pot of tea. Within a few minutes, they were sitting on opposite sides of the table, each with a cup in hand.

He took a sip of his tea before looking at his wife. "I've missed you," he offered, like a child longing for mercy during a just disciplining.

"Stop it, Hamaraz. You have earned everything you are getting. Tell me about your dream."

Her constant deflections at his weak apologies were beginning to wear on him. If his horns were truly evidence of his strength and virility, they would be dangling by his cheeks. Hamaraz took a deep breath and another sip of tea.

"I dreamed of a thick darkness, blacker than the blackest night and thicker than the thickest fog. In the midst of that darkness was a void of light. Within the borders of that light was a Man. At first he stayed in the center of that light because he was afraid of the darkness. He feared the source of light also, but it gave him peace. As time went by he went closer to the edges of the light and even began to tip his head out into the darkness. The more he did this, the more he felt it was his own strength that kept him safe. Horns of pride grew heavenward from the sides of his head."

Hamaraz was pleased his wife was listening so intently. It was the most she had paid attention to him in days. "The horned man began to build great structures that would protect him from the darkness. These buildings were massive yet ornate. The day came when the horned man paid no more attention to his source of light, but only marveled at the work of his own hands. Soon after that, the horned man began to claim that he was the source of light and made plans to wipe out any that still revered the light. When that day came, the void of light left him and the darkness overtook him. His mighty structures were destroyed. The horned man became a slave to darkness for the rest of eternity."

"What do you think it means?" his wife asked, feeling more puzzled than afraid.

"I do not know for certain. I am not trained in these things. What a shame we did not hold onto those men a few more days. Something about the eyes of the shorter one makes me think he might have helped." He pondered this, and then offered his explanation. "I think it is the story of our people. We have built up for ourselves buildings of great architecture and beauty. Nothing in all of Nold competes with our design and strength. We have put so much trust in our design and intelligence that we have conspired with the Nemarians to wipe out the people of Bachar. Perhaps they are associated with the light."

His wife took a long sip of her tea and pondered what Hamaraz said. She found herself agreeing. "What are you going to do?"

Hamaraz knew what he had to do. He just did not want to do it. "I must leave tonight for Isarnorn. I must speak to King Berogeis."

"To tell him what?"

"That the Mugaal must surrender or be destroyed."

16 SHACKLES

The journey north was treacherous. There were constant ups and downs. Onero had recalled seeing the thousand hills when he was on the mountainside, and now he was feeling them. If there were roads that stuck to the valleys, their captors were not letting them experience those. At all times, they were either doing a fast walk or a jog. The only hope they had was that some of the soldiers were also on foot, so the caravan had a limit to its maximum pace.

The first ten miles were sustainable. It was around this time—having gone up and down about five hills—that Wylm started to become petulant. He had maintained his composure to this point, but had always required the utmost discipline to hold his tongue. History had revealed that only a limited level of fatigue is necessary loose the chains that bind it. Wylm began to taunt and bait the soldiers. They rewarded him with swift beatings.

Onero and the young lion-man became fellow recipients due to Wylm's persistence.

For further sport, the soldiers would spur the horses on to a gallop. The three wounded warriors would lose footing and be dragged behind the cart. Wylm never lost heart and never seemed to consider what effect the punishments had on his comrades. For the first day of travels, Onero and the warrior from the village kept quiet and took what was doled out to them.

The villager had spoken only once. He said his name was Jugel of Herr's Cove, and the one who had taken the arrows for him was his uncle. With much prodding, he went on to explain that the woman was his betrothed. They were in the middle of their wedding ceremony when the soldiers attacked. Her father and mother had died trying to stop the first soldiers. After this, Jugel said nothing else. Out of grief or disdain, Onero did not know, but as they traveled the young warrior often shot looks of wrath at Wylm.

Twenty miles had been covered that first day, as they were marched late into the night. The next day was more of the same. It was at this point that more garrisons of soldiers began to join them on the road north. Three garrisons of fifty to one hundred soldiers had joined in front or behind them. Each garrison had a cage full of young women. One garrison had a male captive as well. Tied to the women's cart was an older boy, not yet a man. His hair was scarlet, and he carried an air of disrespect and defiance about him.

By the fourth day, twenty garrisons of soldiers had come together for one large caravan headed north and then west. They were on their way to the capital city of Kefeer. Eventually the group came to a great plain, the only plain Onero had seen in this hilly land. The male captives were all herded together and placed in a single cage in the back of a cart. The soldiers made camp in a circle around the cage. A score of other cages filled with young women and older girls also filled the center of the camp. The women were tended to and fed well. The men did not experience the same luxuries.

Onero, Wylm, Jugel, the scarlet-haired boy, and ten other men were crammed into one cart. The boy and other males all stared at the two friends. They marveled at their pale skin, short hair, narrow pointed noses, full upper lips, and dull teeth and fingers. The young boy came and sat near Onero. Being a boy of twelve or thirteen, he was about Onero's size.

The largest male in the cage spoke first. "My name is Tofir of Meona." He turned to the other lion-like men in the cage. "Peace to you, my brothers. May the strength of Emabbir find us this day." Then he turned to Onero and Wylm. "Concerning you, my peace will stay with me. I do not know who you are or what you are. Living in Meona, at the foot of the mountain, I have seen many strange and foul creatures come out of Lylyth's Hill. I have never seen a people so pale and weak as you. My mind says to kill you now and spare myself future pain, but my heart says to wait and hear you speak. Lucky for you, I am a man of my passions. What manner of sprite or wraith are you. Speak quickly, lest my heart has a change in purpose."

Tofir was an immense creature with a long, dark beard and longer tawny hair. Four complementary scars marked his face, through his left eye to the right side of his neck. Tofir was a person of great reputation. One of the young women in the cart, to which Onero, Wylm, and Jugel had been chained, had recognized him the day before, when the different garrisons were forming a caravan. She had seen him in her local tavern. The trio had heard her mention that when under the influence of too much spirits, Tofir had boasted that his father had given him those facial scars when Tofir was only seven years old. The inebriated Tofir had boasted that he had taken his own claws and drove them deep into his father, killing him.

Even without that story, Onero was awash with intimidation because of the size of this creature. Of course Wylm had no such feelings. He never cared about the size of the opponent. Wylm had never doubted his own ability and training, and he had never been wrong. He sat in the corner of the cage, knees to his chest, increasingly annoyed with the words of this brute.

"Whether you listen to your mind or heart matters little to me," Wylm retorted. Then he continued in the only manner of speech that he knew, inflammatory. "If you raise your hand at me, I'll blind your good eye and hit you so hard you'll beg for your father to resurrect and start beating you again just so you get some relief."

Onero cast a look of caution at Wylm, but Wylm scowled back. Tofir rose quickly to his feet, his right eye burning with anger. Onero was struck with curious nausea at the sight of that eye. Tofir's eye flickered orange in his wrath with a thin black shaft of a pupil running from top to bottom. It was similar to the mountain face at the mouth of the pass in Arogan.

Tofir took a step toward Wylm, but paused. The cage was not big enough to withstand a brawl. He was not afraid of Wylm, and thus tried further taunting to intimidate the man. "What strong words for such a small creature. What deeds have you done to back them up?"

Onero tried to save the moment. A quiver betrayed his voice and he regretted it. "If you want to know his deeds, ask Jugel."

"Hah!" scoffed Tofir. "The baby speaks. When I want your opinion, I'll—"

He never finished the sentence. Wylm sprung from his corner and grabbed the bars across the roof of the cage. In the same motion, he brought his right knee up into Tofir's solar plexus. This pitched the lion-man forward, and Wylm responded by releasing his left hand and punching it square into Tofir's eye. Wylm did a full twist and brought the heel of his boot into Tofir's throat, knocking him back into the corner, unable to see and unable to breath. Tofir landed on another captive.

Wylm stood there and took a breath. As he turned to head back to his corner, another began to rise to challenge him. Before he got to his feet, Wylm twisted around and drove his boot into the other's temple, knocking him unconscious. Keeping his head low, he casually glanced around. No one else was challenging, so Wylm went back to his corner.

Onero looked to Wylm. Wylm had a shallow grin hiding at the corner of his lip. It was so subtle Onero hardly noticed. Wylm was not like this one month ago. His life was structure and soldiering. He lived always to please his father and to be the greatest warrior. He trained hard and beat his body and lived every day within the regiments of military life. That life was not merely on hold, it was over. Now, Wylm was a man without an allegiance, an explorer, a pioneer, a dangerous warrior on the frontier of a new world. This was a world where he did not know the rules or the players in the game. He did not know the law; he was an outlaw.

Onero knew that until they knew the law, the rules, and the game, they were going to be challenged. With Wylm, Onero's livelihood in this country would likely be constantly in danger. Without Wylm, he might not survive that danger. As Wylm continued to look at him with that subtle grin, Onero began to interpret its meaning. *I'm protecting you again. That's one more point for me.* Onero had to find out more about the game. Wylm's foolhardy strength could not be relied upon forever.

Tofir was beginning to catch his breath, but his bruised throat made it a painful recovery. While some of the others were distracted, Onero took the floor. "My name is Onero Seon. This is my friend—" Wylm grunted, halting Onero's sentence. He stammered to resume his story when the young boy spoke up.

"Shachal! Shachal! It's Shachal!" The young boy beside Onero could not contain his joy. "The White Lion has returned! He has."

Onero was shocked. Wylm looked amused. Onero asked the necessary question. "Young man, who is Shachal? Who is the White Lion?"

"Do you really not know Shachal? He built Kefeer. He did. He was the first king of the Emari. He was. Some said he was a god. My father told me he would return one day. He said it was prophesied many years ago when Kefeer was destroyed. My father used to say, 'Goor, listen to me,' he said. 'Shachal will return, and when he does, he will rebuild Kefeer. You must unite yourself with him, Goor. You must bring honor to our house.'"

Turning to Wylm, Goor said, "Am I right? Am I? Are you Shachal? Are you the White Lion? Are you going to rebuild Kefeer and restore your kingdom? Are you?"

Wylm looked at the young boy. He was enjoying this and hated to deny the lad the joy he seemed to have in thinking he was Shachal. To be fair, he hated denying himself the idolization he was receiving. So, he kept silent.

Onero took advantage of the pause. "What is this prophecy?"

Goor did not hesitate.

> *"The White Lion will come from mountains south, black panthress at his side;*
> *'Rebuild Kefeer,' ordered from his mouth, 'my glory to abide.'*
> *The stones will rise, a kingdom to build, and people filled with dread;*
> *His enemies slain, by the cougar killed, alas his right hand red."*

Jugel spoke up for the first time in days. "Shachal was an albino Emari who walked these lands a thousand years ago. In those days there were many tribes that warred against each other. Shachal gathered a band of outcasts around him and raided many villages and tribes and made them pay him tribute. His band of ruffians and scoundrels grew larger and stronger and he began to take over a village, then a town, then tribe after tribe. He had set himself over enough of the country that he declared himself king of all Geongalann, north of the mountains. He built for himself the city of Kefeer. He reigned in fear and terror. Eventually his lust for power escalated to the point that he declared himself a god."

"What happened?" Onero asked. "How did his reign end?"

"He died," Jugel answered bluntly. "He grew old, like we all do, and died."

"No, he did not. He didn't," cut in Goor. "He travelled south by night and was carried over the mountains by the ravens. He was. His prophets said that he was going to establish his dominion over the rest of the world. They said he would be coming back, and the whole world would be prepared for his eternal reign. It would. "

"Tales for fools and drunkards," dismissed Jugel. "The reign of Shachal was a mortal and blasphemous reign. Any Emari who claims to be Shachal is wicked and has only evil in mind for the the rest of us. Consider Regeldam, who has now set himself up as king in Kefeer. He wears the fur of a white lion as a cloak; he crowns himself with the head of the same lion, and wears a red glove on his right hand. He has already set about the rebuilding project of Kefeer. In fact, we are likely being taken to the Pit of Bor where strong and able prisoners are sent to work in the quarry."

Goor was becoming furious. His long, scarlet hair was standing on end. Onero noticed his claws starting to extend from his fingertips. "That Emari that I will not name is not the White Lion! He's not. He is an imposter. He is. My daddy told me. He came from the north, not the mountains. He is not even really white skinned. He wears a costume to fool people into believing. He does. That imposter on the throne in Kefeer is not Shachal. Shachal would not steal all the women from the villages. He would not cut off the hands of the men. He would not have killed my daddy, no way; an Emari who has spent his life waiting for Shachal's return." As he mentioned the death of his father, his tone died down, and his shoulders began to drop. "He is not Shachal." Then looking to Wylm, he asked, "Are you the White Lion? Are you?"

Nobody knew it at the time, but what Wylm did and said next changed the lives of everyone in that cage. His actions appeared harmless and his words seemed innocent. He rose from his corner, stepped to the boy, and crouched down beside him. Putting his arm around the boy, he spoke softly in his ear, "Don't worry, young one. They've taken your father, but I'm here."

Onero had never felt more confused in his whole life. They were in a strange land with strange people. Women were being taken, and men were being maimed and killed. Most bewildering of all, Wylm was showing compassion to a young child. More concerning, though, was that he was allowing this boy's fantasy to continue. It felt dangerous to Onero. He intended to put a stop to it and was about to open his mouth to declare that

Wylm was not Shachal. At that moment, the serpent around his waist constricted, halting his words.

He chose a question to ask instead. "Why are the women being captured and taken to this King Regeldam? Why are the men being relieved of their left hands?"

Another of the lion-men, an Emari, spoke up. This one had a dark beard and dark hair. Onero noticed a leaf here and a twig there, scattered within his hair. "My name is Kahya of Nachal. May the strength of Emabbir find you. I'll take a shot at answering why my here brothers are losing their hands. When that there Regeldam declared himself king, a prophet came to pay him a visit. It's said that no one ever seen this prophet until a couple of years ago. That there seer is shorter than most Emari. He has long white hair and thick gray beard that covers most of his face except for his pointy nose. On his head he wears a shaggy fur of some creature I'm not familiar with. That there fur covers his eyes."

"The stories I heard," Kahya continued, "say that he was reckoned to be just a crazy old fool until he started making them there predictions that kept coming true. Others said they seen him perform some wondrous signs. These started in our small towns of the Southern Foothills. As his fame grew, the prophet was bound by Regeldam's guards and taken to Kefeer so Regeldam would have his own personal seer. The king figured that if he seen into the future, he could stay one step ahead of his enemies."

"You seem to know a lot about this prophet," stated Onero in a tone that requested more information.

"I reckon I do," confirmed Kahya. "I seen him two years ago. He came to my home."

Many of the captives had lost interest in Kahya's unrefined speech until he said those words.

"My wife—may Emabbir guard her—had just prepared her famous rabbit stew, but my children—protect them—had picked the wrong herbs. Those there ones they picked were poisonous. Now my Sweetie always lets me have the first bite at dinner, and when I swallowed that there spoonful I could immediately feel death rising up inside me. At that moment, our door swung open and I seen this prophet enter our home.

"He wore an animal-skinned cloak over his head. It was marked with some symbol like a bow and arrow, nocked and drawn, and aimed at the sky. He had a staff in his right hand and some herbs in his left. The man walked right up to that there kettle, tossed in his herbs, stirred the stew, and pulled out a hot mouthful in the ladle. He then rushed up to me like a scared deer and forced the stew down my throat. I reckon it burned away half my stomach."

"The whole time he was saying, 'This will not do. This will not do. The Lion has made plans, and you should really not be trying to foul them up. The bow of the great hunter will be needed in the end.' Then he up and walked out of our house. Pert-near immediately after I swallowed I began to feel death leave me. Within a couple of minutes, I was like my old self again. I tried to find him to thank him, but this here seasoned hunter couldn't even find his tracks."

"As I said," Kahya began to conclude, "This same prophet came before the king. He stood before him and proclaimed that there imposter to be wicked and unjust. A prophecy of doom was uttered:

"The Warrior will arise from the southern foothills, uniting the South against the wicked King of the North. The Prince will join this insurrection and drive his sword through the heart of the Queen. When the Prince is revealed, the Warrior will strike with his left hand, killing the King who is white as snow. Because of his actions, the Warrior will become defiled, but his seed will rule all for a millennium.'

"That there is word for word. My father heard it for himself and told me by letter."

"Did you know of the attack?" Goor questioned.

"I did," Kahya confessed. "And I got my wife and kids off to safety. I told them to head toward the stronghold of Tetemek, but to not enter except in dire need. I stayed behind to help protect the men of Nachal, but them there soldiers eventually caught me."

Jugel spoke up again, bringing the prophecy back to attention. "You can see why he has sent his soldiers to cut off the left hands of the men of the South. If no man has a left hand, then the prophecy cannot be fulfilled. But Regeldam is foolish. He is also trying to rebuild the city of Kefeer. He needs workers to build and to quarry the rock. He believes that the prisoners cannot escape from the prison at Bor. Thus, he captures what he believes are the most capable and strongest willed men to put to work in his pit. He is foolish because he leaves them both of their hands."

No one else was speaking on the matter, and Jugel turned to Onero to explain to him a brief history of his people. None of the other Emari stopped him. It seemed that listening to Jugel's words brought some clarity to all of them, even though they had lived there whole lives in this land.

"Concerning the women," Jugel began. "A desecration by our people has led to great iniquity. It was through this iniquity that Regeldam came into power. In the ancient days, there were many more women than men north of the mountain. Men took more than one wife to provide for the women and to give them love. In doing this, our people expanded quickly. What began as a decision of compassion and the strengthening of our people turned into an abomination. Eventually, the number of women being born began to equal that of the men. In the North especially, the men take many wives. An Emari's status in the North is determined by his wives: how many he has, how long their hair is, and how well they are dressed.

"The wealthy stayed north and those who were poorer moved south. Regeldam began as a man of great wealth. He had a few wives who were very well dressed and with long, flowing hair. One day, his business took him south. At the base of the mountains, he met a woman who was more beautiful than any he had ever met before. Her father gave her away for a lowly bride-price. When he came back north, all were amazed at her beauty, and Regeldam's status rose in the community.

"This woman then inspired him to take more and more wives," Jugel continued. "Then she persuaded him to surround himself with the strongest men of the kingdom and to give them additional wives. He heeded all her advice. Soon he was sending his men out to find young women from all over the kingdom. They were payment to his men for their loyalty. The number of his faithful followers grew for the promise of a wife. Rebellion or betrayal meant that your bride would be taken from you and given to another."

Onero listened and shook his head at the depravity of all creatures under the sun. Jugel went on. "Like Shachal of old, Regeldam became so powerful that he set himself up as king. His seductive bride from the base of the mountains then fashioned for him a cloak and crown from the hide of a large snow cat from Melkorak. She pronounced him as the Great White Lion, and they moved to Kefeer and began to rebuild it. "

Kahya interrupted Jugel at this point. "How do you know all of this? That there is more detail than I have ever heard of Regeldam."

"My father used to be Regeldam's business partner," Jugel answered. "My father loved my mother solely and uniquely. At first, Regeldam only teased my father about his devotion to my mother, but eventually he began to persecute all who had only one wife, especially if that one wife was not a gift from Regeldam. My father fled to the South when I was a boy. He fled a free Emari."

Tofir had fully caught his breath and moved into a sitting position. He recuperated against the bars of the cage. "And now you are being dragged to the North like the rest of us—"He groaned as he rubbed his chest with one hand and his throat with the other. "—In shackles."

17 BARDAZ BEROGEIS

Bardaz Berogeis was an impressive creature. He stood a head taller than any other Mugaal in his court. His chest was as massive as a bear's, and his arms were as thick as most other's thighs. His horns pointed skyward at twice the height of any in his kingdom. In hand-to-hand combat, there was not a king in all of Nold that could best him, except for maybe the Pytecki king. Not a single Mugaal could overcome him, and likely not twenty. His physique was of great renown.

Yet it was not by strength that he became leader of the Mugaal. He had a brilliant mind for strategy and war, though the Mugaal had not fought a war in his lifetime. He had great foresight into the events of the future. That was how his people had recognized the Nemarian spies. That was how he saw an impending Nemarian invasion as a chance to finally free his people from the fear of Rhumaiv.

Bachar had fallen just over a week ago. The last of their forces had made their final stand in the plains of Katalalo, near the watchtower. His spies reported it was annihilation. Now, his forces could finally leave Arogan Forest and attack those fertile lands, the lands that had once belonged to the people of Rhumaiv, the Bacharites. Long he had told his counselors the Bacharites no longer served Rhumaiv and that the sorcery of that martyr from half a millennium ago would no longer cover them.

His counselors had been cautious. "Your words may be true, oh wise King Berogeis," they had flattered him. "But if you are not correct, then we risk losing ninety percent of our people, as it happened in the Decimation of Rhumaiv." With hesitancy, they had asked, "What of the small chance you are wrong, Oh great king?"

That counsel had always stayed his hand in the past, but the Bacharites were a defeated people. The Nemarians now ruled south of the forest, and they were a heathen nation who followed no individual deity. *No power now prevents me from leaving Arogan.* Bardaz Berogeis stroked his thick, coarse beard, which started at the corner of his lips and hung to the top of his abdomen. His generals were preparing their forces for an offensive within the next week or two.

His thoughts were interrupted by one of his guards. "My Lord, General Hywel from the Ostmark is here to see you."

"What is Hamaraz doing here?" Bardaz Berogeis boomed. "He should be preparing his company for the upcoming offensive."

"He would not tell me, my king," the guard pronounced. "He said he left the Ostmark before the sun rose. He rode all day to bring you an urgent message."

The word *urgent* appeased Bardaz slightly. "Send him in."

General Hamaraz Hywel strode into the room and stood at attention before his king.

King Berogeis waved off the formality. "Be at ease, Hamaraz. What is this urgent message that takes you away from preparing for war?"

"I have had a dream, my king," Hamaraz stated.

"A what?" the king asked, not trying to hold back his anger at what he thought was a less-than-adequate response.

"King Berogeis, when you were commander of the Horned Army, I served as one of your captains. You will remember the story I told you of my childhood dream. In those days, you were interested. You thought highly of the words I spoke, and even brought me into your counsel after I told you."

Bardaz waved his hand, as if to try to hurry Hamaraz's words. "Of course I remember, the mighty ram leading a victorious army. It is because of that dream that I have raised for the Mugaal such a grand army. It is also because of that dream that I have not ordered you to receive lashes at this moment." Truly any other officer would have been whipped or worse for such a dereliction of duties, but Bardaz had never before heard of any other Mugaal having a dream. When he first heard Hamaraz's boyhood dream, he had been filled with pride and purpose. Now he hoped to feel the same. "Go on, Hamaraz, tell me your dream."

The general went on to express his dream. As he described it, the face of King Bardaz Berogeis began to grow red. When General Hywel finished telling what he had seen, there was a long, awkward silence.

Finally the king broke that pause. "That is it?" he fumed. "You left your troops in the Ostmark to tell me about a child's tale of woe?"

"It is not a child's tale, my king. I believe it is about the Mugaal. I believe it is about the Nemarians." General Hywel was showing great courage in front of the king.

"You believe?" King Berogeis raged. "Is that all this is, a belief? What happened with your first dream? Did it ever come true?"

"Not yet, my king, but I belie—"

"You believe," the king interrupted. "Once again, you believe." He gathered himself for a moment before continuing. "Do you believe yourself to be a prophet? Perhaps you are a witch? Do not get me wrong, General, I would be impressed with you having had one dream, let alone two. The thing is, I am not sure I even believe you had the first dream. How convenient that the first dream brought you into my graces. Some might say you gained your position as general because of that vision. And now you bring me this one." Again the king paused. He would give Hamaraz the chance to save himself. He truly did like the general. He had been a good friend and counselor for many years. "Now that you have presented me with this new dream, what is it that you suggest?"

General Hamaraz Hywel knew what he needed to say. He also knew what would be the best response to maintain his livelihood as he knew it. King Bardaz Berogeis provided the official question, but the real question was "which answer would he give?"

"King Berogeis, I know in my heart that we Mugaal have become too enamored with our own greatness. No longer do we even consider from where that greatness comes. I believe the survival of the Mugaal depends on the decision you make this day. I believe the Mugaal will be destroyed by the Nemarians. They are a formidable foe. Even the fortress of Sardis has fallen."

"You disgrace to Arogan..." the king began, but Hamaraz kept speaking.

"I believe the only way to save the Mugaal would be to surrender to the Nemarians—"

"You are a coward of the highest order and are not worthy of your horns..."

"If not surrender, then we should flee, as a nation." Hamaraz was done. He had stated his case and recommendations. Now he would stand there, like the soldier he was, and await what orders the king gave.

"By your words and by your counsel, you are stripped of all that you have. No longer are you a general of the Horned Army. No longer are you to bear arms in the service of Arogan. No longer are you a citizen of this great Realm. You will be banished to Libbiorn Prison, you and your whole family. Anyone who swears allegiance to you will join you. There you will stay in the darkness until the Mugaal are victorious over the Nemarians. On that day, the day of my great victory, I will drag you back into the sun. You will be executed; first your servants, then your children and your wife, and finally, when all has been stripped away, you too will go to your eternal torment under Ivveleth's Mountain with the rest of this world's cowards."

18 WORDS OF LAYISH

After breaking camp the next morning, the caravan of soldiers and captives set out for another day's journey heading west. The soldiers split up Wylm and Onero when Captain Pilesar had decided "the two pale foreigners" should not be together. Wylm had been shackled alongside Kahya of Nachal and Goor of Koor. Onero was chained alongside Jugel of Herr's Cove. The latter two had considered it the providence of the Creator. Of the captives from the other night, they were the only ones that the other really trusted.

Each one told his story. Onero started with the invasion of, and resounding defeat by, the Nemarians. He told of the tunnel and prison escape. He told of the Mugaal and the mountain pass. Surprising himself, he even told of finding the body of his grandfather and the snake that turned into his staff. Jugel recalled the staff and lamented that it was surrendered when

Regeldam's soldiers captured them. Onero did not mention that the staff was still traveling with him in the form of a serpent. Finally, Onero told Jugel of his oath and wavering friendship with Wylm. He was surprised by how much he shared, but he felt nothing in his spirit telling him to stop.

When Onero was done, Jugel told his story, making Onero realize that only part of the truth had been told a few nights earlier. "Regeldam and my father were not only business partners but best friends. When Regeldam began to take on many wives, my father—named Jugel of Kefeer—was initially jealous of his status," Jugel of Herr's Cove said, not shying away from the past faults of his father. "Then my father took a wife for himself, but unlike his associates, he saw her for the soul that she was."

Jugel became wistful at the mere mention of the word *wife*. His bride had been stolen from him, ripped from his arms by that wretched Regeldam. The lord of Kefeer had taken his love, and for what? Another night of his own pleasure, as a purchase price for some new sycophant? As he ran alongside Onero, his teeth clenched and his claws extended. Onero could tell that this was more than just anger. Some purpose wrapped in confidence fueled the look in his eyes.

"He will pay for what he did," Onero said, trying to console his new friend.

Hearing Onero's words brought Jugel back. His claws retracted as his jaw relaxed. "I am sorry, my friend. Where was I?"

"Your father had taken a wife," Onero reminded him.

"Oh yes. Jugel of Kefeer, my father, took for himself a wife, and they loved each other solely and desired each other's company. Those around him had encouraged him to take more wives to increase his status and his wealth. He could not fathom sharing himself with another."

Onero stopped Jugel. "You are confusing me by calling your father *Jugel* as well. Do you have the same name?"

Jugel flashed annoyance at such a childish question, then realized that their customs might be quite different than those south of the Great Mountains. "In Geongalann, one's name declares his lineage. If a firstborn son is worthy, he will take on his father's name when he comes of age. The father then will take on another name. Sometimes with Emari of prominence, the father will keep his name until death, at which time his heir will take his name. Many times the son is not deemed worthy, or another child is deemed more worthy. There are many other *ifs* and *buts* and *whens*, but I am not a scribe who can explain them all. Needless to say, when the time came, I took on the name Jugel, from my father."

Jugel of Herr's Cove continued his story. "When Regeldam began to come into power, my father began to speak out against his actions. At first he spoke directly to Regeldam as a friend, suggesting that what he was doing was not right. This progressed to blatantly telling him that his actions and decrees were evil. 'Judgment will come upon you, and darkness will take you forever,' my father had prophesied to his former friend."

"Regeldam had been taken aback by my father's words and challenged him to a duel. I was nine years old at the time and had not yet taken my father's name. When the challenge was issued, my father accepted. He was a strong and deft warrior. I still remember the day he came home and announced the duel to Mother and me over dinner." Jugel paused as if wishing for those days when the three of them dined together.

"That night, the Lion appeared to my father in a dream," Jugel said. "He told my father to flee to the eastern foothills at the base of the mountain.

He said the fight would not be fair, and my father would die along with my mother and me."

"The Lion?" Onero interrupted. "Who is the Lion?"

"He is Layish, the counselor of our people, sent by the God of Emabbir to deliver the Emari." Jugel was in wonder that Onero did not know him.

"After this vision, my father fled. My mother loved him for it. Regretfully, I thought him a coward and told him this to his face many times. We travelled east and then south, along the same road they have led us captive these past days. On the third night, on the eastern shore of Eastern Lake, Layish, the Lion, appeared to my father and blessed him. He told him that he must 'persevere in the face of adversity' then gave him a magnificent sword. It is called Shawag, *The Lion's Roar*. With that sword and the blessing of Layish, Jugel of Kefeer went with confidence and rested in the town of Herr's Cove. He took on a different name and gave me the name Jugel when I came of age. Eventually my uncles joined us, and we lived a peaceful and quiet life."

"That is a fascinating story," Onero remarked. "It is as if your family has one of the great tales as written in the Book of Prophets."

"What is the Book of Prophets?" Jugel asked.

"It is the stories of the ways our Maker has guided and directed and corrected men, whether it be nations or individuals." It was Onero's turn to become wistful. "I used to have access to the book and read it often."

"Used to?"

"I was a prophet in training, but I was banished from the order five years ago."

"What happened?"

"It is a painful story that I do not wish to retell, but your story reminds me of the life I had always hoped to have. That was when being a prophet was a possibility for me. You speak of spiritual beings presenting themselves to your family, and prophecies being spoken over you. It seems that the prophets are alive and well north of the Great Mountains. You are fortunate to have such an experience in your family." Onero was excited for Jugel and the people of Geongalann, and melancholy that this level of spiritual greatness could now never come to him. "Take comfort in the fact that a being such as this Layish has presented himself visibly to your own father."

"Not only to my father," Jugel said. "He also came to me. It is a tragic story, but one worth telling.

"My father had been an older man when he married and was nearly sixty when I was born. He died five years ago on the northern slopes of the Fortress Peak. For five hundred years, the kings of Geongalann had kept a small garrison of men to guard the mountain pass there. The soldiers would serve a six month stint before they were relieved by the next garrison. The people of Herr's Cove kept an eye on the road from the pass to their village. If any soldier passed along that road, a call went out, and my father and uncles would hide.

"One day, my father was watching the road when a commotion was heard at the pass. He went closer for a look and saw a horde of foul, mannish beasts with bent backs and crude weapons. They had fallen upon the garrison of soldiers and were killing them. My father had no love for the soldiers of Regeldam, but they were Emari and in need. He drew Shawag from its scabbard and let out a terrible roar. It was heard for miles around. The beasts shuddered, but then attacked.

“My father attacked the horde, his seventy-five-year-old body remembering the art of battle. Forty of these intelligent beasts fell to Shawag that day, but eventually my father was overrun. The men of Herr’s Cove and my uncles arrived just in time to see him fall. As his youngest brother came to his side, my father handed him Shawag and made him vow to pass it on to me.

“I had come late to the foray, as I had been hunting five miles to the north. When I heard my father’s cry, I came swiftly to the mountain. He never saw me. My uncle gave me Shawag, and I was overcome with justice. I bounded after the remaining beasts and followed them to Lylyth’s Hill. Many were overtaken and killed by the power of Shawag in my hand.” As Jugel retold the story, the ferocity of a warrior flashed across his eyes. ”But a remnant remained and crossed a narrow bridge over a large canyon. My father had warned me to never approach that mountain, so I stayed and waited there for a whole week. The beasts never came back out.

“As I made way home, a failure and fatherless, I cried out in grief. I mourned to Layish over the loss of my father.” Jugel paused and looked to Onero. His eyes were filled with wonder, as if he had seen something more perfect and beautiful than life itself. “Then, Layish appeared to me. When I saw the Lion, I was terrified and fell to my face. With a voice like the multitudes, He spoke to me. Then He said my name.” Jugel paused again and closed his eyes, causing him to stumble on the rough terrain as they were being nearly dragged behind the cart. Despite this, he kept them closed. He was reliving the sound of his name as spoken by his encourager.

“When I heard my name, Onero, an unexplainable calm swept over me. Layish told me that I must lead the people of Geongalann. He said, ‘I give you the same admonition I gave your father. You must persevere in the face of adversity. You must stay in the South and never set out for the northern kingdom, but on the day you are brought north of the Eastern Lake—where your father first met me—on that day you shall be the King of the Emari.'"

Onero was amazed by this story. It was fascinating and nearly unbelievable. Or was it truly unbelievable? He had just met this Jugel. The warrior fought valiantly and seemed truthful, but he was Emari, and Onero did not know the ways of this strange people. He wanted to believe Jugel. He wanted to help him become king, but he held back his full belief. He considered the words of his grandfather. *A liar's words are like guju berries: sweet on the tongue, but death to the body.*

Jugel of Herr's Cove looked at Onero as they ran behind the moving cart, now doing well to keep stride. Onero, on the other hand, seemed to be processing all he heard and was thus stumbling more often than not. "We passed Eastern Lake right after we broke camp this morning," Jugel informed his new friend. "And the only person that knows that I am a king is you. Of course, you are not Emari."

19 IN A PIT

The long caravan of soldiers and captives came to a stop. All fourteen of the male captives were once again loaded into a single cage. Two garrisons of soldiers surrounded the cage of the prisoners. The rest went with the women captives as they were transported west to Kefeer.

The tops of the tallest buildings in Kefeer could be spotted from where they were. Unfortunately, Onero did not know where that might be. He had heard the name Bor in context with a prison, pit, dungeon, and quarry. As he looked around, he saw no landmarks, workers, or other captives. All he saw were the soldiers who surrounded him and his fellow captives. An Emari soldier leapt onto the top of the cage and fed a rope through eyelets on opposite sides of the cage. Then he tied the rope upon itself. Forty soldiers grabbed that rope and began to slide the cage off the back of the cart. The three foot drop was jolting.

One edge of the cage rested on the ground, and the other was on the cart. The soldiers dropped the rope and moved to the front of the cage. As they approached the elevated side, the captives moved away from that edge, expecting ill treatment. The soldiers tipped the cage on end and knocked it to its side. The captives fell upon one another. Onero was on the bottom and suffered more than a little under the tremendous size of the Emari.

The soldiers turned the cage around and began to push it along the smooth rock. Wylm strode to the edge of the cage that faced his captors and grabbed the bar with his left hand. With his right, he grabbed the wrist of the nearest soldier. The same soldier reached to his waist for his sword, but at the same moment his comrades gave the cage one final push. For a moment in time, the fourteen people inside the cage became weightless.

The captives were falling off the edge of a cliff. Fear began to rise in Onero until he was suddenly hurtled to the floor. The rope had gone taut after a fifteen foot drop. Only Wylm did not join the heap of bodies on the cage floor. He was still holding onto the top bar. The soldier whose wrist he had grabbed had initially been on the top of the cage. When their drop came to a sudden stop, the cage swung and the soldier fell.

What shocked most of the captives was how far the soldier fell. Two hundred feet above the quarry floor, the cage swayed back and forth through the air. It clanged against the sheer rock wall, jostling the captives every time it did. Onero glanced around. Below him and around him was a large pit, a maw spanning about a half mile front to back and side to side. Nearly every wall was steep and sheer. On one side of the pit was a quarry lake. Its waters lapped at the base of the rock wall on either side. Beyond the lake was the only wall that had any real forestation and maneuverable terrain.

Jugel saw Onero glancing at the lake and wall beyond. "There will be no escape beyond that water," he cautioned. "The deep waters of this land are filled with Lylyth's monsters."

As they continued to descend, Onero continued to survey their new surroundings. He noted that every fifty feet along the quarry wall, halfway down the rock face, was a railed platform. It was like a nest of some great bird on a craggy ledge. A rope ladder descended from the cliff edge above to the platform below. Stationed in each were two or three archers. Like a kettle of vultures, these archers encircled the quarry floor and watched the prisoners.

Dozens of Emari were laboring below. Each prisoner was armed with a tool. Some had pick axes, others hammers, and some chisels. There were many crews. One crew was hewing the rock from the face of the wall on the east end of the quarry. This was the only attainable location where the rock wall was not a sheer face. There were about ten ledges from top to bottom. Each ledge was three times the height of an Emari. There was only one ladder that was moved from ledge to ledge. This whole section gave the only possibility of escape that Onero could see. Fifty archers were at the top of the quarry with arrows nocked and aimed, ready to stop any plan of escape.

Once the rocks were hewn, the large chunks were lowered to the floor where they were squared by another group of prisoners. Guards with whips surrounded these prisoners. As Onero watched, one prisoner chipped a corner of the rock and ruined the finish. A guard began to beat him mercilessly. Other guards joined in. From the other side of the block, another prisoner leapt, chisel in hand. He buried it into the back of one of the guards.

Instead of attacking the second prisoner, the guards all backed away. As soon as there was distance between them and the aggressor, three arrows sunk into the chest of the Emari that held the chisel. The guards then converged on the slain prisoner and dragged his body to the water. They paused by a large wooden scaffolding with a platform on top. It had two stilts on the quarry floor and two in the water. From that point, they threw the body into the lake.

Onero watched as the body began to sink. At first a bubble or two escaped to the surface, and then the water began to churn wildly and vehemently. For a brief moment, what looked like a thick brown sea snake slithered over the body then both the snake and the body disappeared. The water slowly stilled. Onero stared in awe. The others just turned their head in sorrow as if they had seen this before. *What devilry lurks in the deep waters of this world?*

"No wonder they need fresh workers," grumbled Wylm.

Whether it was lack of food, too much running, or the violent death he just saw, Onero's stomach churned. He turned his head and looked back to the prisoner's work. They had just finished squaring one of the quarried blocks. It was then rolled on sticks to a platform. The platform was suspended from the top of the quarry's edge by four strong ropes. A large pulley system was at the top, and the guards slowly pulled up the platform.

The cage of captives struck the rock floor, bringing Onero's thoughts back to his current situation. They were immediately surrounded by thirty guards with clubs and whips.

Their chief came to the door. "Your work detail will begin tomorrow. First you will spend a day and night in the Oven."

The guards lined up on either side of the door and made a path through which the captives were meant to walk. They stood a fair distance from the captives and marched them to the far side of the quarry. Having seen one prisoner skillfully eliminated by the archers, none of the new prisoners chose aggression.

They were marched to a point on the north of the quarry. A cave was cut out at the base of the wall, beneath two hundred feet of rock above. Thick iron bars covered the mouth of the cave from top to bottom and some went side to side as well. The cave was large and could hold many prisoners. As they neared the entrance, an increasing wave of heat bellowed from its mouth. One of the guards unlocked three thick chains that secured the door. He swung the door in, and all the new captives were ushered inside.

It had already been very hot that day, and the heat from within the cave made it unbearable. Within minutes, they all were sweating profusely. This was obviously a tactic to exhaust and weaken the prisoners to make their chance of escape less likely. The young Emari, Goor, was able to stand closer to the back of the cave than any of the others. As he stood near the heat source, his hair looked a deeper scarlet. The light layer of hair on his arms made his whole body look red. He smiled.

"It's like the furnace in Koor! It is," he said excitedly. "Only this one is not as hot. My daddy told me the furnace in Koor was a gift from Shachal to his helpers. They had provided Shachal with strong weapons of war. They did. And, in return, he gave them an eternal fire. As a thank you for the gift, the black smiths of Koor gave Shachal koorore. Yes, they did."

Goor's excitement was very much out of place considering the captive's situation. Onero recognized this, but anxiety, like the heat, was beginning to overwhelm him. He needed noise, conversation, anything to take his mind off his ever-worsening situation. So he prodded the curiously excited Goor. "What is koorore?"

Goor was all too ready to explain. "It is a metal that gets stronger as it gets hotter. It does. Only the most skilled of smiths can fashion it and bend it. On a normal day in Geongalann, a sword made of koorore is stronger than any other blade. It is. In a place like this cave, the sword would be harder than a diamond. It would. Only when water turns to ice does the metal become weak. Yes, sir. You might have noticed that the bars of our prison are also made of koorore."

The young Emari paused and thought about their situation. He still stood fifteen feet closer to the source of heat than any of the other prisoners. Goor brought his eyes up to meet Wylm's. "Only Shachal could break us out of a prison like this. Only Shachal could."

Wylm felt sorry for the boy. The hope he put in Wylm and the despair he felt at possibly being wrong about him made Wylm feel like he had to do everything he could to help this young boy through this terrible circumstance. Forsaking the pain and discomfort from the heat, he stepped forward and approached Goor. He stood beside him and put his arm around the young lad who had lost his father only a few days ago. Goor leaned in and rested his head on Wylm's shoulder.

As much as Onero was confused by it, seeing Wylm show compassion to anyone warmed his heart. He had always been a loyal and dutiful friend. Wylm would lay his own life down to save the life of those he loved. In fact, he had done this many times for Onero. He had rescued him from the Pytecki raiders, traitorous soldiers, waterfalls, smugglers, and wolves.

Despite Wylm's great loyalty and bravery, though, Onero had never seen him compassionate.

Maybe it was this place, not so much the pit, but the land in general. It was different than any of the lands he had seen south of the Great Mountains. Those lands, back home, seemed more advanced and older. The people were governed by rules and laws and religion. This land, Geongalann, seemed younger and more innocent. The people seemed ruled more by duty and honor. Here the words of a prophet were honored and feared. Miracles were more prevalent. Even their deity walked among them in the form of a lion, according to Jugel.

Of course, it was not a perfect analogy. Geongalann still had its governments, and Bachar had its miracles. However, even the government of this young world seemed like the stuff from legends and children's books. The miracles of Onero's homeland were far too few and seemed to only surround his family. At least they did, once upon a time, before he was banished, his father scandalized, and his grandfather dispensed on a fool's errand only to die within the mountain.

Onero realized he was no longer thinking about Wylm and Goor. He stared past them, to the deep recesses of the cave. He thought back to his childhood, when he would sit before the fireplace at his grandparents' home and just stare into the coals, letting the heat wash over his face. His grandfather would sit on his chair, a few feet behind Onero, and read a book.

On. That's what his grandfather used to call him. *On.* His name begins with a long *O*, but his grandfather would shorten his name to 'On', and say it like using the *O* from the word *joy*. Onero never understood it, but he cherished the way those two letters sounded when spoken by his grandfather. "On, come over here," his papa used to say. "I have a wonderful story to tell you."

20 ON

When evening came, the rest of the prisoners were returned to their heated cave. The recently captured were too fatigued to attempt or even consider an escape. None of them were used to so much heat. Even Goor had made his way toward the bars for some fresher, cooler air. After the prisoners' long day of labor, they were fatigued beyond the physical. Their cat-like eyes were lifeless and hopeless. It did not require a great stretch of the imagination for Onero to see how they had gotten to this point. These were farmers and hunters, simple men whose lives and freedom had been stolen from them. How long until hope was drained from his eyes as well?

Onero watched as six guards ushered the laborers into the holding area. As the gate swung in, they dragged themselves through one by one. They ranged from boys slightly older than Goor to elder Emari with long white beards. Like most Emari, they were tall and muscular, and even the boys were taller than Onero. Toward the back of the weary crowd was one who stood out by the fact that he was consumed by the relative giants around him.

Where all of the prisoners were tall, he was short. Most were wearing minimum clothing, such as tattered trousers and absent or shredded shirts. This one was robed from head to toe with old, well-worn fabric. A fur mantle was over his head and around his shoulders. Many of the grown Emari had a one- to two-inch beard that lacked a mustache. The hair on their face was soft in appearance. This shorter one had a long gray beard that was ragged and coarse and uninviting.

His head was down, and he was dragging himself toward the gate. When he was still five steps away, he stumbled and fell to his hands and knees. The Emari prisoners around him sidestepped him in a curious display of callousness toward their fellow captive. Onero wondered what evil this one had performed to deserve such indifference. The older one was slow to come to his feet. It seemed to Onero that no one but he cared about the lone straggler.

But someone else did care. One of the guards, named Bagad, drew a whip from his side and flogged the old man across his back, causing him to fall prostrate as his back extended and his arms gave out. The other guards looked to their aggressive comrade with disapproval and fear. They slowly stepped away from the one bearing the whip. Bagad showed no fear as he whipped the old man again, yelling obscenities at him. "Get to your cage, you lapdog of Lylyth. Your cunning tongue cannot save you in Bor."

Though no one else seemed to care, Onero felt a deep compassion for this helpless captive. He looked to Wylm, who shook his head and turned his back, drawing back into the cave with the others. Onero did not expect Wylm to do anything. He could not count on him for all acts of heroism. Something had to be done, though. He reached for the gate, pulled it a little more open, and began to take a step.

He was blindsided and slammed to the ground. Onero looked up to see Wylm on top of him. To his side, a step behind where he had been standing, he saw an Emari with an arrow buried into the back of his thigh. Surely that dart had been meant for his chest.

"Rhumaiv curse you, Onero," Wylm spat in anger, as the wounded Emari cried out in pain. "Carcasses. Can't I go a week without saving your life? This isn't a place for heroes. Even if it were, you're not a hero." Wylm dragged Onero deeper into the cave, out of shot of any armed guards. "Didn't you see how everyone else ignored that old man? Why are you trying to save someone who everyone else thinks isn't worthy of being saved?"

By this time, the old man had made his way into the prison. His robe was sliced across the back, and he was bleeding. He stopped just inside the gate before it was slammed shut and locked. Onero pushed away from his friend. "Thank you, Wylm, but in this country, we do not know the definition of *worthy*."

He moved toward the old man who was hunched by the gate. The other prisoners, though, were pressing toward the bars to escape the intense heat and feel the cooler outside air. Onero grabbed the man and dragged him farther in, staying along the rocky wall. He propped the man up on the rock. Fatigued beyond measure from the laborious day's work, the wounded prisoner could not help Onero. Instead, he took advantage of the rare act of kindness being shown to him. He twisted to his right, bringing his bloody back off the wall and exposing his acute wounds to his helper.

Onero surveyed the raw flesh. There was not much he could do except keep the man's garments out of the bloody tissue. "Your mantle is rubbing against your wounds, dear sir. Would you mind if I moved its lower edge higher over your shoulders?"

"Whatever works for you, my child," the old man replied. His voice was weak but full of awareness.

Onero found there was not much to do for the man, so he merely rubbed his shoulders in a compassionate gesture. He found himself with so many questions. Why did no one else help the man? Why were the other guards afraid of him? What did the guard mean by *lapdog of Lylyth* and *cunning tongue*?

The old man slowly turned and faced Onero. His mantle was low over his eyes, and the glow from the furnace cast a shadow on his upper face. "So many questions, my child, but I will do my best to answer them."

Onero began to stammer a response, but the man raised his hand and stopped him. "To start with the last question on your mind, the reason the guard mocked me is because of my reputation. I used to give the king advice, very accurate advice, until one day he no longer wanted my advice. Heh. Such is the way of kings."

Onero was about to speak, but the old man continued. "The reason the other guards were afraid to hurt me is because speaking the truth is not my only set of skills. Let me just say there have been signs that I can be a little more... hmm... flashy."

"You are a prophet!" Onero exclaimed in realization.

"So some have called me," the old man replied. "Others call me a wizard or sorcerer or crazy old man."

Onero looked the man over: long white hair and thick gray beard that covered most of his face except for his broad nose. "You are… are you… of course, you have to be. You are the prophet that foretold the downfall of Regeldam. Is that not true?"

"Is that what I foretold?" the old man asked, not waiting for an answer. "Well, apparently that's at least how Regeldam perceived it. That is how I got my bumpy and hasty ride here to Bor, as well as my, Regeldam-approved, *special treatment* from the guard, Bagad."

"Wow." was all Onero could manage. In that one word, he was expressing his honor, respect, appreciation, and sorrowful envy. He was in the presence of a man who prophesied before kings. That was everything he had wanted to be before it was all torn away from him.

The prophet seemed to read all these emotions and a whole lot more. "I was told someone would be coming to take my mantle, but I was not told whether I would be giving it willingly. Let me see you." He grabbed Onero's chin with his right hand and lifted Onero's head so his eyes were illuminated in the light of the furnace.

He stared at Onero for an extended moment, then let go. Onero thought he heard a quick but muffled intake of breath. The prophet placed his hand on his own face and dropped his head. Onero noticed the man's shoulders began to shudder. Was he afraid or sad? He could not be sure. The prophet was obviously restraining himself, but the occasional whimper or giggle escaped. Onero was not sure if the man was sad or laughing.

For a long time, the man sat quiet. With his head down and face still in his hand, he said in a whisper, "My child, you had one more question you wanted to ask me. In fact, it was the first question that came to your mind. You are wondering why no one else has taken the time to help me or show me any compassion or care. I will answer that question now. The others in this prison do not accept me for the same reason they do not accept you."

The prophet lifted his head and, for the first time, allowed his eyes to come to the light. What Onero saw would have been expected south of the Great Mountains, and thus it took him a bit longer to realize how monumental of a moment it truly was. The old prophet's eyes were round! They were full of wisdom, and full of pupil, and full of tears. "You are a Man!" Onero gasped in amazement. "I do not mean you are a male, but you are a Man, as in from south of the Great Mountains."

"That is right, my child," the prophet said. His eyes were still damp, but a familiar grin peaked through his excessive beard. "And now there are three of the race of Men north of the Mountains: you, me, and the son of Hamyn Kanu."

"What? How? Who? What?" Onero had been amazed nearly every day since falling into that hole only a couple weeks ago, but this moment outweighed all the others. The emotion it roused thieved all rational thought from his mind.

"My dearest On."

Onero froze. A tingling ran from the nape of his neck to the corner of his lips. His muscles quivered and his heart quickened. This could not be. Only one person in the world called him that, and he had not heard that name since he was a young child. Was he really hearing it again? Could this really be the man who prophesied before the kings of the southern kingdom? Could this really be the man who was sent into the Horned Realm on a death errand, the one whose body he had presumably found in the mountain pass? Could this really be Hugla Seon, his grandfather?

"Papa!" Onero regained his strength and hastily embraced his grandfather with a hug that had been a couple decades in the making. He had forgotten the fresh wounds his grandfather had sustained.

Hugla Seon grunted in discomfort, but did not pull away. "You would think that an old prophet would have seen an embrace of that magnitude coming." He pulled Onero close, and the two wept and laughed and forgot the pain, fatigue, and heat of their current circumstances.

Before long, they fell into the shadow of a visitor to their side of the cave. The old prophet, Hugla Seon, addressed the newcomer before he even lifted his head. "Wylm Kanu, it brings great joy to my eyes to see you again."

Wylm's response was not as hospitable as the greeting he had received. "Carcasses, Onero. Did you tell this old fool my name? You have not heard the words these Emari are saying about this delusional sorcerer. Do you not know who this is?"

"Of course I know who this is," Onero said with a smile. "This is my papa."

"Are you really so weak that you are already hallucinating after only one day in this furnace, or has this wizard bewitched you?"

"It is Papa, Master Prophet Hugla Seon. He made it through the pass. He is the prophet who healed Kahya of his sickness. He is the one who foretold the end of Regeldam. He is alive, Wylm. He is alive."

Wylm still had doubts, but a strange hope rose within him. "And my grandfather, did he survive as well? Or was that really his body we saw in the pass?"

Hugla looked deep into Wylm's eyes, and a tear began to form at the corner of his own. "I am truly sorry, young Wylm. I know you have mourned for your grandfather for years, and seeing me renews in you a false hope. You have truly lost the greatest of ancestors.

"Yuri Kanu was the greatest warrior I have ever seen and I am proud to have called him my dearest friend."

"How'd he die?" Wylm asked.

"That, my dear Wylm, is a mystery with which I still wrestle," Hugla lamented. "Our march through the pass had been unimpeded most of the way. We had passed many bodies and had just come upon the last one, a poor soul with an arrow sunk deep between his shoulder blades. It was at that very moment that my staff went limp. A snake's head formed at the top, and it coiled down to my hand and bit me right above my right thumb. The poison took affect almost immediately, and I slumped to my knees, my vision hazy. In that moment, I saw an arrow sink into the chest of my dear friend. He reached for his sword, but by the time he pulled it out, many more arrows had found their mark. "

"He died a hero," Wylm said, mostly to himself.

"He lived a hero," Hugla amplified. "He did so much for me my whole life. He laid down his reputation for me, and it was my hope that I would one day be able to repay him. Alas, he got the upper hand and laid down his life for me as well."

"So seems to be the way with the Kanus and Seons," Wylm muttered, having heard enough. He turned abruptly and walked away, back to the other side of the cave. He did not know how to take the story. It seemed convenient that the old man would be bitten just as an arrow was released. His story did not explain how he did not die from the bite or how he got out of the pass once he came to. "Sounds like another excuse for Seon cowardice," he thought to himself.

Goor, Kahya, and Tofir stood together watching as Wylm approached them. "Is that who I think it is?" Kahya asked.

"No," was Wylm's answer. "That's just a cowardly old man who thinks of nothing but himself. I'm not surprised that not a single prisoner from this haggard bunch made any attempt to rescue him when he was being flogged."

"How can you say that?" Tofir inquired. "You were only over there for a couple moments."

Wylm turned his head quickly to Tofir and shot him a look of ire for daring to question him. The impressive and intimidating Emari took a step back in caution. Wylm relished the control he had over Tofir. After establishing his dominance, he answered him, "I know him, and I know his son. They've betrayed my loved ones to death, and there's no place in my heart for them."

"Do you want me to kill him, lord? Do you? " Goor looked to Wylm. He yearned so much that Wylm was Shachal returned. He would not give up on this dream.

Wylm wished Onero could have heard that. He knew it drove Onero mad to hear Goor laud him with worship and servitude. Why did he allow this young boy's words to continue? Was it because it irritated Onero, or because he did not want to break the lad's heart? Perhaps he was truly only basking in the glory of his praise.

Wylm's father, Hamyn Kanu, Commander of the armies of the southern kingdom, had little opportunity to praise his son. He was often with his troops or officers. Wylm had served him well and rose in the ranks quicker than most, but Hamyn never wanted to be accused of using nepotism. Thus, he gave commendation to Wylm only as much as any other soldier, and maybe less.

Wylm ruffled Goor's red mane. "No, my child, killing the old wizard will not be necessary. Besides, that's a job for soldiers and scoundrels, not innocent children like you."

Goor pulled away slightly at being referred to as an innocent child. He could hold his own. He was not afraid to take the life of those who betrayed his lord and would prove it before this was all over.

Kahya concealed his disagreement with Wylm's words. He was sure that this was the prophet who had saved his life. He recognized the cloak with the mark of the heaven-aimed bow and arrow. Kahya believed the prophet to be good, and he felt similarly about Onero. He really did not know Onero, but what he had observed was a small man who seemed to lack in aggression. He did not believe that the two of them were making plans on how to exploit and destroy everyone else.

Of course, Kahya did not make his thoughts known to Wylm. *That pale devil has a fuse as short as a Lylyth's tail.*

21 MY PRIVILEGE, MY BURDEN

The heat in the prison never relented. It was more than just temperature. The air was thick and difficult to breath. The fact that a cooler evening had fallen helped as much as acquiring one more soldier in a battle against thousands. What helped more was the fact that Onero was with his grandfather again after decades of absence.

"What happened after that, Papa? How did you make it out of the pass?" he asked, never in his life having been so alert in a conversation.

"That is a story of which I only know pieces." Hugla leaned his back against the rock behind him. His body had been shielding the rock, and it felt a little cooler than the air around him. He winced in pain for a few seconds. When it subsided, he told Onero the details he could recall. "I remember beginning to pass out, thinking that my staff had betrayed me to my death.

Before I did, I saw or imagined a great flash of light followed by screams of terror. Soon there was silence. I suspect at that time I had fully passed out.

"When I came to again, I was in the presence of a great amber light." Hugla leaned forward. The coolness of the rock had been absorbed and the relief it had given was overwhelmed by the pressure on his tender wounds. "Soft words were being spoken over me, like those of a woman, but not one that walks on this earth. They were beautiful words that I did not know. If there is any jealousy in my heart, it is that I do not know how to speak in that melodious tongue. Still weak from the poison, I could hardly open my eyes, and every time I tried, the same amber light filled my sight to the point of glorious discomfort, so I kept them shut.

"Soon the words stopped, and I began to sink into a deep sleep. Not a fitful or fevered sleep, but a restful and healing one." Hugla remembered that sleep and wished he could experience it now. "While I slept, I dreamt I was flying through the clouds. When I awoke, I was in a small hut near the top of a mountain in the southwest part of this country. I could see a T-shaped valley below me and a thousand hills stretched out before me. There were lakes and plains and, beyond that, ice. Childlike emotions ran over me, like…"

"Like when your parents first took you to see the Eternal Falls?" Onero interrupted. All children in Bachar talk about the wonder of the Falls the first time they see them.

"Hmm." Hugla looked into Onero's eyes with curious amusement and smiled. "It's as if you are descended from a family of prophets."

Onero faked a smile, then dropped his grandfather's gaze. "Hmm, indeed."

"Oh dear!" Hugla distressed. "The Maker has shown me many things involving the future of this realm and even the last days, but He has hidden my own family from me. Even now, with you here before me, I cannot see what is causing you such pain, nor do I know how you came to be in Geongalann."

"The name of Seon does not carry with it the same reputation it did when you were home," Onero lamented. "Circumstances and choices have turned good deeds into scandal and respect into derision."

"On, I do not care about reputation. Character is all that matters." Hugla began to rub his grandson's back. "Reputation is what the masses think about a person. Character is what the Maker sees in a person." He grabbed Onero by the chin and lifted his head until their eyes met. "Has the character of the Seon's been tarnished or just the reputation?"

"I think it has only been the reputation. At least, I can say I know my father's character stayed true. But I do not know about myself. I do not know what the Maker sees in me. He does not speak to me." Onero paused in introspection, then spoke the first emotion that came to him. "I am the son of a prophet and the grandson of a prophet, but I have no idea what it takes to be a prophet. What do I have to do to hear the voice of the Maker?"

"Listen," Hugla responded.

Onero stopped and listened. He waited for his grandfather to finish his statement. The elder Seon did not speak. He only looked at his grandson with another amused smile, clearly enjoying the opportunity to teach simple life lessons. Onero could not wait any longer. "I'm listening, Papa. What do I have to do?"

"Listen."

"I am, but..."

"Listen, Onero," he said with a little more emphasis. "My young and curious On, all you have to do is listen."

Onero tilted his head back. "Oh." He finally grasped what his grandfather was telling him, but he was far from understanding. "Listen to what?"

"Let me tell you a story. Or rather, let me complete the story I have already started to tell." Hugla leaned farther forward, not because of pain, but because what he was about to tell moved him to do so. "When I was a prophet in Bachar, I relied on my training and the power of my staff. I was more of a wise counselor to the king who occasionally performed some sign from the Maker. Not until I was brought into Geongalann did I truly become a prophet.

"For two days I sat on the precipice of that mountain, sleeping most of the time. When I would awaken, there would be a loaf of bread by my head, as well as a portion of roasted meat. I would eat the meal and drink from the small spring, then fall back to sleep. With the food, drink, rest, and thin air, I finally recovered. It was then that I began to get up and look around. The small hut sat on a piece of grass-covered land that was thirty feet wide and twenty feet deep. I looked for a way off and found none. It was a small outcropping on the side of the mountain. The rocks below me were steep and mostly sheer. I began to panic.

"As soon as those anxious thoughts arose, a hawk with a dark-red tail flew toward my precipice from below. I could see that its flight was labored, as it was carrying something. In one claw it grasped a loaf of bread, and in the other, a portion of roasted meat. For two weeks, three times a day, the hawk would provide sustenance to me. In between those meals, I would look north, out over the world before me. I would ask myself how I had gotten here, what I had done wrong, why this was happening to me. Finally, after two weeks, I got tired of thinking." Hugla paused to make sure Onero was listening. "That is when the hawk stopped coming.

"Days went by and still the hawk brought me no food. I had only the spring to provide its ice-cold water. I became weak and faint. I became too exhausted to think, so I just sat in the hut or near the edge of the precipice and listened. After a few days, I began to have vivid dreams and visions. At first, I thought I was hallucinating, but then I realized I was being shown something important. Vision after vision passed before my eyes. Something impressed upon me that they were visions of the future of this world.

"What is most important to remember, On, is that I did not see any visions until I stopped constantly thinking, and I started listening." Hugla Seon turned his eyes to his grandson who had been getting so wrapped up in the story that he had forgotten there was a lesson to learn.

"Is that it?" Onero asked. "Is the only thing I have to do is listen? Listen to what?

"Close your mouth, Onero," Hugla answered with a little more force. "Rein in your thoughts. Listen to what the Maker is trying to tell you."

"What did the Maker tell you, Papa?" Onero asked to an increasingly exasperated Hugla. "What visions did you see? What happens to this land? Did you see me? Did you see Wylm?"

"I remember a boy who used to come home from school twice a week with a note from his teacher. I think I'm beginning to understand what happened in that classroom." Hugla was experiencing peculiar blend of frustration and amusement. He had felt a tugging in his spirit that this conversation was of dire importance to the lives of the people of this land. What Onero grasped could change the fortunes and wellbeing of the people of Geongalann for a decade and a half.

"On, listen to me. Look into my eyes and listen to me. Many of the visions I saw I have already spoken, and many others were for my eyes only, but one thing sticks out to me. In many visions, and especially in many of the significant ones, this one thing was consistent: a sword and a shepherd's staff, crossed at their centers, played a vital role."

Hugla paused to let that sink in. He continued to look Onero in the eyes. He could see Onero had broken eye contact and was searching his mind to understand this. When Onero finally formed a question, Hugla cut him off and spoke first. "The house of Kanu is very important in shaping the future of this world. I knew this as a young prophet in Bachar. That is why I made an oath to protect them. That is why I made an oath that my descendants would protect them. This is our privilege. This is our burden."

"Why did Master Kanu make the same oath to you?" Onero asked. He had wondered about the oath most of his life. It would be refreshing to get an answer of any kind.

"Yuri loved me. We were closer than friends. We were closer than brothers. I made the oath because I was led to make this oath. Yuri repeated the oath to me because he loved me. It was a statement born by devotion, but conceived in haste."

Onero thought about the oath between him and Wylm. "Wylm has denounced his oath to me. He is angry at me. Actually, he is angry at you and my father 'New world, new rules,' he said to me as we exited the mountain pass. He has lost his love. He has lost his devotion."

Hugla brought his hands up to Onero's face, turning his grandson's gaze up to his own. "Listen to me and do not forget this. You must *never* break your oath to young Master Kanu. No matter what the circumstances, you must hold on."

Just then, one of the guards clinked his sword back and forth against the koorore bars of their prison. It was Bagad, who had whipped Hugla Seon earlier. "Alright, maggots, new and old, the day is done and tomorrow is coming. You fresh recruits are going to learn what a hard day's work really is." He snapped his whip and it moved deftly through the bars and cracked against the cheek of one of the Emari who had made the long trip with Onero and the others. "Better turn the lights out." At this, the guard began to chuckle at his own sadistic humor, for the deep fire of this cave was the cause of their misery, and there was no power known that could nullify it.

22 A RIVAL

Regeldam sat on his throne smiling. Magnificent news had just been received from a messenger. A large supply of virgins had just arrived at the Bride Market. From girls to young ladies, they ranged in age, size, and ferocity. Emari women of the South were not as docile as those in the North. They made better sport for their suitors.

The timing was perfect, and the numbers were just about right. According to the briefing earlier that morning, there were already four hundred future brides in waiting, finishing their preparations. The messenger from the southern raiding band said that another one hundred and twenty-two had just arrived this evening. Regeldam beamed. That was over five hundred girls.

"With the new arrivals, that should cover the new cadets and add another wife for each of my faithful commanders, as well as the nobles on our northern borders who are repelling Melkorak and the Roes," Regeldam said to his queen.

She was dressed in black silk, with a sash of deep purple crossing her left shoulder. Her long hair was pulled together and draped over her right shoulder. Her pale, unadorned neck was exposed to him, contrasting with the purple sash. His eyes followed that contrast until the sash and her hair met in the middle of her plunging neckline. His stomach churned in desire. She had bewitched him. He knew it, and he did not care. She got everything she wanted in the kingdom. In return, he got everything his heart desired.

"We have more than enough," the queen said. "In fact, you should take two or three of the young ones for yourself. Bring them in tonight before they have been prepared. Let them feel the power of the White Lion."

"Not tonight," Regeldam said. He looked his queen in the eyes then again dropped his gaze to follow that purple sash, placing a hand on his abdomen to calm the acidic torrent. "Maybe tomorrow," he said as he took her hand. "I had other thoughts for tonight."

At that moment, a cautious rapping came to the chamber doors. Affairs were supposed to be done for the evening, and Regeldam was irritated. "Come in, attendant."—Regeldam no longer bothered to learn the names of those that kept his schedule. He was continually dismissing them for incompetence or for looking too long at his queen.—"What is it?"

The attendant, a tall and lean Emari who had recently completed cadet training, opened the door and stepped cautiously into the throne room.

"Captain Pilesar of Kefeer has returned from the mission to the Southeast, and he has urgent news for you."

"See him in," Regeldam stated with a wave of his hand. Pilesar of Kefeer was one of his oldest friends. They and another had been business partners long ago, before Regeldam had met the queen. As Regeldam rose in power and stature, Pilesar tried to catch a ride on the train of his robe. He offered too much advice, and this annoyed Regeldam and his queen even more so. She had counseled to have him killed because of his constant begging for more power, but because of his past friendship, Regeldam had actually gone against the advice of his queen. He instead gave his friend the title of Captain and stationed him far from Kefeer to keep him away from the throne.

Now here he was again. Pilesar always felt the need to personally report after each mission. It irritated the queen, and Regeldam always hoped that his captain would not say something inflammatory enough to stir her wrath.

Pilesar entered the throne room proudly, with his helmet in his left hand and held against his flank. His right hand gripped the pommel of his sword as it rested in its scabbard. He strode into the chamber and stopped twenty feet from the throne. He dropped to his left knee before Regeldam. "My lord. My queen."

"Rise, Pilesar," Regeldam spoke as he motioned. "What urgent news do you bring that your messenger has not already told me?"

"It is concerning the captives that we brought to Bor, Highness." Pilesar stood and squared his shoulders before the king. "Most of the men of the South are either dead or nursing the recent loss of their left hands. Fourteen captives were brought to Bor. Eleven strong and able Emari, one fiery lad, and two pale creatures, the likes of which I have not seen before."

The last part grabbed Regeldam's attention and got the queen to sit up in her chair. He had never seen her actually attentive when Pilesar was speaking. "Tell me more about these pale creatures," he commanded

"They are shorter than Emari, with pointy noses, dull fingers, round eyes, and hair only on the top of their head," Pilesar said, summing up what he considered the obvious differences.

"Men!" the queen spoke up.

"What? Are you sure?" Regeldam was horrified. "Does that description fit what you saw during your travels over the past year? If so, how did Men get into my kingdom?"

"They said they came from the mountain, Highness. I suspect they came through the pass," Pilesar answered the question as if it were aimed at him.

"Why aren't your men guarding the mountain pass?" Regeldam knew the answer, but was flustered by this news.

"The guard was abandoned years ago after the beasts attacked. We send a scout crew there once a season. There has never been any sign of sentient life." Pilesar gathered himself before speaking again. "Your Highness, that is not all of my report."

Regeldam was fatigued from the first report, but allowed Pilesar to continue.

"You asked me to keep an eye out for any leaders among the people." Pilesar dropped his voice a little and spoke the next line with hesitancy.

"You ordered me to look for any person who might fulfill the prophecy of that wretched wizard, may Lylyth take his soul. Two of the fourteen may fit the description. One of the Men seems to lead and demand respect. Despite his size, he is a brute and a pest. He managed to best one of the largest Emari I have ever seen. The other Emari seem to cower before him, despite all being larger than him."

Pilesar paused. He was hesitant to identify the other leader. Regeldam was petulant. "Well? Spit it out, Captain. Tell me about the other one."

Pilesar obliged him. "The other one we encountered in Herr's Cove. He had a small band and put up quite a fight against our soldiers. It seems our men attacked during his wedding ceremony. His bride was yet unspoiled and was whisked away to the Bride Market ahead of all the other girls. He was able to lead his villagers in taking many of my soldier's lives. In fact, the two men from the mountain joined him in this fight. This Emari fought with confidence. He had a kingly sword and spoke with the authority of ten thousand lions. What is more, my lord, is that he resembles our former business partner, Jugel of Kefeer."

Regeldam was speechless. He started to speak, but he had no words to say. Silence permeated the chamber as the king pondered this news. Not sure what to do with this information, he turned to his queen. "What do you suggest?"

The queen gathered herself and rose to her feet. "Send all three to Lylyth. Make it a spectacle for all the workers. Place them on the platform at the water's edge, and let the Lurker gather them and take them to his dark queen."

Regeldam felt the resolve of impending satisfaction. For years, he had wished evil upon Jugel and his family, ever since the coward had run from his challenge. Sure, he had planned to have Jugel of Kefeer and his family killed that morning, all those years ago, but that satisfaction had escaped him. Tomorrow he would retrieve it.

The thoughts of unfulfilled suffering that he had long hoped on his former business partner washed over him. He looked at his queen. "Tonight, I will have you join me in my chambers. Tomorrow, I will defile the bride of my enemy's son, while her husband is introduced to the fury of the Lurker."

23 OFFERING

Wylm awoke in a sweat. He had drifted off for a short while after their evening meal of bread and broth. They had worked hard all morning and all day. At what Wylm had guessed was the eleventh hour, the guards ushered the prisoners back to the Oven for their dinner. Wylm had wolfed down his food and dozed. He encouraged those around him to do the same. In these conditions, food and sleep would be important whenever they could be had.

Unfortunately for Wylm, he rarely slept well any more. Though he would never tell Onero, that night in the woods with the witch of Embor still haunted him. The things he had done that night, the words he had said, he could not take them back. There had been no real peace in his life since that day. Any love the Maker had for him was surely gone. How could He forgive what Wylm had done?

He never told Onero. His friend's response would have been predictable. He would have sympathized with him and talked him through it. *Always wanting to talk about love and forgiveness*, Wylm thought to himself. *Onero can keep those womanly actions to himself.* Wylm considered himself a man amongst men. He would not feel bad for himself or cry for himself. He did what he had to do for duty to a fellow soldier. *And one time friend*, he thought.

This evening, though, the sweat was not from a fitful night. In fact, he had slept well considering his imprisonment. This was not the first time he'd had to find rest while in the holding of the enemy. It was the heat of the cave that was getting to him. Despite this, and despite being surrounded by dozens of a fierce and able people, he actually felt quite secure.

Wylm opened his eyes and looked around. On his right slept Tofir of Meona, the biggest non-Pytecki Wylm had ever seen. Wylm was glad he had taken Tofir by surprise on their first encounter. *Hand-to-hand combat on an open field may have been more challenging.* On Wylm's left was Kahya of Nachal. He was not an enormous creature, but his arms and legs were tight and lean. No movement seemed to be wasted with this forester. A twig and leaf still clung to his ragged mane and beard.

At his feet was the young lad, Goor of Koor. Never had Wylm seen such blind devotion to a dream. Wylm truly believed the child would do anything for him. He realized he had unwittingly replaced the role of the child's father. It was not a role he relished, but he did not want to abandon this young lad during this adventure in the way that Wylm's father had always left him behind.

Onero looks at this child in the way my father's friends used to look at me. The thought irritated him, and perhaps that was why he cared for the lad. Perhaps that was another reason he found himself progressively more frustrated with Onero lately. Where was his former friend? Wylm saw Onero on the other side of the cave. He was sitting on the floor at the feet of the old man, just the two of them, likely discussing their cowardice. Wylm was lying with the rest of the Emari, as one of the people, but the Seons were outcasts even among the desperate.

That's the way it should be, Wylm judged. He no longer had any respect for the Seon family. Hugla Seon was a scoundrel who betrayed Wylm's grandfather to his death. Burd Seon was a coward who ran from the coming battle to escape with his harlot mistress and his illegitimate son. Onero Seon was essentially a woman. He talked too much, mostly about feelings and emotions, and was always needing rescued. The grandfather and father both betrayed their oaths, and he was sure Onero would do the same as soon as he had the chance.

As he thought about Onero, Wylm gazed around the room again. Most of the captives were haggard and weary. Even in their sleep, they looked fatigued. Of the new prisoners, most looked scared. Many were curled up in a protective posture, like a small child clinging to a dolly or blanket, trying to find rest as Wylm had suggested, but most were not successful. Even Tofir and Kahya were not sleeping soundly. Only one was different. Only one other stood out.

Jugel of Herr's Cove was sleeping amongst the Emari. He was not near the wall or hiding in the middle of the pack. He was sleeping between the majority of the captives and the bars that held them. It was as if he were trying to protect the group from the guards. He was lying on his back with his feet to the bars. His legs were uncrossed. What caught Wylm's attention was that Jugel's hands were behind his head, exposing his entire abdomen and chest to any guard or archer who might desire him harm.

Wylm did not like this Emari. He despised the air of confidence that he displayed even as he slept. The other Emari were all impressed with Wylm when he bested Tofir. They all deferred to him even now, but not Jugel. He feigned indifference in the presence of Wylm, and Wylm would even argue that the warrior from Herr's Cove detested him. *I slew dozens in his presence, and he doesn't even give me the respect of eye contact.*

As Wylm stared at Jugel in disgust, he noticed movement on the quarry floor. The soldiers and guards were coming down into the quarry via the pulley system. A great many of them were convening at the far end. Many more archers were climbing down ladders into their lookouts. Three to four archers were stationed on each platform. Whatever was about to happen had their captors nervous. Wylm looked to the top of the quarry but there was no cage full of prisoners to be seen.

What he found curious though was the action by the water's edge. Many guards and soldiers were reinforcing the wooden scaffolding that the captives had passed the day before. From who knows where, a tall flight of wooden stairs was being rolled to the platform. Many of the captives were awakening now from their brief naps. A hum of unanswered questions began to permeate the Oven regarding the preparations made by Regeldam's minions.

They all watched as a young guard climbed fearfully up the stairs. He was being forced to climb at the demand of a soldier. He got halfway up the steps, then turned to come back down. The soldier drew his sword and roared another order. The guard turned and climbed to the top. Hesitantly he stepped onto the platform. The soldier bellowed more commands, and the guard began to jump up and down and rock back and forth on the platform.

While he was doing this, Bagad—the guard who whipped Hugla Seon the night before—picked up a large rock and tossed it into the lake behind the platform. When the rock hit the water, the guard on top screamed. Wylm could see the front of his trousers darken in hue. In full terror, the young guard jumped off the twenty foot platform onto the hard floor below.

It appeared his landing broke his leg, but that did not stop him from moving. He crawled as fast as he could with two arms and one good leg, as far from the water's edge as he could get. Many of the guards chuckled while Bagad laughed violently. The soldier was not amused, but his task was finished, and he turned to a group of twenty soldiers and a guard carrying a set of keys. He spoke another command and pointed his clawed finger at the bars running across the cave entrance.

"They are going to summon the Lurker!" one of the prisoners yelled out in dread. Wylm turned to look at the one who spoke. The Emari was gaunt and faded. Wylm supposed he had been there the longest and seen the most.

"What is the Lurker?" Onero asked as he stepped up beside Wylm. Wylm cringed in annoyance at the familiar tone.

"It's a monster of the deep." Jugel said as he stepped to Onero's other side. "I knew it was foolish for Regeldam to keep us alive. He's apparently realized this as well."

A guard arrived at the gate with the keys. "Back away from the bars," he commanded. Everyone obeyed except Wylm and Jugel. "Back away now!" he said more forcefully. Archers in the company behind him raised their bows and pointed arrows at the chests of the two defiant prisoners.

Wylm and Jugel backed away, and the guard unlocked the koorore gate. Two soldiers opened the gate. The bars seemed heavier that day than the night before. The heat of the day was much greater than the day before. As Goor had informed them, koorore becomes stronger in the heat. Based on the efforts of the soldiers, it apparently got denser as well.

The officer of this group of soldiers stood at the open gate. "Alright you scum. Everyone step out here in single file. If you step out of line, you will be shot. If you stumble, you will be shot. If you speak, you will be shot."

From the back of the cave a came out, "Sir, my father's foot is lame from yesterday's work, he cannot—"

An arrow flew from the bow of one of the soldiers and sunk deep into the chest of the one who spoke.

"Let me repeat," the soldier said. "If you step out of line, you will be shot. If you stumble, you will be shot. If you speak, you will be shot."

The captives began to file out. Tofir went in front of Wylm to protect him from any incoming arrow. Goor followed right behind. Onero went over to help Hugla to his feet. The old man grabbed his mantle and flipped it over his head. It dipped over the front of his face, covering his eyes from anyone standing over him. They followed the other captives. Slowly the procession of prisoners dragged themselves toward the other side of the quarry. The Emari with an injured foot brought up the rear.

The soldiers stood to the left, on the lake side of the procession. The archers were positioned in their perches along the wall to the right. When the company was alongside the wooden scaffolding, the officer called for them to halt. The captives obeyed, even Wylm. The soldiers to the left bracketed the prisoners on either side. The officer called for them to face the water. They did.

From their right, a decorated soldier strode in front of them. He stood alone between the captives and the water. Jugel recognized him as the captain that reinforced the garrison in Herr's Cove a few days ago. He could not shake the thought that he recognized him.

"My name is Captain Pilesar," the soldier began. "By order of King Regeldam, this morning there will be an offering to appease the Lady of the Night. By her grace, Geongalann has come to good fortune. By her mercy, the city of Kefeer grows stronger. By her love, Lord Regeldam reigns secure on his throne, with his queen at his side."

Captain Pilesar began to pace back and forth, looking at the captives as if he were inspecting his troops. "It has come to the attention of the king that there are some among you who consider themselves leaders of the masses. You are wrong. There are no leaders except for those that Lord Regeldam has deemed fit to lead." He continued to examine the captives. Nearly all cast their gaze to the ground. The ones who did not were those for whom he had come.

"For those of you who fear the power of Regeldam, it will go well with you. You will serve your king here in Bor with your sweat and your blood. Your service will make Kefeer a beacon of hope to all the nations." He paused in front of Wylm, standing just far enough away that Wylm could not grab his throat without having to first adjust his balance. "For you who consider yourself leaders and rebels…" He turned to face the prisoner's right and strode in that direction. "You will meet Lylyth this night as an offering."

His about-face turn must have been a signal. Two soldiers grabbed Wylm's arms, one on each. Another soldier shoved the point of a sword into his back. The same happened to Jugel and Onero. The three of them were being marched to the platform over the water. Goor began to whimper. He wanted to yell and fight, but the arrows of the archers had proven to be quite accurate.

The soldiers forced Wylm onto the steps first. After him went Jugel. The soldiers were lifting Onero onto the first step when a voice rang out from behind them. "Stop, there is one more. There is one more insolent fool amongst this sorry lot." Onero turned to see Bagad grabbing Hugla from behind and forcing him to the steps. "This sorcerer has no love for Regeldam. The idiot wizard belongs up on that platform as fodder for Lylyth's pet."

Captain Pilesar stepped up to the scaffolding and reprimanded the guard. "How dare you interfere with my orders? This is not a democracy. We do not vote on who occupies the platform. Take that prisoner back to the line."

"But, sir," Bagad begged—his mistreatment of Hugla had begun as an order from Regeldam, but was becoming a manifestation of his own hatred—"this is the worst of scoundrels. This is the prophet that foretold the death of King Regeldam. May his words die with him. He deserves this death."

Pilesar of Kefeer, Captain of the White Regiment, was furious. He strode up to the unruly Bagad and drew his hand back to teach him a lesson of respect.

"In the same manner did you strike one of Regeldam's wives when she threatened to expose your adultery," Hugla quietly spoke. His hushed words stopped Pilesar's arm midswing. The soldier looked to the short elderly prophet and wanted to speak, tried to speak, but was too shocked, embarrassed, and exposed to say a word. Hugla Seon took advantage of the awkward silence. "On the third day of the fifth month of this year, during the Festival of Winged Lions, you excused yourself from the king's table and snuck into his harem. The guard, Sesto of Hebel, owed you a favor…"

"Enough," yelled Captain Pilesar, striking Hugla with the back of his hand. The old prophet stumbled and would have fallen had not Bagad been holding him. "This one goes on the platform with the others."

"Sir, there is only room for three on the platform," the soldier holding Onero's right arm protested.

"Take your man and place him here, in front of the platform," Pilesar commanded. "When the Lurker has taken his offering, we will run this one through with arrows."

The soldiers holding Onero brought him before the platform. Onero stood on the quarry floor, twenty feet from the scaffolding. The soldiers turned him to face the platform.

Pilesar and Bagad grabbed Hugla firmly and marched him to the steps. Jugel and Wylm were already on the platform, mesmerized by the ordeal taking place below them. "Let's see you speak your way out of this one, wizard," Bagad gnashed in his ear.

"I'll bet you regret your words now, old fool," Pilesar spat as he pushed the prophet onto the steps.

Hugla fell onto the wood plank and bloodied his knee. This did not slow him as he came to his feet, climbed one step, and turned to face Pilesar, Bagad, and the rest of the soldiers. "I will always speak the truth given me to speak. By the grace of Rhumaiv, in the power of Layish, and with the counsel of Ergo, the words of truth will never return void. I am not afraid to make spoken what is given to me." He paused and took an easy breath. "I have seen the last days, the end of all things. On that fateful day, the wicked and vile will not survive. Alas, the events of today are so integrated to those of the last, that it would be folly for me to not speak the truth."

He backed up a couple more steps and spoke again. "The Truth says that on this day many will go to Lylyth, but I will not be counted among them. Kingdoms will fall, heroes will rise, and hearts will be changed because of what takes place here today. This day is counted greatest of all in my difficult life. Today a power will awaken, a king will roar, and I will walk hand in hand with Rhumaiv through fields of golden wheat."

24 THE LURKER

King Regeldam called over one of his guards. This one was new. Regeldam did not know his name. It was not unusual for the king to not know the names of his guards, nor was it unusual to have a new guard protecting him. What was unusual was that the opening of the position had actually occurred because the previous guard was promoted to the chief of labor over the mining pits in Bor. Most previous openings had been due to one guard or the other being on the wrong side of their king's ever-more-frequent fits of rage.

Those fits of rage were going to be coming to an end, Regeldam knew. They had increased in earnest a few months ago when the short, pale prophet had been brought into his kingdom at the suggestion of one of his attendants. At the recollection of this, Regeldam realized that he had not terminally punished the attendant for his misinformation. Perhaps he would be lenient. That prophet had spoken words of doom against him, the White Lion. Those words had sent the king into a fury. From that moment, citizens of his kingdom had begun losing their lives, beginning with that back-woods guard, continuing on to many of the people in the South, and all of his many sons.

He missed his sons, but they were not essential to his joy, nor did his legacy depend on the heir to the throne. Too many heirs foul up the kingdom that their fathers have prepared for them anyway. Regeldam intended for his legacy to come with the glory of the city which he was building. But how could he build his city with the threat of an impending prophecy lying on the horizon?

Regeldam told himself and others that the glory of Kefeer was the thing that he strived for. He had convinced the others, but he knew better. What really brought him joy was fulfilling his nearly insatiable appetite for passion. To satisfy this ravenous hunger, he had his wife, his expanding harem, and tonight he would have the daughter-in-law of his former nemesis. This is why he now beckoned the guard.

"Guard," Regeldam uttered as he pointed to the new recruit. "Has there been any word about my festivities for tonight?"

The guard hesitated before stammering. "Ah-are you referring to the girl or the actual feast, m-my lord?"

Regeldam liked this one. All other new guards would have naturally assumed he was talking about the feast, and they would not have been far off in doing so. The feast tonight was going to be excessive. All of the nobles from the city would be there, as well as governors from throughout the kingdom. They all believed they were celebrating the plans to rebuild the palace, which would start the next morning. They did not realize that Regeldam's true inspiration was to celebrate the establishment of his throne.

It would have been natural to assume that the word *festivities* referred to the feast, but this guard seemed to have an eye right into the king's heart. Feasts came about whenever the king desires, but the opportunity to impose his will on the new bride of a hated family had the king in a truly festive spirit. Regeldam considered asking the guard for his name, then realized he still did not care.

"Is the girl ready?" the king clarified.

The nameless guard betrayed a subtle smile and answered, "The young bride from the South has been taken to your bedchambers. She is currently chained to the bedpost and awaiting your arrival after the feast or whenever it is that you arrive."

"Thank you, guard. That is all." Regeldam turned from his servant.

"My lord, if I may say one more thing?" the suddenly brave guard offered, with more resolve than he should have had.

Under normal circumstances, speaking up after being dismissed would have led to another opening for a royal guard, but Regeldam had already determined that he liked this one. "You may proceed."

"The young lady, my lord, she's…," the guard paused, searched for the right words, then grinned. "She is a wild fire."

Regeldam could not contain his joy. "Bring me my goblet. Tonight is going to be a triumphant night."

****

Onero watched as Hugla climbed to the top of the stairs and stepped onto the platform beside Wylm. He hugged the grandson of Yuri Kanu and whispered something in his ear. Wylm looked at him with a raised brow then cast a confused and obstinate look back to Onero. Next, Hugla leaned forward and whispered something to Jugel. The proud Emari stood taller on the platform in response. Then Hugla turned and faced Onero. He pulled his mantle back a little from his head.

Drums began to beat behind Onero. It startled him at first, and he wanted to turn around, but the eyes of his grandfather held him fast. The beating of the drums became rhythmical, *Boom, Boo-Boom; Boom Boo-Boom BOOM.* The prisoners behind him began to murmur in fear. Wylm and Jugel began to scan the horizon of the lake. Onero just looked at his grandfather. The old prophet stared at his grandson and beamed with pride.

Onero could not understand why his grandfather would smile in such a situation. He could not understand why he would choose to be on the platform. They were both going to die. He was still looking at Onero, but Hugla was trying to say something to his grandson. The drums drowned out his voice, and Onero leaned forward to try to hear him.

What was he saying? Something starting with an *L. Lion*? Onero shuffled a couple steps toward the lake. The water behind the platform began to churn and bubble. "What are you saying, Papa? I cannot hear you. Speak louder."

Then he thought he heard it. *Listen?* He yelled back to confirm. "Listen? Did you say 'listen', Papa?"

"Listen, On. Just listen."

So Onero did.

Everything went quiet around him. No longer could he hear the murmur of the captives or the barking and nervous commands of the soldiers. No longer could he hear the water as it began to churn behind the platform. No longer could he hear the drums. Onero just listened. When he did, all fear and anxiety left him. He felt the peace of silence comfort him, then he began to hear the gentle hum of a melody. It was quiet, very quiet, as if someone was humming softly on the other side of the lake.

What his eyes saw was anything but quiet. When the humming started, a long, thick mass of brown flesh appeared from the water. It was scaly and muscular. It was what Onero had seen when he entered Bor the day before. He had thought it was a sea snake of some sort. Soon three of these massive serpents were writhing and coiling over each other. Behind the coiling snakes, another object began to break the surface. It was much larger than a snake. It was about six feet from side to side and eight feet from front to back. As it rose, the snakes began to move their long bodies out of the water in large loops of movement.

All at once from the water emerged a large body, grotesque and misshapen, like the underside of a decaying log. At the same time, the snakes all leapt out of the water. They were not snakes at all, but the large elongated arms of Lylyth's monster. As the coiling arms began to swing around and search the air, the creature opened its mouth. From deep inside that hideous flesh came a shrill and terrifying scream that caused soldier, guard, and prisoner alike to all cower. Some of the soldiers left their post and ran. Some of the captives began to cover their ears and pull at their hair. At some level, the sound terrified all in Bor that day—all, that is, except the family of Seon.

For perhaps the first time in his life, Onero was truly listening, and what he heard was altogether different than what he saw. Three voices began to make a gentle melody. It was a soft song, carried by winds of an unworldly peace. One voice soared high over the others, singing of the glory of the Maker. Another roared a deep tone, bringing power and richness to the song. The third voice was somewhere in between. It was the softest of the voices, but Onero related to it the most. It conveyed grace and mercy and met Onero right where he was.

The music surrounded him and comforted him. He still saw the fury of the monster of the lake, but he was not frightened. Hugla Seon had his eyes closed, seemingly listening to the same song. He did not appear frightened either. Not even when an arm of the Lurker wrapped around him and jerked his relaxed body off the platform. The other two arms found Jugel and Wylm as well, but not before Wylm ducked the first advance of the limb that sought him. The three people Onero cared most about—his grandfather, his best friend, and his newest friend—were all being swung around in the air, soon to be the Lurker's next meal.

Jugel was calm and discerning. His muscles were tensed, waiting for his chance to escape. Wylm was fierce and furious, fighting every second to force his escape. The arms of the Lurker seemed unyielding, but he managed to get his right arm free. Hugla Seon seemed indifferent to the danger, indifferent to the arms around his waist, and indifferent to the large gaping maw of the Lurker.

The monster had been twisting and swinging its prey. Now it began to bring its victims closer to its ravenous mouth. All three were pulled down at the same time. The only question was which of Onero's loved ones would it choose first. The lot seemed to fall to Jugel. The Lurker pulled him close. In a moment of desperation, Jugel opened his mouth to let out a battle roar as he had done in Herr's Cove not many days ago. The Lurker tightened its hold on the Emari's chest, and only a whimper escaped.

The monster continued to pull in Jugel, but the one who proclaimed to be king was not going down without a fight. The warrior from Kefeer was a survivor. He managed to place either foot on the top and bottom of his predator's mouth. He had the strength and flexibility to at least make it difficult for the Lurker to swallow him whole. The Lurker was not used to fighting with its meal; it pulled Jugel back and went to its next course. Wylm.

If Jugel was a survivor, then Wylm was an overcomer. Life-and-death situations were becoming common place for him. He had been held captive more than most men had been held by a lover. He was a captive inside his captivity. The overheated maw of the Oven was much more survivable than the rancid maw of this lake monster.

The Lurker pulled him in. As he began to enter the mouth cavity, Wylm threw a forceful punch to its upper lip, or to where the lip would be if it had a lip. The Lurker let out another hideous scream as wind and spit flew out of its mouth. Its rancid breath nearly made Wylm swoon. The Lurker pulled him in again, only lower. This time Wylm forcefully kicked its lower lip. Where Jugel was defensive, Wylm was offensive. He was always offensive.

Onero continued to watch this whole event with the sweet song of peace embracing him. Though he did not understand the words of the song, something told him to not fear for the lives of his friends. When the lake monster had first attempted to feed on Jugel, the song seemed to dwell more around his grandfather. Onero could no longer hear the foreign words, but only the sweet melody.

Hugla heard everything, and what was foreign to Onero was understood by him as he closed his eyes in understanding. When Wylm kicked the Lurker's lower jaw in his aggressive desperation, Master Prophet Hugla Seon opened his mouth and spoke. *"Shemita melek asa melkama."*

The Lurker pulled Wylm away from his mouth. It brought Hugla before his face and seemed to stare at him.

The prophet repeated his words, this time with more force. *"Shemita melek asa melkama."* The tongue in which he spoke was unknown to all except the Lurker, but all could hear the authority the words possessed.

The Lurker resisted the words charged at him. It screamed at Hugla, saliva and bile again flying from its gaping mouth.

"Laqach shote ruuts a sar shalam," Hugla retorted at the Lurker's protest.

The monster of the lake was furious. It drew Wylm and Jugel close and continued to object to the prophet's words. It squeezed the two warriors tighter. They grimaced and fought. No air could enter their screaming lungs. There ribs were on the verge of fracturing.

"Shemita melek asa melkama." This time Hugla bellowed his words with such authority that the Lurker seemed to jump back.

It squeezed Wylm and Jugel one more time before throwing them to the quarry floor. Then it lunged forward. With its two free arms, it knocked over the wooden scaffolding. Now nothing stood between it and the onlookers. The prisoners did not know whether to fear the Lurker or the arrows more. The monster of the lake scanned the crowd with its solid black eyes. No one moved. Whether in fear or by some bewitching, everyone stood still.

With the quickness of an illusionist, its arms shot out and grabbed two more victims: the wicked Bagad and Captain Pilesar. There was neither drama nor time for dispute. The Lurker immediately engorged himself, nearly stuffing both in its mouth at the same time. But the monster of the lake was not satisfied. It protested again to the aged prophet still in the grip of its mighty arm. This time, its complaint was a guttural sound mixed with its scream.

"Lylyth yalad ata, Tannim. Yarad sheowl, im eda okol ra nephesh." Hugla commanded with more authority than any of his previous words. He pointed at the monster, then pointed to the southwest foothills.

The Lurker shook Hugla in defiance.

"Yarad sheowl," the prophet repeated.

Again the monster shook him. Hugla's mantle flew off of his head and shoulders, landing at Onero's feet. Hugla turned his head, observing where his mantle lay. He closed his eyes and bowed his head, as if acknowledging a command given to him. He turned back to the fierce monster of the lake.

"*Az aniy chedel hayah acharon arucha attah ad akal.*" He paused then repeated his words in a tongue that all could understand. "Then I will be the last meal you ever eat."

In victory, the Lurker squeezed the prophet and let out a triumphant shriek. Its terrible arms quickly brought Hugla to its mouth and devoured him.

Onero's heart ripped in grief. *Thank you, Papa*, he eulogized.

Onero was not afraid. He had known that his grandfather was going to die. The music had told him. He did not understand the words, but he understood the song. Similar melodies had been heard around campfires in his past, songs of heroes giving their all in battle, lamentations that sang of the noble deeds of the dead.

The Lurker writhed in front of him. It had come too far onto the quarry floor. Half of its body was out of the lake. With its stomach full, it was unable to return. Clouds had been hiding the sun up to that time. Now they parted, and the full force of the mid-summer sun beat upon the monster's body. Without water, it could not keep cool, nor could it float. Soon it became overheated, and breathing came with increasing difficulty.

Despite the Lurker only a few feet from him, Onero had no fear of the massive beast of the lake. He bent over and picked up his grandfather's mantle. It was made of coarse hair and smelled like honey and sweat. He held it in his arms and began to walk back to the prison cave. As he did so, the Lurker came to its last moments in this world. Onero ignored it and kept walking.

As the lake monster struggled with its last breaths, its arms flailed about in panic. The guards and soldiers fled to the far wall, while the captives fled back to the safety of the Oven. At first, they were all safe from any arrow volley because the archers on the wall were shooting at the Lurker's arms to try to save their comrades. A few captives tried to escape, though, and the archer's killed them quickly. At this, the soldiers composed themselves and ushered everyone into the cave and locked the gate.

25 A SNOWY DAY

The collective pounding of hearts was nearly audible. Ten minutes had passed since the guards had locked the gates of the Oven. It seemed no one had yet recovered from what had just transpired in the Pit. All the prisoners were murmuring about what had taken place. Some were rejoicing over the death of Pilesar and Bagad. Some were mourning the death of the prophet. Others felt the prophet had it coming to him. The general sense was one of awe. All of the soldiers and guards were still stationed on the quarry floor or on the rim above. None had left to take word to Regeldam about the events at Bor.

Onero stood at the gate of the Oven, staring into nothing. His thoughts ran to his grandfather and the sacrifice he had made. *But why?* he wondered. *What hope does a dead monster and two dead Emari bring?*

A chill ran across his neck. He had previously taken the cloak of his grandfather off his shoulders due to the heat. As the chill came over him, he instinctively reached for the cloak and draped it around his shoulders. His eyes closed.

A moment later, he opened them and was startled by what he saw. Everything around him had turned white. The prisoners backed deeper into the cave and gathered together as one. The bars shattered into pieces. Lightning bolts shot out of the depths, and white lions with red right paws scattered to the wind, while some piled into a heap as if dead.

Onero closed his eyes again. When he opened them, he was back in the intensely hot prison. He calmed his mind and listened. "Say it," a voiced whispered in his spirit.

The short man with the fur mantle called for the attention of all the prisoners. "All who live through today will have their freedom. In a short time, these doors will open, and the soldiers will scatter. By the grace of Rhumaiv, we will all be saved."

"What're you doing, Onero?" Wylm hurried to his friend's side. "Have you gone mad? Do you fancy yourself a god that you can save us? You may have your grandfather's cloak, but don't go mad like he did."

Jugel approached. "What do you have planned, my brother? May Layish strengthen you."

Wylm was annoyed by the trust that Jugel showed Onero. His stomach soured at the words *my brother*. He sensed a betrayal by his friend. He had distrusted Jugel since their capture. The cat-eyed warrior had given him no attention since his village was slain, as if he blamed Wylm for their slaughter. Wylm knew he was not to blame. It was the weakness of the villagers that was to blame. He grunted to himself in contempt.

Onero turned to Wylm first and then to Jugel. "Behold the power of our Deliverer."

At that moment the serpent that had been dormant about his waist slid up his abdomen, across his chest, and around his arm. It exited the sleeve of his tunic and slithered through his hand, where it became a solid wooden staff. To all who watched, it appeared as if a staff formed out of the palm of his hand.

Onero spoke again, only this time for all the prisoners to hear. "Behold the power of Rhumaiv!"

A strong rushing wind could be heard a distance off. In the quarry, they could not tell from where it came, but soon they could see its effects out of the southwest. In an instant, a deep chill came upon them, and it only grew colder. Thick snow began to fall and immediately accumulated on the midsummer ground.

Off to the side, the prisoners could see the soldiers and guards running for cover. Two archers climbed up the ladder out of their posts. They both lost their grips and fell, hitting the platform before tumbling over the edge. Many of the guards along the top of the cliff could be seen scattering. The temperature continued to drop. All of the prisoners backed deeper into the cave, where the Oven provided them with unfathomably needed warmth.

Onero turned to Wylm who was still by his side. "According to Goor, this metal is weakening as it gets colder." Ice had started to form on the bars of koorore. "Do you think you can kick your way through?"

"My pleasure," Wylm said with a grin. It was the first he had felt appreciated by his friend in quite a long time. Wylm proceeded to the gate and began to drive the bottom of his foot at the latch and hinges. The bars gave and bent, but they did not break. He continued to wail on them, and they continued to flex toward freedom. Nevertheless, they did not break. Wylm clenched his fists and let out a yell of rage and frustration.

At that exact same moment, Jugel felt a stirring inside himself, like a royal lion released from a pit. He believed today was the day that Layish had foretold. He had waited for five years. Now he would take hold of the authority granted to him by the Great Lion. As Wylm clenched his fists in frustration, preparing to yell, Jugel stepped forward. With one foot in front of the other for balance, he unsheathed his claws, swung his tensed arms behind him, and bellowed a wonderful and terrible roar in the direction of the bars.

Young Goor had been watching Wylm the whole time. He was of course startled to learn that Onero was actually a wizard. He was even more shocked when Onero had produced a serpent staff from his arm. Goor's excitement grew, however, as snow fell into the quarry. What better platform for the White Lion to come into his kingdom than the purest white snow? Goor marveled at the strength of Wylm as he bent and deformed the koorore bars with the power of his blows. Goor's eyes were focused solely on Wylm. At first he was disappointed when Wylm's strength did not break through their prison, but when he heard the roar, that he thought had come from Wylm, he was giddy. Surely Shachal had returned.

The bars shattered! The strength of Jugel's roar had broken not only the prison door, but the whole grid that kept them bound, and the ground jolted in a tremendous quake, shifting the earth from Bor to the Great Mountains. Wylm was dumbfounded by what he experienced. Onero was not.

Jugel turned to the two hundred prisoners and gave orders like a warrior king to his troops. "Tofir, take three Emari and head to the terraced east wall. Use the ladder and climb to the top. Once you make it to the rim, run to the other side and let down the platform. Kahya, find yourself a bow and cover them. Everyone else, find a guard and strip him of his weapons. Help your brothers. Now move, for your freedom is at hand."

The authority that Jugel bore seemed unquestionable. Most of the prisoners moved immediately, invigorated by adrenaline and the cold refreshing air. Tofir, however, looked to Wylm for approval, which he received in the form of a nod. He chose three of the largest and most able Emari. They would need the strength for any of the soldiers that remained on the outer rim. They moved quickly and scaled the multiple terraces within minutes.

Kahya sprinted out of the cave with a destination in mind. When the snow had blown in with a fury, he had seen a bow fly out of one of the archer's hand. With the speed he normally used to run down a deer, he raced to the jettisoned bow. He brushed away the inches of snow until he found it, and then rubbed the string to warm it. No arrows had been dropped, so he grabbed a stone, fixed it to the string, and shot it at one of the archers.

The archers on their perches were not prepared for this weather, nor had they spent two years hunting in Melkorak like Kahya had. When the stone hit the archer, he was knocked unconscious. He tumbled over the side rail and landed with a mortal thud. Kahya relieved the body of his quiver and strapped it to his own back.

The wind was fierce, even in the quarry. The archers were volleying arrows as quick as they could at the escaping prisoners. None of them were hitting their targets, but there were enough prisoners dashing here and there that some were randomly struck.

Kahya reached back and counted the arrows in his quiver: nine. Then he counted the remaining archers on all the platforms: ten. "Creator of Emabbir, be with me," he said aloud. One by one, he picked off the four nearest him who had been doing the most damage shooting stray arrows in the crowd.

There were three archers on the next perch. He pulled hard on the arrow and sunk it deep into the chest of one of them. It flew with such force that it pierced the guard behind him as well. Both bodies fell limp in the direction of the arrow's flight and struck the third archer, knocking him off the balcony. "I reckon that there had a little of the Almighty in it," he mused.

Three archers remained, and Kahya had four arrows. As he looked to the top of the rim, he saw Tofir and his helpers tossing guards over the edge into the quarry below. Kahya noticed a large soldier sneaking up behind them. He glanced to the tree tops. The canopies of the western trees began to sway farther than before. Kahya aimed high and left and loosed his shot. Snow drove the arrow low, and it began to head right for Tofir, but at the last moment a massive gust pushed it to the right, directly between the eyes of the onrushing soldier.

Tofir looked up in surprise and saw Kahya waving at him. He gestured back then urged his small band on to the far west side of the quarry. They got to the platform and began to let it down with the pulleys. The descent started smoothly. As he looked over the edge to monitor his progress, he heard a cry of wrath behind him. He turned in time to see another soldier's head snap back at the force of an arrow to his head. "That's got to be a quarter mile in a snow storm," Tofir guffawed. "I'm glad that back-woods Emari is on our team."

The platform reached the quarry floor. The three remaining archers were close enough to it that their volleys were keeping Jugel, Onero, and Wylm at bay. Kahya sprinted toward them, but one of the archers turned and fired his way. He shifted his weight and avoided the arrow before releasing his shot. The arrow flew wide to the right of all three archers.

His shot alerted the other two, and all three archers took aim at Kahya. He was a quicker draw, though, and released his final arrow. Again, it went right of all three archers and hit exactly where the first one had. The iron chain that secured the balcony to the side of the wall broke loose on the second strike. The whole perch dropped on the one side, spilling all three archers. If they did not die in the fall, the prisoners on the ground ensured their demise.

Jugel, Onero, and Wylm climbed onto the platform. They and the other prisoners had fought and killed most of the guards and soldiers that were still on the quarry floor. The ones that remained were in the process of coming to their end by the hand of other prisoners. Kahya and another escapee joined the three warriors on the platform heading to the top. As they began to lift to the surface, Goor came running.

"Wait for me, Shachal!" he begged.

Wylm reached down, grabbed him by his hand, and pulled him onto the ascending platform. When they reached the top and stepped onto the rock ledge, Jugel turned and looked west toward the lights of Kefeer.

Onero smiled at Wylm. "That may be our most exciting escape yet."

Wylm returned the smile and began to respond, but Jugel interrupted with urgency. "I travel to Kefeer, and my heart fears the grief I may face. But beyond all pain, success will be affirmed when the Imposter pays for his sins. The reckoning of Regeldam has now come."

26 UP THE HILL AND DOWN

I Kefeer was a five mile journey from Bor. The road was a good one with well-packed dirt and no intrusive trees. Wylm could see portions of Kefeer ahead. It would be a perpetual uphill run. The moon was high, and it highlighted the city on the hill. From this distance, the construction and scaffolding that was scattered about the city could not be seen.

Jugel and Wylm had armed themselves with the swords and scabbards of fallen soldiers, while Onero was carrying only his staff. Jugel looked to Onero and waved him along, and the two of them ran ahead together to Kefeer.

Wylm had been irritated when the Emari from Herr's Cove interrupted his talk with Onero. He was about to finally have a nice exchange with his friend after many days of tension, but the golden warrior had stepped in as if with some ordained authority. Wylm watched as his most trusted and dearest friend, the son and grandson of two cowards, ran ahead with a new friend.

Onero still ignores all that I have done for him. He shuddered as he thought back to his encounter with the Raven Witch of Embor.

That Onero would abandon him like everyone else in his life stung him. Now the prophet's son clung to another warrior who was less damaged than Wylm. Those two had spent a day together running behind one of the carts. Apparently Jugel had stolen Onero's loyalty in that time. Even with that trickery Onero used in the prison, Jugel had been trusted with his confidence more than Wylm. As soon as Jugel announced he was going to Kefeer, Onero left his conversation with Wylm and stepped to the Emari's side like a dog to his master. This sickened and angered Wylm. Surely Onero intended to disregard his oath like his father and grandfather before him.

Does he not realize what I did to save his life?

Wylm had made his own friends, though. Running alongside Kahya and Goor had been informational. Kahya lives near the small town of Nachal, which sat on a hillside at the foot of the mountain. It was west of the Mountain Pass, a little farther than Herr's Cove was to the east. Nachal was a wooded town near the edge of a thicker forest, through which ran a deep ravine. The town itself was surrounded by trees and had a single narrow road leading into it. The road was not much more than a forest path. Not even a horse-drawn cart could maneuver it. The people were foresters and hunters and had never been bothered by the soldiers of the North—until recently—because the town was so hidden.

Goor was from the town of Koor. Koor was north of Herr's Cove. It started as a settlement for the blacksmith guild. A natural furnace had been discovered ages ago in one of the caves near Koor. It was much larger than the one in the Pit of Bor. The people of Koor called it The Forge. As much as Nachal was unknown, Koor was very well known. The smithies worked continually to produce weapons, tools, and any other metal items that Regeldam demanded.

Goor had explained to Wylm how Regeldam always had a soldier posted overlooking the work. Every six hours, there was a change of the guard. The people were not allowed to make weapons, except when ordered. When a bundle of swords or spears or axe heads was commissioned, a full garrison would show up to guard The Forge. They were making sure that no weapons were being put away for the villagers. "What the Imposter's soldiers did not know," Goor had explained while shackled to the cages a few days earlier, "Was that there is a second natural furnace in a hidden cave a half mile from The Forge. There is. That is where my daddy spent long secret hours making better weapons than those produced for the Imposter. Yes, he did."

With that information in mind, and having seen the leadership abilities of Kahya and Tofir, Wylm turned to give them instruction. "Gather all the escapees and head for Koor. I will meet you in a day. We will gather all the weapons there before heading for Nachal. If we are successful in Kefeer tonight, the kingdom will be in disarray for some time. We will strike when the time is right." He then turned to Goor. "Go with Tofir and Kahya and show them the entrance to the secret cave."

Goor protested. "I will not leave your side, Shachal. If you are to fulfill the prophecies, then you must reach the Imposter before Jugel of Herr's Cove and your wizard friend." Wylm turned to see Onero and Jugel, now a quarter mile up the road. Wylm looked Goor over. Though he was strong from his years of swinging a hammer, he was not swift or enduring of foot. Making another quick calculation, Wylm picked up Goor and placed him on his back before running after the others.

Wylm had an ability to see things that he had never seen before. He could read people and situations and make plans that often led to victory. That had not helped him in that final battle against the Nemarians, of course, but no strategist could have overcome those odds. There was a reason, however, that his troops were the last remaining company of the Bacharite army. *It all began that night with the Raven Witch*, he thought.

The bent, haggard woman had been standing right in front of him. Her eyes were strong and evil. Her appearance, as well as her voice, seemed frail, but those eyes struck terror in his heart even now. She had just looked at him and smiled a wicked smile.

It had taken a while for Wylm to muster the courage to speak. "Where is Onero?"

"Is that the name of that helpless man?" she had asked with a patronizing smile. "He was unconscious and nearly dead when I found him, so I never got his name."

"If you've hurt him…"

"Foolish man," she had interrupted. "It is not him that I want. I have caused him no harm… yet."

"What do you mean *yet*, witch?" Wylm had been quite unnerved by this woman and had felt that putting a title to her evil would help him.

"My dogs are hungry. They have not eaten in three weeks and are now too feeble to hunt. A nearly unconscious man should make for an easy, nutritious meal." The witch had answered with great ease in her voice as a howl sounded nearby.

"That's not a dog," Wylm said. "It's a wolf. They can go many weeks without eating and still maintain their ferocity."

"Then you better hurry to save him." Her voice became more guttural and demanding.

"Where is he?" Wylm had tried to affect intimidation but found it difficult.

"Down there." She had creaked dismissively, pointing off to her right through the thick fog. "He is lying on the ground with his eyes rolled back in his head."

"I see nothing, witch, and neither do you." Wylm was getting angry. He had begun to spin the pommel of his sword in his hand.

"Your mind is clouded by the fog of loyalty and honor. You do not see the world as it actually is." This time, her voice feigned seduction. This had repulsed Wylm, reminding him of the gypsies who used to frequent the outskirts of Zakakos when he was a boy. The witch had produced a small vial from some unseen pouch or pocket. "Drink this, and your eyes will be open to see."

"What's that?" Wylm had asked with more curiosity than dismissiveness.

"It is my own brew. Drink it, and you will see the true reality of your situations. You will be able to see all that stands in your way. You will be able to see what honor and loyalty cloud from your mind, and the fog the Maker wraps you in will fade away. Then you will be victorious."

Wylm knew that her offer was evil. He had paid little attention in his religious studies, preferring arithmetic and warfare, but he had learned well that consulting a witch was profane in the highest order. "I just want my friend."

"You cannot see your friend, so you cannot find your friend, and therefore you cannot save your friend." She had caused each phrase to be more intense than the previous. "Very soon, though," she slowed her speech, "my wolves will find him, and there will be nothing but bones when they are done with him."

Another howl filled the air to Wylm's left, followed by ravenous barking and yelping. "It will be over soon," the witch had consigned. "If only your eyes were opened."

Wylm had been torn. He knew what he was thinking was wrong, but Onero was all he had next to his father, and he rarely saw his father. Onero had always been there for him. Even when Wylm was unbearable to all others, Onero had been there. He couldn't let him die, not when he could do something about it. "Give it to me!" he had barked.

The witch had tossed Wylm the vial. He stared at it hesitantly as the wolves continued their feral raucous. Their sounds erased Wylm's caution, and he had downed the contents. Immediately, the fog had dissipated, and he could see. Onero was off to his left, down a steep decline. He was lying in a room in the middle of a labyrinth. One of the walls of the room was wooden, and there were six wolves scratching and gnawing at it.

The voice of the witch had broken through his assessment. "The next time you drink from the cup of my hand, you will belong to me."

Wylm had turned on his heels and pulled his sword. "There'll not be a next time." He had begun to leap toward her, but her next words and actions held him fast.

"There is one problem, master Wylm. In my hand, I hold a lever." The lever had been in a down position, and she lifted it slightly. "As you can see, it controls the wall between the wolves and your friend." Sure enough, when she released the lever, the wall rose slightly. The beasts could now swipe a leg or snout under the wall. "If you take another step, you will indeed slay me, but your friend will die." She released a different lever. "And now I have opened a secondary door into his room. His smell is surely wafting through the corridors as we speak and soon will lead them to him. You better hurry if you plan on saving your Onero."

As Wylm quickened his pace toward Kefeer, with Goor still on his back, he remembered how he had saved Onero. He had killed all six wolves and had been able to negotiate the labyrinth without difficulty. It was as if he could see how it was all going to unfold. Onero had only known of the wolves, and Wylm had never told him about the witch. *He would have shamed me for what I did*, Wylm thought.

Goor shifted his position on Wylm's back. Though Goor was a young Emari, he was large compared to the size of Men. Despite this, Wylm was strong and able to carry him, even though the whole journey was uphill. This was the only way he could keep up with, and catch, Onero and Jugel.

Throughout the chase, Goor was whispering in the ear of his assumed hero and object of worship. "Keep going, Shachal. You can catch them. You can. You are the White Lion. You are the coming king. You are. The unnamed king is a pretender. He is not white of skin. He wears a fake hide fashioned for him by his wicked wife. He does. The Imposter is a false

Shachal. You will take the throne. You will. You have finally come as a god from the mountains. My daddy told me you would return. You would have loved my father. He loved you so much. Oh yes, he did. "

For two miles, Goor praised and gave adoration to Wylm as Shachal. Wylm knew he was not this Shachal of old. He was not even Emari, but never did he stop the boy. In fact, he was starting to be jealous for the magnification he received from Goor. The son of Hamyn Kanu began to feel like he was meant to sit on the throne in Kefeer. He actually allowed himself to believe that he was meant to rebuild the city for his own glory, as the prophecy stated. Somewhere between one and two miles from the city, he decided that the prophecy was truly about him. *I am the new Shachal*, he said to himself, and decided that nothing would stop him.

Wylm saw Jugel of Herr's Cove heading to Kefeer to kill Regeldam. He had essentially announced it when they stood upon the rim of the Pit of Bor. It hit Wylm all at once—the authority Jugel displayed during the escape, the power he had shown in his roar—he was planning on killing Regeldam to fulfill the prophecy and set himself up as king. Wylm let a guttural expression of jealousy and ire escape from within.

From upon Wylm's back, Goor of Koor saw where Wylm was looking and heard the unspoken words of his master's grunting. "That's right, my lord. Jugel is trying to steal your throne. He is. He means to take the glory for himself. He means to lay hold of the Imposter and strike him down. He does. He means to place the millennial blessing on his own descendants." A knot rose in Goor's throat, and like an impotent child trying in vain to hold together his collapsing view of right and wrong, his voice betrayed him with a crack of desperation, followed by a whisper of fear. "You have to stop him, my lord. You have to. Please stop him. Please."

The emotion in Goor's words drew Wylm back to his own childhood. He remembered when his grandfather had left on the mission to the forest of Arogan. Wylm had only been four or five at the time, but he remembered it vividly. He lived next door to his grandfather, who was his hero. Always Wylm tried to be like him, walk like him, talk like him, and even stand like him. He idolized his grandfather.

Every night, Wylm would wait by the window and look for his return. He had always returned previously, triumphant in battle or fearless in adventure. He had always sat Wylm on his lap and told him the stories. When Wylm's father was in the room, he kept the stories simple, but when it was just the two of them, he told every detail. Wylm watched that window every night for six months. Finally, his father sat him down, put his hands on Wylm's shoulders, and looked him in the eye. "Your grandfather is never coming back. He's gone Wylm. He's gone."

In his anger, Wylm had lashed out. He remembered needing someone to blame. For Wylm, it was easy to find that someone. He blamed the man that had always hung around with his grandfather. He blamed the prophet. Master Prophet Hugla Seon had been his grandfather's best friend. In the stories told, his grandfather was always rescuing the prophet from some danger or trial. As a young boy, Wylm figured that the prophet had gotten himself into some situation, and his grandfather died trying to save him.

All these years later, he felt his assumption was confirmed. How many arrows had his grandfather taken for the Prophet? The proof was in the Mountain Pass. Once again Yuri Kanu was a hero. Only at the end did Hugla Seon try to redeem himself. *He's not a hero. He had his death coming to him,* Wylm thought. He considered the words that Master Prophet Seon had told him on that scaffolding: *"My life for yours, Master Wylm. Do well, for the strength of the house of Kanu will turn the tide more than any other name."*

The words had vexed Wylm, but the source of that riddle was now dead. *And I'm glad the coward is gone.* Now, the grandson of that coward was running on ahead, trying to aide an imposter in usurping the throne. *Onero doesn't care about me. The only reason he stuck with me was to save his own life. Now it seems he's moved on to another friend.*

"I hate him," Wylm muttered out loud. With those words, his pace quickened, and he began to close the gap with an alarming speed. Fueled by jealousy and hate, he felt invincible. There was less than a mile to go to the walls of the city, and the tower of the king's chambers was not too far beyond that.

Wylm was right behind Onero and Jugel, coming up on their left side. He reached down to loosen his sword in its scabbard then changed his mind. There was no doubt he could beat them both in battle, but all Onero would have to do was slow him down to free Jugel to run on ahead and slay Regeldam first. Wylm released his sword. Something would be done, though. Wylm would arrive first.

Onero was running on Jugel's left side. They were on a mission, but had no idea they were in a race. Wylm came up on Onero's left side. Onero looked over at Wylm and saw the look in Wylm's eye. Instinctively, he took a defensive grip on his staff. Wylm gave him no time. He dipped his right shoulder and rammed hard into Onero, shoving him squarely into Jugel. They both tumbled off the side of the road and down a steep hill. They rolled and bounced many times, but did not come to a stop until they reached the bottom. It took them another few moments to gather themselves before starting the slow climb up the hill. When they finally reached the road, there was no one to be seen.

Wylm was in the lead, and only the sleeping city of Kefeer stood between him and Regeldam, between him and a prophecy fulfilled.

27 GETTING A GRIP

Adrenaline was coursing through Wylm as he approached the city gate, but the gate was fashioned from bars of koorore and was twenty feet high. The rest of the wall was just as tall. Despite his strength and athleticism, Wylm could not scale this wall or break through this gate. Goor understood his master's limitations. "It's okay, my lord. You will come into you full strength once the black panthress is at your side. You will. Until then, I know another way in."

They traveled north along the wall and came to a spot where it was only nine feet high. Kefeer was still being rebuilt and the entire wall had not yet been completed. At the lower points, Regeldam had stationed soldiers. Goor warned Wylm of this as Wylm set him back on his feet. Physical obstacles were one thing, but a few soldiers were nothing. With a leap, he grabbed the walls edge and quickly pulled himself atop the wall.

Two soldiers stood below, with the tips of their swords in the dirt. One of the soldiers had a horn on his belt. It appeared to the soldiers that a ghost had suddenly materialized above them. The light of the full moon illuminating Wylm's pale skin did nothing to change their interpretation of the situation. After a fearful pause, the one soldier went for his horn, but was already flying off the wall toward him. In less than a minute from when his feet first left the ground, Wylm had dispatched both soldiers and was pulling Goor over the wall and back onto his back.

The path to the tower was easier than the wall. They saw only one other Emari along the way, and he quickly escaped into his house at the sight of Wylm. When they reached the tower, he let Goor off his back. "You will have to stay here. Hide in those bushes. There are likely dozens of guards and soldiers inside, and I cannot protect you and get to Regeldam."

Goor thought about protesting, but then remembered to whom he was speaking. "Yes, my lord Shachal. It is as you command. It is. May the strength of Emabbir be with you this day." He ducked into the bushes.

Wylm realized that the front door would slow him down too much. He looked to the top of the tower and saw an open window which faced the troubling southeast country from where they had come a week ago. Surely a king who reigned in terror always had an eye out for what he fears. *That must be Regeldam's chambers, always looking for the king from the southern foothills.* Wylm purposed to climb the outside of the tower and come upon the king in his sleep.

The tower had been built long ago with large stones. There were many gaps between the stones where the mortar had been chipped away. The wall was scalable, but the ascent was not easy. The window was up six stories. What might have taken an avid climber ten minutes took Wylm twenty. He had to pause often and shake out one hand then the other to get the blood back in his fingertips. Many times his foot slipped out of a gap, or the face of the ancient rock crumbled under his weight. On one of these moments, the stone gave way as he started to push toward a higher grip. He started to fall but narrowly grabbed onto a thin ledge. He tore the skin off his fingertips, but prevented a certainly mortal drop.

The time it took Wylm to climb the wall was the longest he had been alone in a while. The young lad was not with him, speaking in his ear. There were no words of encouragement or effusive praise. He liked Goor. He was a passionate and courageous lad. Wylm was glad he could be there for the child, to help him through the grief of losing his father. He felt so much for the boy that he did not stop Goor from insisting that Wylm was Shachal. He did not want to twist the dagger that Regeldam had placed in Goor's soul when he took his father from him.

"I am not Shachal," Wylm said out loud to himself. He knew the truth. He was a soldier of Bachar from south of the Great Mountains, the son of a fallen general, the lifelong friend of an outcast prophet. "Oh, Onero." His voice was tinged with regret. He had not been fair to his friend. It was not just an oath that had bound them, it was a true friendship. How many trials had they been through? Sure, Wylm had rescued Onero more than the other way around, but Onero had accepted Wylm despite all his faults.

Others followed Wylm or emulated him, but that was because of his heroics and deeds in battle. When the night fell and darkness came over him, it was always Onero who rescued him from the evil within him. *Ever since Embor,* Wylm thought. Wylm had rescued Onero that day, but something had bewitched him in the words the hag had chanted. It felt like evil was crouching at the door since that night, waiting to pounce on him. It was always Onero's words and Onero's presence that kept the door shut.

"I just want my friend." Those were the words he had said to the witch that night, and those were the words that escaped his mouth as he climbed. Wylm found himself shocked by his own words. The vitriol he had harbored for Onero had not actually been stirred by his friend. It had been Onero's father and grandfather who had betrayed the Kanu family.

Their betrayals, accompanied by the trauma of the tunnel, and the mistreatment by the Mugaal general, had set Wylm on edge. Adding to that the lost battle at Herr's Cove, the disrespect of Jugel, the mistreatment by the Emari, and the indescribable sequence of events at Bor, had all kept Wylm occupied, fatigued, and on edge.

As Wylm clung to the side of the tower, with his toes and fingers in gaps wide enough to allow him to rest, he took a deep breath to cleanse his mind. He was a man of action. Stressful events were not new to him, so why did he place so much blame on Onero? Was it the praise of Goor that kept him from thinking straight? Was it the curse of the witch? Perhaps it was his own unfiltered pride that kept him from clearly seeing the heart of his lifelong friend.

Wylm considered for a moment that he was not being fair to him. He wished to hear Onero's voice, even it was in anger, scolding Wylm for his actions. Onero had never abandoned him before. Wylm wanted to look below him, to see Onero pleading with him to stop this madness. If he was there, Wylm would descend this wretched wall and apologize for his actions.

He glanced to the ground in hope. Onero was not there. There was no one to be seen, not even a wandering citizen. Then a voice came from a bush below. "You must hurry, Shachal. Jugel and his lackey are fast approaching. They are. Climb, my lord. Take what is yours."

Wylm returned to the task at hand. Another ten feet and he would be at the window. Onero was following that lunatic, Jugel. *Carcasses.* That Emari had eyes for the throne, and Onero was helping him. Wylm kept climbing and finally got both hands on the sill of the open window. Fatigued as he was, he had enough reserve for another burst toward the final ascent. When his head finally cleared the bedchamber window, he was dismayed by what he saw.

Across the room was the king's bed. Regeldam lay fast asleep on his back, hands crossed over his abdomen. His face betrayed no sense of anxiety or alarm. There was no suspicion of rebellion or insurrection upon his countenance. There was no fear of assassination, no distress that the avenger had arrived to his bedchambers.

It was not the king lying peacefully in bed that distressed Wylm. Standing to the side of the king was Jugel of Herr's Cove. He was gripping his sword, blade down. A prayer, or oath, or declaration of some type was spewing from his lips. Onero stood behind him, head bowed and eyes at his feet, apparently waiting for Jugel to finish his words. *How did they get here first?*

28 A KING'S CASTLE

When Wylm had knocked the two of them off the road, Onero and Jugel had been quite startled. Initially Jugel thought to question Onero about why he had waylaid him, but, as he tumbled down the steep hill, he had seen Wylm fleeing, and the sudden change in situation had made sense. It took Onero longer to realize what had happened.

"Your friend is intending to make himself a king this night," Jugel said. "He has finally believed the adulation and fawning of young Goor."

When Onero finally put the pieces together, he was flush with anger. The audacity, the arrogance, the foolish pride that his friend was showing was more than he could accept. Wylm had been flirting with betraying their oath for days, ever since the tunnels by the watchtower near the Forest of

Arogan. Now he had finally done it. At this point, Wylm was quite far ahead, and the flatterer, Goor, was whispering in his ear.

"Come, master Onero, the strength of Layish is with us," Jugel encouraged.

"By the grace of Rhumaiv," Onero responded.

They slowly, but resolutely, made their way up the steep hill, then continued running along the road to Kefeer. Their pace was quick, but the athleticism of Wylm was too much to overcome. Finally, they came to the locked city gate. Wylm and Goor were nowhere to be seen. As they approached the bolted doors, Onero pulled his mantle over his shoulders. Immediately, a jolt shot down his right arm. In response, Onero held up his staff and touched its tip to the gate. Like shutters in a strong wind, the doors swung open wide. The guards on the other side of the gate were struck by the massive swinging doors and rendered unconscious.

Having just experienced the miracle in the Pit of Bor, neither Jugel nor Onero questioned what had happened. Jugel did allow a quick smile to invade the corner of his mouth, but he quickly squashed it. The ruler in Kefeer had to account for his sins. After that, Jugel would go and find his bride. For too long he had missed Shoshanna. Now that he was in Kefeer, he longed for her even more. Just assuming he was nearer to her filled him with passion that he fought hard to control.

Onero and Jugel ran through the city gate and saw the tower sitting on the high hill at the center of the city. Their pace quickened due to the adrenaline pulsing through them. As they stayed in the shadows, taking back streets when necessary, Jugel began to make impromptu plans of how they would enter the royal house. Each had its flaw, but there was little time for strategy. By the time they were only a block away, he still did not have a plan. They paused behind an old building, Regeldam's house in view.

"If we can accost a couple soldiers, we could put on their uniforms and sneak our way in through a side door," Jugel said aloud.

A chill blew across Onero's neck at Jugel's words, like a remnant of the earlier blizzard. Onero readjusted his cloak. "A king enters his castle by the front door. Only a usurper sleeks in the night."

Jugel stared at Onero. "That sounds like a proverb of old, nice to quote, but not going to work in our situation." He looked in Onero's eyes, and saw he was unflinching. Jugel considered the gates of their prison in Bor. He considered the flash blizzard and the serpent-turned-staff. "Of course, with the way things have gone tonight, why not follow the prophet's advice?" He nodded to Onero, deciding to trust in his new friend.

As they approached the tower, Onero saw Wylm four stories up the wall, gripping precariously to the brick and mortar. He watched as Wylm brought his right leg up, seeking to find another footing. When he did, the block crumbled under his foot and, for a moment, he was holding on only by his fingertips. Onero stepped to the wall to catch Wylm if he fell, but looked to his left and saw Jugel running to the tower gate.

Onero's thoughts and emotions warred vehemently, like a warrior and his adversary battling to the death along the brink of a fiery chasm. *Jugel is to be the rightful king of Geongalann. At least, that is what Jugel claims. How do I know he was not lying to me? I have only known him for a week. I have known Wylm my whole life. But Jugel had that majestic roar that had to be a sign of his authority. But why would I follow a stranger over my friend? Because Wylm is an arrogant hateful fool.*

That's why. He is yielding to the fairy tales of a young sycophant, thinking only about his own glory. He abandoned me a week ago. He cannot be rewarded for that.

In a decision that would haunt him until his death, Onero turned his back on Wylm and ran after Jugel.

They came to the front doors. Like the city gates, Onero held his staff before him and touched the doors. They opened slowly and with a peculiar grandeur. Onero marched through the door as a silent herald. Jugel followed behind him. Guards were stationed along either side of the door and along the walls on either side of the entryway. Each looked straight ahead, never acknowledging the presence of the two intruders that marched into their master's home.

Throughout the center of the room were many tables covered with food. Along the sides of each table were finely dressed men. Though Onero knew none of these men, he had spent enough years walking among nobility and dignitaries to know that these were likely the most politically powerful Emari in Geongalann. What was odd about each was their lack of movement. Like the guards, all seemed to be frozen in place, as if under some enchantment.

Some were previously engaged in conversation with the person across from them or beside them. Others, including one particularly fat dignitary, were in the middle of taking in large mouthfuls of food. A few were facedown on the table, and Onero figured that the power of the staff had somehow knocked them out. As he more thoroughly glanced around the room, he figured the abundance of wine had likely incapacitated these few before Jugel and he had even arrived. None of the dignitaries were aware of their presence or that they intended justice upon their lord this evening.

Onero and Jugel began to move more quickly. They realized that Wylm was likely only a story or two from the king's room in his climb, and they had the whole tower to ascend. Onero kept his staff before him. Jugel began to give orders as to which direction to go and what stairs to take. Soon they had ascended to the highest room at the top of the last stair. Two guards stood abreast in front of door to the Regeldam's sleeping quarters. In a bewildering confidence, Jugel stepped in front of Onero and ordered them to stand aside. They did as commanded.

Jugel was amazed at the ease of their infiltration. Surely Layish had gone before him. Surely the Maker of Emabbir was blessing him and establishing his rightful calling as king. This night, he would avenge the death of the innocent and remove Regeldam from his throne of immorality. Once that was done, he would rescue Shoshanna. All had gone well to this point, and surely no evil could thwart his plan. With that in mind, Jugel of Herr's Cove entered the king's bedchambers as the lord of the city. Onero followed as his prophet.

29 THE RECKONING OF REGELDAM

As Onero entered, he surveyed the room. Another door was on the left side of the far wall. The furniture, he noticed, was not as lavish as he had expected. The pieces were few and worn. No drapery or articles of wealth or affluence could be seen in any corner. The only exception was the king's bed. It sat in the center of the room. Four posts reached up from its corners and sheets and fabrics of many colors draped across it. It was apparent that, to Regeldam, this must have been the foremost thought of his kingdom.

There, on the left side of the bed, lay the king. He was on his back in a deep sleep, his abdomen rising and falling peacefully. Beside him laid an Emari woman. Onero could not tell if she was sleeping. She was not tucked in or sleeping comfortably, if in fact she was even sleeping. Her left wrist was held fast by a chain. The other end was fastened to a metal ring on the far right bedpost. Her position in the bed suggested that she had been trying for some time to break free before relenting and collapsing.

"Shoshanna!" Jugel exclaimed in a forceful whisper that nearly gave their presence away.

The Emari woman stirred and was immediately awake. The look of exhaustion she had previously bore was instantly washed away as she saw her lover. "Jugel! Oh Jugel. You are alive." She sat up quickly, her left wrist still chained. "He was drunk, my love," she explained in shame as she crawled out of the bed of her adversary. "He fell asleep before he could touch me." Then she ignored her shame and looked at her lover. "He told me he had killed you, but you are alive. Oh, Jugel."

Jugel rushed to her and held her tight. She buried her head in his chest and wept tears of joy mixed with exhaustion and relief. As Onero watched the lovers embrace, he noticed keys on the unvarnished desk near him. He grabbed them and rushed to their side. With only three options, he quickly found the right key and released Shoshanna of her fetters.

She grabbed Jugel's hand and began to pull him to the door. "Come, my love, we must flee before he awakens."

"I have come not only to rescue you, my beloved, but to rid Geongalann of this filth." He turned his head to the still sleeping Regeldam. "His soldiers brought me north of the twin lakes without my consent. By the words of Layish, that makes me king, and I will remove all imposters."

"If we will not run, then at least kiss me," she begged. "I have been without you for so long, I am undone."

"You must wait, Shoshanna." Jugel gripped her lovingly by the shoulders and held her at arm's length. "If I kiss you now, I, too, will be undone, and my wits will leave me. There is nothing I want more, but there is one thing that must first be done."

Jugel released her and approached where Regeldam lay in unbroken sleep. He raised his sword in his right hand, cupping his right hand with his left. Bringing the grip to his head, he turned the blade down, pointing it at the king's heart. "You have killed many innocent Emari, Regeldam, all for greed and power. By the word of Layish, I shall send you to the Maker, and He will judge your actions." With that, he lifted his tightly gripped hands to prepare for the fateful blow.

At that moment, Wylm flashed across the room with amazing speed. Jugel saw Wylm and the glint of his jealous blade, but he began the downward thrust as Wylm swung his sword in an upward motion at him. Wylm connected first. His blade made contact with Jugel's right arm midway between the wrist and the elbow. Jugel's bone and flesh were severed from his body. By the resolve of a prophesied king and by the strength of Layish, Jugel continued his downward thrust. His left hand gripped his lifeless right hand, still holding the sword. He powered through Wylm's upward thrust and drove his sword through the heart of Regeldam.

Shoshanna screamed.

Onero was speechless.

Wylm was furious. How could this be? How could this Emari have beaten him to the kill?

Jugel stumbled, nearly going into shock at the amount of blood he was losing.

Shoshanna rushed to his side and began to rip shreds off her dress to make a tourniquet.

Onero came to himself, furious. "Wylm, you fool! What are you doing? You are not Shachal. You are not the White Lion. What have you made of yourself? You were a good soldier. You were a noble warrior. You were my friend."

Wylm pointed his sword at Onero. "That's right. I *was* your friend. But you turned your back on me for a chance at glory. You betrayed me for the hope of riches at the hands of him." Wylm pointed his sword at Jugel. Jugel had dropped his sword and was holding back the blood from his mutilated arm while Shoshanna tended to him. "But how can he be king if I kill him where he stands?"

Wylm took a step toward the unarmed Jugel.

Shoshanna screamed again and tried to step between them.

Onero moved quicker than he had ever moved before and came and stood between Wylm and the injured Emari from Herr's Cove. He held his staff in front of Wylm. "Stop this madness, my brother."

Wylm still burned with anger. With his left hand, he reached out to push the staff aside in order to strike his childhood friend. As he grabbed the staff, his hand instantly became leprous from the tips of his fingers to his elbow. The skin was white with a sickly gleam. Pain rushed into the joints of his fingers and wrist. He stepped back and dropped his sword in horror, staring at his white arm.

Regeldam's queen burst through the door on the far side of the room. She immediately grabbed Shoshanna, pulled her to her feet. "What have you done?" she demanded, as she pressed a knife to Shoshanna's throat. The queen saw her husband slain in his bed, Jugel pale and holding what remained of his right arm, and Wylm grimacing in pain from his transformed hand. Onero stood off a little to the side, but she paid him no attention, not even looking at him. "You all will suffer for what has been done here," she cursed.

She pressed the tip of her knife more firmly against Shoshanna's neck. Blood oozed out and dripped to her blouse. At the sight of his bride in distress, Jugel reached to retrieve the sword on the floor. It felt heavy and awkward in his left hand, but he raised it at the queen.

"Let her go," he managed to say, slowly regaining strength in his movement.

"Foolish son of the South," the queen scoffed at Jugel. "You have the touch of Layish in your eyes, but you lack what it takes to stop me. Put your sword away before you get everyone killed." She then looked to Wylm.

Wylm did not care for Jugel, nor did he care for his bride. He had plans of rescuing the other maidens stolen from the southern foothills, but the fate of Jugel's woman was inconsequential to his plan. This queen now stood in the way of completing that plan. He considered escaping and leaving this hostage situation to Onero and Jugel. What held him fast was the memory of the prophecy. He knew that the queen must also be slain in order to completely fulfill what had been foretold.

The queen smiled at Wylm. "So you are the brute and the pest of which I heard? I have looked in your eyes. I have seen your black heart." She positioned Shoshanna between her and Wylm. "What exactly is your plan, brute? One move and she is dead."

"You are not the first woman of evil that I have faced in a battle of wills such as this. I have a clearer perspective this time around." Wylm confronted her with great resolve. "My eyes have been opened."

"And what is it you plan to do?" the queen asked.

"Destroy the evil one." Wylm deftly flung his sword at the queen. It struck her in the head, and she fell. Her knife slipped across Shoshanna's neck as the young Emari woman fell forward and stumbled to Jugel.

Jugel caught Shoshanna in what remained of his right arm, causing pain to shoot up to his shoulder, but it was not the worst pain he felt at that moment. The cut across Shoshanna's neck was long and deep, and she was losing blood fast. Jugel tried to put pressure on it, but to no avail. "Shoshanna," he called out to her.

She opened her eyes weakly. They were beautiful and without fear. "I see him, Jugel. His mane is vast; his fur is shining. He is calling to me." Her head dipped for a moment in fatigue before looking to Jugel again. "Kiss me, my lover. Will you give me a kiss goodbye? He is calling to me. I must go now."

Jugel cupped her face with his left hand and kissed her. She returned in kind for a moment, and then her lips went cold. He wept. Huge tears rolled off his cheeks and mixed with her blood. His heart was broken. He was truly undone.

Onero grabbed his shoulder. "Come Jugel, we must go."

Jugel nodded but did not move.

"Jugel, we must hurry." Onero glanced at Wylm, who still bore the look of hate, but was not showing any signs of killing them. Nonetheless, he did not trust that leniency to continue.

Jugel held the body of his lifeless bride and tried to stand. He lacked the strength to do it. "Help me up."

"I cannot carry both her and you, Jugel. We must leave her here." Onero hated the words that came out of his mouth, but he knew them to be true.

"I will not leave the body of my beloved to be ravaged by these debaucherous savages of the North." He raised his voice to a threatening tone. "I can handle myself, but I beg you to carry Shoshanna."

Onero lifted her and placed her as gently as he could over his shoulder. He did not want to offend Jugel in the way he carried her, but it would be the only way he could manage her. He offered Jugel his left hand, and the Emari from Herr's Cove pulled himself up. They both stepped to the bedchamber doors and looked back at Wylm before exiting. Unspoken oaths were declared by all as they exchanged foreboding glances. Then Onero opened the door, and the two of them disappeared into the dark.

30 BRIDE PRICE

As Wylm watched Jugel and Onero flee like cowards, he stepped over to where the queen had fallen. He had considered ending their lives in the chaos before they left, but a hint of compassion remained for Jugel at the loss of his love. Also, the constant ache in his white left hand reminded him that while Onero had his staff, he was not as feeble as he appeared to be.

Wylm stood above the silky black robes of the fallen queen and reached for his sword. He grabbed it, lifted it over his head, and brought the blade down hard to ensure her death. The blade struck only garments and the floorboards beneath. No body was present within the pile of clothes. The window shutters flew open, and the sound of a soft cackle could be heard in the breeze. Wylm marveled for a moment, then heard the bedchamber doors swing open behind him. Goor entered the room and saw Wylm standing before Regeldam's bed. "My lord?"

"I've done it, my servant," Wylm said. "The imposter's dead, and the usurpers have fled. I've killed Regeldam by my white left hand. I have fulfilled the prophecy."

He turned to face Goor. The young lad held a blood-drenched sword over his right shoulder. The warm substance oozed over the crossguard and down the hilt, covering his red right hand. Blood spatter covered his torso, face, and scarlet hair. Wylm was in disbelief. "What happened, child? Are you alright?" Goor just stood there staring at him.

Goor was in shock, but not because of the presumed battle from which he came. He looked to the man across the room. Sure enough, just as he said, the man had killed the imposter. He was holding the baneful weapon with the grip of that glorious white hand. Already his left arm was as white as the peaks of the southern mountains. "You truly are Shachal. You are," Goor said.

Wylm stepped closer to the traumatized boy and lifted his chin until their eyes met. "Are you okay, Goor? Are you hurt?"

Finally, the initial shock of witnessing a fulfilled dream was fading. His devotion toward that dream, though, did not fade. Goor dropped to his knees and began to kiss the feet of his lord. "You have slain your enemy, my lord, and I have executed his followers. I have. When I entered the palace, your friend, the wizard, had bewitched the people. None of them moved. They were like statues."

Goor rose to his feet and looked to his White Lion. "None who served the Imposter are worthy of life, so I took it from them. I did. I took it from all of them."

Wylm had fantasized about this moment ever since Goor first began to proclaim him as the returning king. The calculating warrior had considered what would have to be done to thin out the competition for the throne and what would be needed to garner the support and love of the fighting men and the people. Forging the strategy had merely been an exercise to keep his mind off the physical strain of being shackled to a moving cage. Those mental practices had become reality, and Goor had already completed the first phase of his plan.

"You've been a loyal servant, young Goor of Koor," Wylm invoked with a tone of lordship. "Now, you'll be my herald. You'll tell the world that the White Lion's come. But first, we must win the people."

Wylm told Goor of his plans, the plans that he had never intended to carry out. As Goor searched the nearby rooms for a washbasin and a change of clothes, Wylm scoured the bedchamber and surrounding rooms for supplies, as Goor found a washbasin. He had found rope and plenty of sheets deciding to make their escape through the window. By now Onero's magic had surely worn off, and a changing of the guard or a random passerby would easily cause a stir among those who had been loyal to Regeldam. He likely did not have long until someone came to check on their king.

One day, Regeldam's soldiers will obey me as their king, Wylm thought. But this night they would fight for the honor of their recently fallen lord. The odds of escaping the palace were negligible.

Wylm and Goor worked quickly to make the long cord. Six stories was a long distance to repel. Goor had found a couple sacks for Wylm. If they were to carry out their plans and flee Kefeer safely, they would need proof and deceit. Wylm grabbed Regeldam's white-lion cloak and red, right gauntlet. He also grabbed the lion's-head crown and shoved them into one sack. In another sack, he placed evidence of Regeldam's death.

They secured one end of the cord to the bed and descended the window. Goor went out first, and Wylm followed with the two sacks tied around Regeldam's sword. They reached the bottom safely. The city was still sleeping, and no alarms were going off. Wylm would begin phase one of winning the people's hearts.

Goor had passed along his knowledge of the layout of the city. They hurried, unimpeded, to the part of the city known as the Bride's Market. This was where all the women captives were being held. There was usually a refinement period that lasted three months before Regeldam would auction the women off or give them as gifts in reward for allegiance. If Wylm could free the women, it would endear the men of the South to him and inhibit anyone from securing undue loyalties through the Bride's Market.

The Market was a large building surrounded by a small open field. A high wall secured the perimeter. There was one entrance, and it was nearly as guarded as the gate to enter Kefeer. Goor went ahead of his king by fifty yards and came to the gate. "The White Lion approaches. Take your posts. Stand at attention. Open the gate. Your lord approaches and wishes to see his resources. He does."

The guards came quickly to attention and to their posts. Weapons were in hand and at the ready upon the first syllable from Goor's mouth. They did not recognize Goor, of course and the first guard questioned him. "Who are you? What happened to the other guy?"

Goor answered with conviction, because he fully believed what he was saying. "I am the king's herald and devotee. I am the first and greatest and carry with me the full authority of the approaching king. I do. Open the gate, or face the White Lion's wrath."

The guard stepped in front of Goor, lowering his weapon. As he did, he saw past Goor to the approaching man. The man was draped with the hide of a white lion. His head was crowned with that same lion's head. Upon his right hand was a red gauntlet. The guard stepped to the side and bowed his head. "King Regeldam, my deepest apologies." As he lifted his eyes to look at the face of the White Lion, he saw that the man before him was not in fact Regeldam. "Imp—"

The word *imposter* nearly escaped his lips, but Wylm was anticipating his discovery. He punched hard at the man's throat with his open palm, stopping the word where it started. He then squeezed the man's throat. Within moments, the guard's windpipe was shattered, and he fell at Wylm's feet. Wylm did not look at the second guard but turned and faced the still-closed gate.

Goor feigned impatience. "What are you waiting for?" he barked at the second guard. "Do you still make your lord wait at the gate like a peasant or thief? Do you?" Hastily and clumsily, the guard opened the gate and let Wylm through. Goor gave another command. "Send some men on ahead to the house to prepare for the White Lion's entrance. Send them. Do not let his step be impeded again this night or great punishment will befall this whole company."

Goor was enjoying this moment. The words he was using were not in his normal speech, but he had read many stories about kings and heralds. Before he could read, his father would read or tell similar tales of adventure. The words he used now were of the manner of speech used in those stories. He had been practicing for this moment his whole life.

As a few more guards ran on ahead, casting sheepish looks Wylm's way to make sure they were getting far enough ahead, Goor turned back to the guard. "The king is moving the girls to the city of Adom Mirbats. He is. Prepare twenty-five carts with cages. Each is to be driven by two horses. Once they are prepared, you and your men must inform the soldiers at Kefeer's eastern gate that a caravan of cages will be coming through.

"We will be leaving the east gate, we will. Then we will encircle the north of the city and head west to Adom Mirbats. The king suspects a traitor is starting a rebellion. He does. He wants to throw off their trail by heading east first. Before you leave, send another man to the guardhouse and prepare twenty-five uniforms. The White Lion's personal guards will wear these as we transport the girls. They will."

The guard was overwhelmed and perplexed. He found the whole ordeal dizzying and hard to follow. As he glanced down at the lifeless body of his former partner, fear overtook logic, and he got to the task as ordered.

Within an hour, the guards had all left their posts and headed to the east gate of Kefeer to prepare for the king's departure. The women were all in the rolling prisons being pulled by two horses each. The cages were unlocked. Each of the carts was being driven by one of the women dressed in the guards uniform with her hair pulled up in the helmet or covered by a hood. By the beginning of the fourth watch of the night, all the women had escaped Kefeer and were heading east.

Goor had his own horse and was ordered to ride ahead to Koor. Great news was to be proclaimed. Regeldam was dead. The prophecy had been fulfilled. A new king was coming, bearing gifts. Wylm knew that returning sisters and daughters would be the price for their loyalty. Give him a year, and he would truly reign in Kefeer as king of the Emari.

31 THESE THOUSAND HILLS

There had been little talk between Onero and Jugel. Each had come to the brink of exhaustion. They had been moving all night at the swiftest pace they could manage. Their flight had begun near the end of the second watch, and they had run as far away from the city as possible until the first light of day.

Onero had born the body of Shoshanna. In an attempt to honor her and soften Jugel's pain, he had tried cradling her body in his arms. Within a half mile of their escape, he had realized this could not be maintained and moved her over his shoulder again. He had never been the strongest or most fit soldier, and though Shoshanna had been thin, the Emari people were larger than Men. That extra size had had its effects on Onero. In fatigue, he had continually switched her body from one shoulder to the other.

Now he was free from that burden, but that did not provide him any relief. A few hours earlier, a red sunrise had emerged along the eastern horizon. As the foreboding sky glowed threateningly, Jugel had made a request. It had been only the second time he had spoken in the previous six hours. He had pointed to a southeastward facing slope and asked that Shoshanna be buried there.

Jugel had had his own difficulties through the night. He had lost a significant amount of blood at the palace. Onero had placed a tourniquet to stop the bleeding, but the amount lost had diffused his strength. Onero had watched him struggle through the night. Jugel had taken every step as if it were twenty. He approached every log as if it were a boulder. He was the one who had made the plan to flee until daylight. Onero had not been sure Jugel would make it.

Of course, loss of blood was not what had slowed him down the most, nor was it the reason he and Onero had hardly spoken. The pain of loss at the brink of hope had been overwhelming for Jugel. He had most assuredly felt these emotions before: grief, fear, hate. But he had never felt all three so bitterly and with such combined intensity. Onero wondered how Jugel could bear it. What was worse, he knew that all of these emotions could be blamed on one person: Wylm Kanu.

Four hours after they stopped, Onero had nearly finished burying Shoshanna. It was not the first time he had buried a body, but at his level of exhaustion and without proper tools, it took him twice as long as usual. At the break of dawn, Jugel had pointed out the hillside. He had seen something in the distance and knew that this hill looked toward Herr's

Cove.

Jugel had wanted to help with the burial, but Onero refused to allow him. While Onero labored, Jugel slumped beneath a tree. Onero was not certain the warrior from Herr's Cove would be alive when the burial was complete. With only a few handfuls of dirt remaining, Onero went to wake his friend.

"Jugel, it's time."

Jugel lifted his head and grabbed Onero's left forearm, allowing Onero to pull him to a standing position. Jugel slowly made his way to the low mound of dirt. He knelt and grabbed at the loose earth beside him and sprinkled it over the mound.

As Jugel moved the last portions onto his beloved's grave, he began to sing. The unexpected richness of his voice was touched with the depths of authority and a quiver of sorrow. The song he sang was sad and beautiful. Onero assumed it was an old burial song of the Emari people. It overwhelmed him.

"Your child passed this life through the trials of Geongalann,

Over the thousand hills, till she lies weary in the ground.

Oh, Great Layish. Oh, Great Layish.

Do not pass her by, but smile and take her hand.

Fly past these thousand hills, till she sings merrily o'er the clouds.

Oh, Great Layish. Oh, Great Layish."

He began to sing the lyrics again, but as he sang, he began to make marks in the dirt.

"Your child passed this life through the trials of Geongalann…"

His finger drew a simple horizontal line from left to right.

"Over the thousand hills, till she lies weary in the ground."

Starting a little back from the right end, he curved a line up and down until it crossed over and past the horizontal line near its left end.

"Oh, Great Layish. Oh, Great Layish.

Do not pass her by, but smile and take her hand."

From under the current symbol, he started a vertical line that rose and stopped at the midpoint of the horizontal line.

"Fly past these thousand hills, till she sings merrily o'er the clouds."

Finally, he finished with a short vertical line from the top of the curved line rising above the symbol for a short span.

"Oh, Great Layish. Oh, Great Layish.

Oh, Great Layish. You are great, Layish."

When Jugel called to Layish, it was with absolute pain and complete trust. Onero remembered his father and grandfather similarly crying out to Rhumaiv in times of great despair. Onero felt that same despair now.

He had gone over the events of the previous night countless times during the past hours. Of everything that he had done, he kept coming back to something that he did not do. He did not stand below Wylm to protect him from a fall. It angered Onero that his conscience kept trying to put this on him. *Wylm was the one to blame here, not me.*

The prophet's son put forth his argument, hoping to alleviate his guilt. Had he stopped below the palace wall to guard Wylm, what would have happened? From Wylm's height on the wall, they likely would have both died, had he fallen. Besides that, Jugel would not have been able to make it to Regeldam's bedchambers without Onero by his side. Wylm would have arrived first to fulfill the prophecy on his own.

That argument was not enough to put Onero's heart at ease. He tried again. This time, he considered Jugel. According to Jugel, he had been considered king of Geongalann from the day they passed north of the Eastern Lake. Onero's oath to Wylm was always to guard and protect his friend above all else, *"save the king."* Onero reasoned that since Jugel was now king, his place should be at Jugel's side, no matter what.

Onero knew that argument did not hold up either. In Bachar, the Seon and Kanu ancestors were not always at the king's side. They had just vowed to protect his life over each other's if that situation arose. Also, he had never pledged his allegiance to Jugel as his king. He was still a citizen of Bachar. While Onero had stood below Wylm at the palace wall, Jugel's life had not needed saving. Had Onero decided to try to guard and protect Wylm in that moment, Jugel's life would not have been in any greater danger.

What it came down to was that Onero had abandoned his friend. He had broken his oath and committed a grievous sin. How many times had he defended his own honor to Wylm. How often had he declared that he would never break his oath? The doubt that Wylm had had in him had been proven correct.

Onero could hardly bear the guilt. His feelings of worthlessness were returning. The depression that had been stalking him had finally overtaken him. He despaired of life. He hoped for death, to sleep forever beneath these thousand hills of which Jugel sung. He longed to be back in the tunnels beneath Arogan Forest. Onero cursed the Mugaal for ever pulling him out.

This land would be in a lot less pain without Wylm and me in it, he thought as he raised his eyes to watch Jugel.

The Emari from Herr's Cove had just finished his song of prayer and was lying on his back beside Shoshanna's grave. His left arm rested on the new dirt mound; what remained of his right was wrapped to his chest. The forlorn warrior looked to the far horizon, to Fortress Peak. Its snow-capped ridges glistened in the mid-morning sky.

A gentle breeze blew up the hillside and bent a tuft of high grass into his face. He reached up with his left hand and pushed it aside, letting out a brief laugh as he thought he was pushing away Shoshanna's long, bountiful mane. Mournfully, reality struck him, bringing with it more pain than he had experienced just seconds ago.

He remembered the last time he had rested on a hillside beside his beloved. He had become entangled in her hair.

"If I spend the rest of my life entangled in that bountiful mane, it will be the sweetest imprisonment a husband could want," Jugel had said to her.

"Now how are we supposed to get out of this?" Shoshanna had pretended to be a damsel in distress.

"I have my sword," had been his joking response.

"You always have your sword. Sometimes I wonder if you love it more than you love me."

Her response had been in jest, but it no longer mattered. The thing that he had loved most in this world had been taken from him by the evil wife of the Imposter. The promise of authority, from the mouth of Layish, had been usurped from him by the treachery of a covetous Man.

Jugel rose to his feet with more strength than he had shown just moments earlier. He began to stride down the hillside, descending in the direction of Fortress Peak.

"Where are you going?" Onero asked.

"I am going home," he said, not looking back. "I am going to get my sword."

EPILOGUE

Fifty-one weeks after the death of Regeldam.

He stood on the edge of the precipice, high up on the northern face of the mountain. All of Geongalann spread out before him. The sun was rising far in the east, casting an eerie shadow on most of the land. He surveyed the scene before him. It looked peaceful and glorious from this height. The rolling hills of the South nestled up against the Great Mountain. The large Twin Lakes of the central country were massive guardians for the growing city of Kefeer. The lower hills and plains of the West were tucked in between the lesser mountains of Tetemek and the wasteland of Khamer. On this morning, even cast in shadow, all looked peaceful.

It was truly the most beautiful land in the entire world of Nold, and he knew that from experience. How many years ago had it been that he chose to protect these lands from evil? How many years had it been since the promotion of good had become his utmost call? He was tired. His efforts were too often in vain, and he could hardly stand against the weight of his impotence.

As he stood on that edge, thinking about all that he had done with little effect, an amber light settled behind him. He was not startled or dismayed. Instead, he let the warmth of that light bathe over him. As always, it refreshed him. He would need more than that, though, to lift this hopelessness that had him bound. He would need the counsel and touch of the radiance he loved.

"I have been looking for you," sung the sweet, soothing voice from within that light. "How long have you been up here?"

The man was not surprised by the woman's words. In fact, he had hoped for them. "I came up last night. Esteg brought me."

"Did any one see you with him?"

The man shook his head but did not turn to face her. Despite her warmth and peace, the burden he was carrying was still so much that he could not even shift his weight.

The woman of light approached him, and he could feel it. "What is troubling you, Henyr?" She asked laying a loving and soothing hand on his shoulder.

Some of his tension began to release, her healing touch restoring him countless times over these many long years. "Esteg brought me a report from his scouts. I'm beginning to wonder if it all has been worth it." He paused before finally turning to face her. Seeing her brought more relief, but the ever-present worries that beset him began to slowly weigh him down again. "The people think everything is better. They think the tide has turned. Many, if not most of them, are excited. In fact, I have overheard much talk of wanting to travel to the North. They think the hard times and persecutions are over."

"And you do not?"

"Not after Esteg's report," he answered, too overwhelmed to elaborate.

The woman of light brought both her hands to his shoulders. Her touch was usually more effective, but his fatigue was too overwhelming. "What was Esteg's report?"

"Kefeer is in chaos." Again he turned to gaze upon the façade of beauty which was Geongalann. From this height, the pain, sorrow, and oppression could not be seen. "The generals and commanders there are jostling for leadership, but none of them have enough support to take or keep the throne." His next thought made his shoulders sink even more. "The people in the South want to follow the Man. All their talk is about him. They think he is the one who was foretold."

"What do you think of him?" she asked, trying to help him verbalize what was truly troubling him.

"I think he has wickedness in his heart." He faced her again, this time frustration propelling his words. "You have seen him: quick to strike; slow to listen; slower to trust." Then exasperated, he added "The old seer had said the Man's lineage was important. The old seer even gave his life for him."

"Not just for him," the woman of light reminded.

"True, for the Left-handed and the prophet also, but it was declared specifically of the Man that his family was integral in catalyzing many of the major events of Tomorrow. The old seer spoke of honor and duty. What does the Man do instead? It seems he is setting himself up to be ruler in Kefeer." Henyr was becoming incredulous. He had loved this land for so long. He had given his own blood and sweat to protect its people for a great many years. Now, he watched as it seemed one tyrant would give way to the next. "I mean, he even has the red boy acting as his herald throughout the North."

"I have seen this," she said, her words revealing that perhaps she had seen even more.

"Have you spoken to Ergo?" His tone was harsher than he intended. He would have normally taken this time to tell her how important she was to him, but he was frustrated, and she did not always tell him everything she knew.

"You know that I have. I speak to him every day."

"Have you asked him about the Man?"

"I have," she answered.

"And?"

"And what?"

"What did he say?" Why did she do this to him, demanding proper etiquette in conversation even in his anxious state?

"He said many things. What do you want to know?"

"Does he win Kefeer? Does he become king of Geongalann?" He wondered, with her elusive answer, whether she was actually trying to help him feel better or worse. To be fair, his depression was lifting as he became more agitated.

"He said that no Man will ever reign in Kefeer."

The answer greatly surprised Henyr, but brought him relief as well. "That is good."

"Is it?" she asked enigmatically.

"Of course it is good," he pronounced. "That Man is full of strife. He would make a violent king. I'm just surprised there is someone who will stop him. Esteg's scouts tell me the Man's forces are formidable and loyal. Even now, he has gathered them to make an advance on Kefeer in the next week or two. Who stops him?

She did not answer, but grabbed both his hands and looked with compassion into his eyes.

"Who stops him?" Henyr asked again with a little more force.

Again she did not answer. This time she had trouble keeping his gaze, but she held his hands tighter, letting him know she was here for him.

He was starting to understand. All these years together, he was slowly learning to realize what her silences meant. "Did Ergo tell you not to tell me?"

She gave a sideways nod. "He told me I could tell you if you asked, but he hoped you would not ask. He has seen your weariness. He knows you are tired." Again she looked on him with empathy and compassion. "But your task is about to get harder."

"Who stops the Man?" Henyr asked again with love, understanding and resolve.

"The abomination is coming."

Her words hit him squarely, causing him to recoil a step. "When?"

"Very soon."

"Will *she* be by his side?"

"Eventually," the woman of light answered knowingly.

"Will he attack us?"

"Eventually." This time she paused before she continued. "But you will not slay him, nor I her."

"Then we will be defeated at last." He was not sure if his own words were a question or a statement.

She answered nonetheless. "Ergo did not tell me."

The hopelessness he had felt minutes ago was now worse. Up to this point, he had fought bravely and with determination. Still he felt all his works

ACKNOWLEDGMENTS

This story has been fifteen years in the making. For over a decade, it was just a group of stories in my mind and on notepads that were shared with no one except my wife, mother, and father. Many times I had initiated the process of turning my stories into a book, to share my creation with whoever would listen. Each of those efforts led to empty results.

A couple of years ago, a coworker of mine, Amy Horn, decided to join a contest to write a novel in one month. She completed her novel and published it in paperback. This motivated me to take the next step. Thank you, Amy, for the inspiration. My story may have never left my yellow notepads had I not seen you do it.

Once I started writing, the story, I would send every chapter to my mother, Julie. She would read each chapter immediately after it was written. It was easy to press on when I had such positive reinforcement shortly after each section of my tale. Thank you, Mom, for your encouragement and motivation.

Once I had my first draft written, I gave it to friends to read and review. They came back with more encouraging words, ideas, and a few edits. Thank you, Kris Clum, Anna Frum, and Amy Horn, again, for being willing to read my story and give me your comments. Thank you also to my aunt, Amy Wentworth, for reading the first draft. All these kind words energized me to keep going.

A very special *thank you* goes to Erin Poulin for providing the light copy edit of my book. Erin, your eye for the minutia amazed me, as well did your attention to detail in finding every missed comma, passive sentence, and character inconsistency. I am truly fascinated by your professional work. Had it not been for you, who knows how long it would have been till this book saw the light of day? May God bless and prosper you and your family

My final statement of appreciation goes to my amazing wife, Carrie. The hours I spent typing, and the years I spent writing, were surely excessive for a man who has a fulltime job and fulltime family. Carrie, thank you for supporting my dream of writing this story. It is absolutely ridiculous how much God blessed me when he gave me you

ABOUT THE AUTHOR

Abram Klaserner is a physical therapist and speaker at his local hospital, where it has been suggested he is too literary in his professional documentation. The son of a pastor, he has spent his life captivated by the stories of the Bible, and he is a sucker for any good adventure on the silver screen. His love of Scripture and movies has inspired much of his stories, and his insistence on romanticizing reality has inspired the rest. He lives with his wife, three sons, and daughter in New Philadelphia, Ohio.

You can follow Abram on Twitter @abramklaserner

The HOUSE OF KANU Series

By Abram Klaserner

Kings of Geongalann

Book 1: *IMPOSTER*

Book 2: *USURPER*

Book 3: *OVERLORD*

Sons of Kerux

Book 4: *THUNDER*

Book 5: *FIRE*

Book 6: *QUAKE*

Voices of Naos

Book 7: *WILE*

Book 8: *WHISPER*

Book 9: *ROAR*

Made in the USA
Lexington, KY
04 June 2015